FINDING FAULT

Praise for Annie McDonald

When Sparks Fly

"This is a slow-burn, gentle romance between Dr. Dani Waveny, and iron sculptor and hockey coach Luca McAffery. Both are well developed characters and have obvious chemistry from their first meeting in the book. I think I fell a bit in love with Luca myself. The secondary characters are equally well developed. All of the characters fit well in their roles. The romance itself is slow and sweet, with a few misunderstandings along the way to add conflict. This story really is delightful. I can't wait for Ms. McDonald's next Canadian romance novel. If you are into tender, slow-burn love stories with a definite Canadian feel, then check out this story."—*Rainbow Reflections*

"It was as if Ms. McDonald knew exactly the type of story my heart was aching for, and sat down and wrote it just for me. Add into the mix the slow romance, the secret and heartbreak that Dani carries, and the shame that weighs Luca down and you have the tale of two complex people that doesn't let go. But the characters that surround them are just as interesting, and I found myself frequently cheering for a couple of them as well."—*Carolyn McBride, Splintered Realities*

Where We Are

"The characters were all fun to read about and very varied, and the plots kept me engaged as well. It was a very very fun read."—*Danielle Kimerer, Librarian (Nevins Memorial Library, Methuen, MA)*

"[T]his is an intelligent enemies to friends to lovers tale...This was my first exposure to this author, and I have every intention of getting every one of her books as she writes them. If I could give her more than five stars, I would. Sharp writing, great characters, dogs, and all that food…This one deserves 8 stars for sure!"—*Carolyn McBride, Splintered Realities*

"I truly enjoyed Annie McDonald's debut novel *Where We Are*…There are quite a few things I love about this book. I love how Canadian the story is with a Canadian author, setting and characters. I love the bits of Canadiana mentioned in the novel such as the group of seven (especially Tom Thomson) and mentions of the First Nations stories…Ms. McDonald mentions in her profile that she plans to write a novel set in each of the Canadian provinces and territories. I will definitely be looking for these future novels."—*Rainbow Reflections*

By the Author

Where We Are

When Sparks Fly

Finding Fault

Visit us at www.boldstrokesbooks.com

FINDING FAULT

by
Annie McDonald

2022

FINDING FAULT

ISBN 13: 978-1-63679-257-6

THIS TRADE PAPERBACK ORIGINAL IS PUBLISHED BY
BOLD STROKES BOOKS, INC.
P.O. BOX 249
VALLEY FALLS, NY 12185

FIRST EDITION: NOVEMBER 2022

CREDITS
EDITOR: BARBARA ANN WRIGHT
PRODUCTION DESIGN: STACIA SEAMAN
COVER DESIGN BY TAMMY SEIDICK

Acknowledgments

Thank you to those who caretake the land where I write, the Acadia First Nations Mi'kmaq (Nova Scotia) peoples.

Thanks to my dear friends and beta readers, Laurie Danowski and Susan Shepherd, who help me stand in different places and see the words through new eyes. I'm ever grateful to Dr. Lori Haskell, whose expertise in PTSD inspired me and pulled me out of a pretty dark place. Sandy Lowe at Bold Strokes Books provided welcome direction during the early stages of *Finding Fault* that helped me craft a better story. I could not possibly end up with a story worth reading, though, without the expertise and humor lent to it by my editor, Barbara Ann Wright. Simply, she makes it all better. Thank you.

The past few years have been hard for so many people. There's a homemade sign I see beside the highway north of Halifax that reads "Just Breathe." I think they got that right.

To Sandy. We're home.

CHAPTER ONE

Evelyn O'Halloran liked hot chocolate. But not this much. Not enough to get her to step into an elevator. But inexplicably, that was what she'd done. In spite of the fact that her favorite stadium vendor was only seven floors up from their fifty-yard-line seats. In spite of the fact that she was in the best physical shape of her life and could have easily managed the stairs. What had she been thinking? Sure, she'd once spent a month sandwiched between layers of sedimentary glacial deposits, gathering evidence for her graduate thesis. Years ago. Now, she could no longer tolerate small spaces. Especially elevators.

This particularly unreliable metal box had come to an unscheduled and unpleasantly jarring stop. The doors would not open. She'd stopped stabbing at the numbered plastic squares on the control panel seconds after she'd realized they were ineffective. She'd held the metal rail beside her to stop the tiny metal box from spinning around her and had waited for her heart to restart. When it did, she'd spent the next five minutes waiting for it to stop relentlessly pumping and pounding blood in her ears. She'd given up trying to discern what the muffled voice on the other end of the emergency phone had said, but at the very least, someone knew she was stuck.

Why an elevator? Why this elevator? She mentally pointed a finger at the generous hot chocolate vendor who'd overfilled each cup. It took only a few searing splashes to convince her that if she wanted to get back to her seat before the game was over, she needed a safer and smoother descent. Mistake number one.

Mistake number two was forgetting how terribly claustrophobic she was.

She desperately wanted to believe that someone was on the way. Hope would calm her. But when the ear pounding mercifully stopped, she became aware of the panting. Alarmed, she tried to slow down each breath. Her face felt like wax, melting. Slowly. Her eyes welled with tears, and every one of the damned numbered dots above the door remained unlit. Her mouth was dry, and the panting was replaced by an onslaught of nausea.

Jesus, get a grip, Evie. Had it really come to this? Was this the way her life would end? In an elevator? At a football stadium? It didn't seem imaginable, let alone fair.

"I'm a good person," she said aloud. "I work hard. I love my family and my dog. I care about this planet. I care about people." Not one in particular more than others, but that was her own failing, and she was sure that didn't require such a dramatic karmic reprimand as this. And working hard? Well, "hard" might have been an exaggeration. One should endeavour to be truthful, she imagined, when conducting a possibly final negotiation with one's maker and taker. Truth be told, then, she had been a workaholic for most of her life. A professional hazard, she'd always thought. As a younger academic, making tenure had absorbed her and most people around her, so nothing except the next publication had mattered. By the time she'd made full professor, though, it had seemed that those same people around her had managed to also find time to pursue additional goals. Love. Marriage. Kids. So that was that.

Evie had her sister and her niece. And of course, Walter, her dog. One needed her now more than ever. *I have to get out.* Another wave of nausea wobbled her knees. She fought against it, knowing in this moment of clarity that the catastrophizing would only making her symptoms worse. She tackled the dizziness first.

She let herself sink down the wall and placed the cardboard tray of no-longer-steaming hot chocolate cups on the floor beside her. Better.

Next, the nausea. In through the nose. Out through the mouth. Or was it the other way around? Why couldn't she pay attention at yoga? Seriously. What did it matter? At least she was breathing. But for how long? How much air was in an elevator? With each intentional breath, Evie felt more able to believe the answer: plenty. *I will not die on this elevator. Evelyn O'Halloran will get another chance.* She would find other ways to live her life. She would set new personal goals. She would change if she had to, will herself all the way there. *What does it mean when you start talking about yourself in the third person? That you're crazy? Egomaniacal?* She settled on alive.

No sooner did her resolve emerge than a grinding, mechanical sound filled her prison cell. Then there was a jolt. Movement slowly up. Then movement quickly down. She fought back a scream. The car moved slowly up again. The damned number five circle blinked tauntingly. She brushed aside her tears. The circle flashed again but stayed lit. She scrambled to her feet and pressed her ear against the door crack. Voices.

The metal doors were parting. Slowly. Very slowly. Every pore in Evie's body was wholly committed to finding space. Sweet, open breathable space. She grabbed the tray of drinks and, unwilling to wait a second more, forced her way through the barely separated rubber door bumpers.

❖

"You were right, Ms. S, the doughnuts were totally worth the walk."

"Jerry, please call me Merr. Can we not take the stairs?"

"Sorry again, Ms., er, I mean, Merr...that's on me. My knees aren't what they used to be, as you might've guessed. Football."

Merritt Shepherd congratulated herself on not rolling her

eyes. She'd hoped that spending a bit of extra time with a couple of the "boys," as Mark Einerson and Jerry Conroy liked to refer to themselves, might prove beneficial. They'd worked for Regina's biggest agricultural nutrition producer, Farmexal, for several years. She was new to the company. *In a way.*

"Spending time" was what had led her to develop a sudden craving for the mini doughnuts found only at the far end of the football stadium's lower concourse. Not because she adored the tiny, baked-on-site treats, especially when warm. *Delicious.* Certainly not because of their powdered sugar cinnamon sweetness. *Irresistible.* Tucked while still hot into a bag she clutched as if it were gold. She did start to wonder five minutes into the walk if the doughnuts were worth enduring Conroy's painfully boring reminiscences of his football years. How he'd toe-dragged a touchdown catch to win the high school city finals. How he'd once had a walk-on with Saskatchewan's football team, the Roughriders, but he'd been nursing a knee injury at the time so couldn't give it his best. To Merritt, it was all, well, numbing.

Einerson, on the other hand, was a seriously closed book. Unlike Conroy, who normally oversaw Farmexal's main facilities' shipping and receiving gates, Einerson was a security guard who worked a circuit. The fertilizer producer had several locations in Regina and a few rural properties just east of the city limits. Einerson's "cushy job," Conroy explained now, was to drive to each and do a visual check.

"And he gets to drive the company truck!"

"Is that such a remarkable thing, Jerry?" Merritt feigned enthusiasm. "I mean, a truck is a truck, no?"

Conroy's eyes widened, and he shook his head. He reminded her of Yosemite Sam in that moment, though she couldn't pinpoint why. In fact, he was quite the opposite of mean, rough, and tough, and Merritt doubted he even knew where the Rio Grande was.

"It's not just a truck. It's a fully tricked out Interceptor.

Tinted windows. Flat-finish paint, rims and bumpers. Anti-ram technology. It's a serious set of wheels, Ms. S. Serious."

Merritt smiled, curious as to why the relatively small manufacturer needed to outfit its security guards with that grade of vehicle. She noticed Einerson smiling and wondered what he found funny.

Conroy continued unfettered. "But I guess now that you've got your own new ride, it's not so impressive, eh, Mark? I guess picking up those extra shifts at the casino have paid off."

Einerson crossed his arms in front of his muscled chest. He clearly wasn't going to be drawn into banter by Conroy. Merritt took it upon herself to try a less confrontational approach.

"Oh," she forced herself to coo, "did you get a new car? Or truck? Tell me about it so I can dream about the day I no longer have car payments."

Einerson laughed. She smiled, hoping she'd secured a sense of camaraderie. Flirting wasn't her forte, doubly ineffectual with men, but if it helped her get a better sense of this strong silent type, she'd bear the embarrassment. She filed away the fact that he moonlighted at the casino for another time.

"It's a Ford F-150," Einerson muttered. "A truck."

He added that last bit as if Merritt had never heard of the model, and for the fifth time in as many minutes, she fought the urge to roll her eyes. Conroy rushed to fill the second of silence, explaining that it was red and had a "sweet chrome package" and could easily tow a boat or trailer or whatever. The level of detail was excruciating, so when Merritt noticed the elevator doors finally begin to open, she could barely wait to step on, hoping that once she did, the doors would close behind her with the boys on the other side.

She lifted her head in time to see that she was just about to walk into someone, or they into her, and before she could react, Conroy charged between her and the person with surprising aggression for a guy with a bad knee. "Heads-up," he said.

The advancing woman reared back, seemingly startled by the onslaught. Merritt watched helplessly as her precious bag of delectable doughnuts launched upward, along with the cardboard tray of take-out cups the woman had been carrying. Doughnuts flew from the bag, lids abandoned their rims, and a rogue wave of beverages and baked goods crashed around with the force of a tsunami.

❖

"Oh my God, I'm so sorry. Jerry, for goodness' sake, move out of the way!"

Evie didn't know who Jerry was. Nor did she recognize the woman's voice coming from behind the inelegant mass of a man before her. She was hard-pressed to focus on anything except the warm, sweet-smelling cascade of milky chocolate that had saturated her sweater clear through to her skin and the remnant of a doughnut perched on her shoulder. The drinks that hadn't landed on her were now pooling at her feet. Tiny doughnuts floated, swelled, then sank into the liquid. *Where did they come from?*

The hulk stepped aside. Evie looked up from the mess and leveled her eyes at the woman in front of her. Not a hulk. Nothing near. Evie was struck with another unavoidable and warm wave. This time, it was embarrassment. "No, no. It's my fault entirely. I wasn't watching where I was going." She surveyed the perfectly tailored woman but failed to find a trace of spillage. In contrast to her relatively shabby self, the woman was spotless. Impossibly immaculate.

"Are you absolutely sure you're not burned?" The woman spoke slowly, almost as if Evie needed extra time to hear. "You are completely drenched."

"They were barely lukewarm. Honestly, the elevator was stuck for so long, they had time to cool." The shouldered doughnut cascaded down her fleece shirt and plopped at her feet, throwing another splash onto her ankles. Insult to injury. The woman pretended not to have noticed, but Evie was sure she had. *How could she not?*

"You'd been stuck in there? How terrible. For how long?"

Way, way too long. "Yes, that's why I was in too big a hurry squeezing out and didn't see you...him...until we collided." For the first time in at least an hour, she was able to draw a breath of relief. "Almost collided. My fault entirely."

Evie noticed a grin begin to sweep across her rescuer's face, but it vanished as she turned to one of what Evie could now see were two accompanying men. In the moment before she addressed the larger of them, Evie noticed her jaw clench as if she was biting back words. When she did finally speak, her cadence seemed notably slower and measured, as if each word was carefully thought out before being freed. "Not the case. Jerry here overreacted to the situation. Let's not debate it. We need to get you cleaned up."

Evie was confounded by the relationship between the three, the uncertainty adding to the oddly vulnerable experience. The sense of panic hadn't entirely diminished, despite the more immediate relief, so she closed her eyes to minimize the sensory input. Within a second, a firm hand steadied her arm.

"Jerry, please take the tray and what little is left of it from..." Strong but gentle fingers squeezed Evie's arm before slowly releasing it.

"Evelyn. Evie. O'Halloran. Dr. Evelyn...um...Evie O'Halloran." Quick and stuttered. Unsure. She stopped talking, embarrassed by her comparatively flustered response, and surveyed the stranger. Even at a glance, there were innumerable differences between them. Whereas Evie was a sloppy mess now, this woman's outfit was on the dressy end of casual and decidedly not as sporty as one would expect at a football game. Yet at the same time, she had an athletic vibe. Neatly pressed gray slacks hung from slim hips, and an equally tailored black shirt was visible beneath a quality, dark gray, wool waistcoat.

Square shoulders. Sharp. She was nicely accessorized, too. Silver hoop earrings showed below an ultra-short and trendy haircut, and a matching necklace softened a decidedly left-of-femme androgyny. She wondered if the attire was true to the woman. If it *fit*. Did it really matter? The overall effect was impressive.

And from what Evie had surmised from her students and the glimpses of pop culture she'd allowed herself, gender was so much more fluid—acceptably fluid—among the younger generations. Not that this woman was that young. Maybe mid-thirties? *You are so out of touch, Evie.* At forty-seven, what did she know about trends and gender-based fashion choices? Not much. Furthermore, her ability to identify who fit and who didn't was astonishingly bad, even when practiced. And she was entirely out of practice.

"Mark, will you please reach out to facilities and let them know about the elevator malfunction?" Ms. Hoops surveyed the area around the elevator and pulled her shoulders back before nodding toward him. "And would you stay near until they arrive so that no one else tries to use it?"

"I called," Evie said. "On the elevator phone. I suppose that was facilities I spoke with. They said they were coming, but that was, well, a while ago."

"Well, Dr. Evelyn Evie O'Halloran, let's see what we can do to remedy this regrettable incident."

Evie hadn't imagined it. There was something quite unusual about the cadence of her speech, as if it was a beat or two slower than most people's. Evelyn wasn't sure if this was Ms. Hoops's normal pattern, or if she was being patronized. She doubted the latter because each word, her name especially, flowed as if it was carried on a river of honey.

"And you are?" Evie managed.

"Merr Shepherd." More honey.

Evie wondered if she'd heard her correctly. "Merr? As in Mary? Or are you a Marilyn?"

"Close, but please just call me Merr."

It was probably a question, but Evelyn detected the polite straightforwardness of the request. No fuss. Easy. Sharp, clear edges.

Merr it is.

❖

The handrails leading up to the eighth floor were unsurprisingly cold. Merritt knew from experience that September in Regina was like the proverbial shot across the bow, and the cold would come. But she'd spent time in much colder locales in Saskatchewan, so she couldn't complain. She could easily imagine that the good Doctor O'Halloran would be feeling the barely-short-of-freezing temperature down to her core. Even if she hadn't been soaked, she wasn't exactly dressed for the weather. Merritt figured that the light fleece pullover had absorbed most of the hot chocolate but certainly not all. Anything beneath it would be equally saturated. She took a moment to appreciate Evelyn's full figure. Shapely top and bottom, with a narrow waist. Was it still okay to think of someone as buxom? *Didn't matter.* Her ample curves totally checked off Merritt's boxes.

"Are you watching the game from a suite?"

"No, I'm at field level."

Merritt held back a gasp. *In the stands? In this weather? Are you crazy?* She glanced over her shoulder, sensing that Evie—a step below—had slowed. She took a second to reassure herself that she'd not, in fact, spoken the words that shouted in her head. Including those about Evie's curves.

"I only ask because you're not exactly dressed for the outdoors. And you were in the suite elevator." Merritt noticed her drop another step. "Not a big deal, obviously, though I'm sure you're regretting the choice now," she added quickly, smiling so that it couldn't be interpreted as criticism.

Evie shrugged and smiled back before catching up on the

stairs. "Not the best of days so far. I'm not a fan of elevators. I only snuck on to the luxury lift because I didn't trust myself on the stairs with the drinks. And you're quite right about my wardrobe choice." She glanced at her fleece and nodded. "It's a long story, but my ride promised he knew about some secret parking spot near our gate, but after circling the stadium for an unendurable amount of time, we ended up at the far lot, and in the rush to make kickoff, I forgot my coat in the car."

"He sounds like a prince." She resisted smiling and continued up the stairs.

"Let's not go there. Robby has time to find better."

Merritt turned. "Robby? His..." She struggled with her guess. Was he the driver's son? Father? Boyfriend? She was rescued before she needed to choose.

"Girlfriend. Robby is my sister Bev's daughter. Great young woman. And smart. But Kevin, who drove today, isn't evidence of that. Hopefully, she ends it before he sticks."

Evie rolled her eyes, and the verdant flash struck Merritt. Set in notably dark and long lashes, the green was fierce but also kind. Keen and gentle. *Interesting.* She waited until Evie stepped up beside her as they turned on the landing to begin the final set of stairs.

"I hate being late," she continued. "When I realized I'd forgotten my coat, I'd hoped for one of the scarves they were giving out today to the first fans."

"Ah, so you're on the Roughriders' side. I might've pegged you for an Argonauts fan."

Evie abruptly stepped back. "God, no! Whatever would make you think that?"

"Er, maybe the 'fashion over function' decision?" She faced Evie and turned her hand toward the still-dripping sweater. It was intended as a light-hearted jab. Toronto's Argo fans were often the butt of many a Western Canadian's jokes.

Evie laughed. It was sweet and unaffected. "Well, I must give you that. Again, though, not by choice."

Merritt was glad she could find humor in the situation. And that she'd accepted the invitation to come up to the corporate suite. The suite had a private bathroom that would accommodate a thorough cleanup, and Merritt was sure she could find something suitably dry for her to change into. Surely, no one in the suite would mind. After all, it was Conroy's overzealousness that had led to the incident, and so it should fall, Merritt rationalized, to his employer to help clean up the mess. Ironically, that was exactly why Merritt was at Farmexal. *Albeit a different sort of mess.* The company's hands were far too full, and considering the odd bits of doughnut debris still clinging to Dr. Evelyn Evie O'Halloran, so were Merritt's.

CHAPTER TWO

Evie was relieved that her heart was back to beating at an acceptable rate and was grateful for her escape from the elevator and for her uncompromising cardio regime. She'd followed Merr and her friend, Jerry, up several flights of stairs to the corporate box level as if on autopilot. Were they friends? No, that didn't seem to fit, even though both he and the man who'd remained to babysit the broken elevator—Mark?—hung on every word she'd said. The power imbalance was curious. Maybe she was their boss? As they arrived at the upper mezzanine, Jerry flashed his lanyard to stadium security staff, who nodded them through the turnstile.

Soon, the cement floor turned to red carpet, and the dull fluorescent overheads turned to indirect sconce lighting that marked each in the long row of identical doors. As they passed, Evie noted the names on the plaques marking the corporate and individual family suite owners. Carts stacked with silver domes rolled quietly past. She had attended a university fundraising event held in one of the elegant boxes a few years ago, and the old-school opulence would have surprised her otherwise. The Saskatchewan Roughriders remained one of very few publicly owned sports franchises, sustained by an enormous and dedicated fan base. When it came to football worship in Saskatchewan, the temple was fittingly grand.

Eventually, Jerry came to a stop and pulled open a door. Evie took one look at the plaque posted near the suite entrance and froze.

Farmexal.

"I can't go in there," she said, her hand flying to her chest as if she was being asked to cross the River Styx.

"I promise you, it's bigger than an elevator," Merr said gently. She seemed perplexed at Evie's hesitation.

Evie succeeded in suppressing her initial response, which would have been far from gracious. Instead, she set her jaw and drew a breath. "No, that's not it. I can't in good conscience go in." She pointed at the plaque. "Farmexal? You work for Farmexal?"

Merr's expression changed from concern and confusion to realization, followed by puzzlement, and ending in conciliation. Evie noticed in spite of herself how each expression was framed within a classically lovely face. Eyes dark like molasses but lightened by gold flecks. High cheekbones etched by deep dimples. Adorably deep. Full lips that required no color or contour, even when pursed in what now appeared to be a look of guardedness.

"Ah."

"Ah?" Evie felt herself growing impatient. Maybe she was being patronized after all. "That's all you have to say? You work for the company that, well, that should be ashamed of itself. In fact, I'm going to tomorrow's meeting."

"Are you now?" Merr was clearly trying to hold back a smile.

Evie shifted and crossed her arms. "Yes. And so are many of my students. Like them, I have some serious concerns about the kind of business you do. Farmexal does." Her assertiveness, usually one of her best weapons in conflict situations, waffled. Merr's accommodating nature was disarming, and Evie's resolve suddenly felt inadequate. Melting. *No, not Farmexal.* She rallied. "I can't go"—she pointed again at the sign—"in there."

"Dr. O'Halloran, I understand, but what choice do you have?" Merr paused as if realizing she'd taken the wrong tack. "I don't recommend people set aside their moral objections without reason, and I understand that people, some people, have chosen to protest. That's important in some situations, in my opinion, for a healthy democracy. Provided it's peaceful. I won't insult you by explaining that the allegations are merely that at this point, and there's no evidence that Farmexal has participated in anything illegal."

Every word was perfectly measured and difficult to refute. Evie had reacted with outrage to the media reports of empty Farmexal totes—square plastic containers used for agricultural chemicals—being found illegally dumped in farm fields neighboring the city. Knowing that concentrated fertilizer, disposed improperly, could create environmental damage, she'd decided to attend the "community information meeting" Farmexal was about to host. The meeting was obviously a PR stunt to stem public pressure, but she'd nonetheless organized students in the university's Planet Change group to bus from Saskatoon to Regina to attend.

Robby's current boyfriend, Kevin, regularly painted Farmexal as akin to an environmental monster. The same Kevin who'd promised a secret parking spot. What was it she always told her students? *Check your sources.*

She still felt strongly that Farmexal was ultimately responsible for the situation, but in the back of her mind, she wondered if she'd done her own due diligence. It was difficult, considering Merr's fair and rational proposal, to maintain her tenuous high ground. Especially when soaking wet. And cold. Resistance was as futile as the Borg made it sound.

She put what energy she had into avoiding what she imagined would be Merr's smug gaze, clenched her teeth, and followed her into the suite.

The room was long and narrow, ending in an open view of

the field below. The walls were cluttered with photographs of various Roughriders together with people Evie imagined were Farmexal employees. Green leather armchairs and couches were tastefully placed so that they had a view of a mounted, large-screen TV, below which sat a table covered with an abundance of game-day food. Toward the open end, high-top tables had a sight line over the four or so terraced rows of stadium-style seats. She grimaced at the opulence. It turned her stomach and set her to wondering, as she often did, if luxury like this had come at an irreversible cost to the planet.

There were twenty or so people in the box, and most appeared intent on watching the game. The one notable exception was a leggy blonde wearing a short black leather skirt and a green sweater. She was almost bouncing as Merr approached, and Evie swore she'd pulled her shoulders back to further accentuate the oversized "I Like It Rough" slogan spread across her equally oversized chest. Evie doubted it was an officially sanctioned sweatshirt. The blonde flitted unwaveringly toward them, but her focus was entirely on Merr.

Merr threw her a dismissive glare that only succeeded in redirecting the chesty stalker's attention to Evie.

"Hi, I'm Kelly," she piped, thrusting her hand toward Evie. "Are you with our Merr?" Her tone was as genuine as her objectionable sweatshirt, and she emphasized the word "our" royally.

With Merr? Our Merr? What does that mean? Before Evie could formulate a response, Merr gently placed a hand under Kelly's elbow and guided her purposefully toward Jerry. She couldn't hear the words exchanged, but Kelly's energy visibly deflated as she pulled sharply away, scowled at Evie, and moved back toward the seated fans with Jerry in her wake.

"I'm sorry about that," Merr said, her words stopping short of describing Kelly.

"What is it exactly that you do at Farmexal?"

Merr shrugged. "It's really quite boring stuff. Process quality assurance, that kind of thing. My brother calls me a bean counter." While explaining, she'd ushered Evie to a large, wood-grain door and pulled on the handle, revealing a bathroom suite complete with a shower and stocked with plenty of thick white and green towels. Evie was again aware of whose corporate box she was about to benefit from, and she hesitated.

As if reading her mind, Merr stepped politely back. "Dr. O'Halloran, I ask that you reserve judgment...in fairness, the court of public opinion has not been presented with all of the evidence." Her words were again thoughtful and clear but not condescending.

Evie held her ground, still wet. "True, though you must admit, it looks pretty bad. It's not like just one empty tote has been found. And all of them have had your company's name embossed on them." Yet here she was, in that same company's corporate box. No doubt ground zero for schmoozing greedy shareholders. A place where executives schemed to keep profits high at any cost.

"I understand. All I can say is that there are things we, meaning all of us, don't know yet. Perhaps in light of that, and that..." Merr pointed to the sweater stains. "You might want to consider a temporary truce? You can't go back to your seat in those clothes. You'll freeze, and then Farmexal will have a whole new legal entanglement on its hands."

Evie loved her humor and hated that she was right. "You're very gracious." *She was.* "Still, it is entirely reasonable to be concerned about the environmental impact of potential spills. And I'm not talking about these kinds of spills." She smiled.

It was obvious how hard it was for Merr to keep a straight face, but she regrouped quickly. "Of course not. We should all be concerned. And I promise you, Dr. O'Halloran, Farmexal is."

"Please call me Evelyn. Or Evie. My doctorate is in geology, not medicine. Only my students call me doctor. Unless they've just failed an exam, and then it's something quite different altogether."

She was delighted to have made Merr smile. The dimples really were adorably deep. And distracting. "If it helps, I'm new with Farmexal and would like to make a good impression." Merr nodded toward the crowd, including Kelly, whose gaze shot back like a laser across the room. "Please, let me help you."

Evie relented, satisfied that her choices were limited, and she wasn't truly compromising her beliefs but rather shelving them until she had more compelling data. That seemed fair. Merr waited until Evie was inside the luxurious room before pulling the door closed.

Evie had peeled off her fleece, now just a hot chocolate sponge, and the shirt underneath. She stared at her reflection, wondering if she should remove her bra, which had sopped up the last bit of drink. She'd celebrated her mid-forties with a revived commitment to fitness, and while there was still an acceptable middle-aged softness, her core was strong, and she'd managed to keep her curvy parts a comfortable mix of high and tight. Decision made, she took the undergarment off and added it to the pile before washing herself down.

The warm water reminded her of Merr's unusual speech pattern. Slow-moving. Deliberate. Comforting. She almost jumped out of her skin at the light knock on the door.

"It's me."

God, did she know I was thinking about her? Evie covered herself with a towel before pulling back on the door enough to allow a still-tagged Roughriders hooded sweatshirt and tee to be passed through.

"I hope you're okay with a bunny hug. It's the warmest thing I could find."

Evie smiled at the local reference. "Bunny hug" was a Saskatonian term for a hoodie, rumored to have evolved when an overpopulation of rabbits in the area resulted in the creation of a furry garment that resembled a sweatshirt. True story or not, the name had stuck. "It's perfect, thanks."

"Just leave your clothes in there, and we'll have them cleaned and back to you early next week."

Evie looked at her bra atop the pile on the floor. "Not necessary, but thank you."

"Of course it is, Dr...Evie. Again, I insist. It's the least we can do, given how you feel about Farmexal cleaning up our messes." Something in Merr's tone convinced her that she wasn't about to give up.

"Fine. Thank you. It's very kind of you." She slid the door closed and pulled on the tee and hoodie. Then she lifted her bra from the pile, folded it in a facecloth and tucked it into the back of her jeans.

❖

Merritt leaned against the wall, waiting for Evie to emerge and taking care not to look in Kelly's direction. A personal relationship with the bouncy coworker would be as unprofessional as it was unlikely. Kelly Paxton was the assistant to the CEO, James Chisley. He was the reason Merritt was at Farmexal. Kelly's duties seemed to exceed her title. She organized her boss's schedule, the company picnic, and managed Farmexal's public relations communiques. Under the circumstances, even if there had been an attraction, which there certainly was not as far as Merritt was concerned, the conflict of interest alone would have made it impossible. Hopefully, now that she'd made her position abundantly clear, her ardent admirer would keep her distance.

Just to make sure, she avoided Kelly's death stare and directed her attention to the chitchat currently being exchanged between Einerson and Conroy. When he'd returned from tending to the elevator situation, Einerson had reported that the facility personnel were on-site and that their delay was because of a more critical scoreboard issue. He'd then relayed each excruciating detail with Conroy, who'd lapped them up as if a burned-out bulb could truly jeopardize the Roughriders' lead. That conversation had pivoted with a poorly executed attempt by Conroy to convince Einerson to lend him his pass for a parking garage near the casino.

"I'll only use it on nights you don't work," Conroy promised.

"No chance, Jer. I'm sitting on gold, and I'm not about to give it away," Einerson countered.

Merritt knew that in the winter, parking garage spots within a short walk of virtually any casino were hard to come by. She didn't blame Einerson for his lack of generosity. But Conroy did not relent, and if only to prevent her head from exploding, she decided to end the relentless banter.

"Jerry, would you mind putting together a few hot chocolates from the beverage bar to replace the ones that soaked Dr. O'Halloran?"

He nodded and eagerly headed toward the beverage bar. Before she could redirect Einerson to something more constructive, he'd already begun chatting with one of the Farmexal executives who'd moved nearer, presumably to wait for the bathroom to empty. She noted how adeptly Einerson had maneuvered. True, he might be avoiding her. Maybe he realized that a contract employee doing a quality audit for the company wasn't worth sucking up to. Fair enough. To him—in fact, to everyone at Farmexal except the owner and his chief officers—that was who Merritt Shepherd was. Regardless, in her mind, she ticked a "follow-up" box beside his name.

❖

Evie was pulling tags off the sleeve of her hoodie as she stepped out of the bathroom and for the second time that afternoon, almost ran straight into Merr. Before she could react, a burly man with an entirely incongruous, and almost comically large, knit 'Riders toque pushed between them and into the bathroom. She shook her head and blushed, feeling far too conspicuous for comfort.

"I am so sorry. Honestly, I've really put you out. And your colleagues, apparently." She nodded toward the door that thudded shut behind her.

"Don't worry yourself. I rather enjoy your commitment."

Commitment? As in, committed to bumping into her? Evie's blush reignited against her will. She still felt rocked by the whole elevator situation and closed her eyes to ground herself. She must have misunderstood. Imagining flirtation now? Ridiculous. She could sense Merr's scrutiny and still couldn't formulate a coherent response. When she did finally look, the dark eyes she'd noticed earlier now seemed edged with an almost ethereal smokiness. *Wow.* It had been a very, very long time since she'd felt the wave of emotion hitting her now. It seeped into her chest, her heart pumping like a puppy's, excited and erratic to the point that when it skipped the odd beat, it didn't set off alarms. Rather, it caused her breath to catch slightly, as if signaling her to ride with the flow of energy. Attraction. A long time.

"Thank you, Jerry."

Jerry?

"Dr. Evie?"

She snapped back into focus, hoping that her mental meandering hadn't been noticed. She also reminded herself sharply where she was. *The enemy camp.* Jerry had magically reappeared and stood beside Merr, handing her a small box filled with insulated, Yeti-style 'Riders cups. He then disappeared as suddenly back into the booth.

"I hope you don't mind, but I feel that, at the very least, drink replacements are necessary. These cups will hold up a lot better than the paper ones, and they're planet-friendly. If you get stuck anywhere between here and your seat, they'll keep your drinks indefinitely hot. Obviously, they're also spill-proof. I trust this

will begin to amend your personal relationship with Farmexal."
She put them gently on a nearby coffee table.

Did Merr just emphasize the word *personal*? Evie's puppy
heart thumped. Or suggest that she was clumsy? Spill-proof?
Damn it. "Let's not forget that manufacturing these cups, reusable
though they may be, has a cumulative impact on the ozone. And
eventually landfills." Evie checked herself, seeing the smile fade
and a perfectly shaped eyebrow rise above one of the wondrous
eyes before her. "If Farmexal really wants to make amends," she
teased, "these drinks would contain a good dollop of Cointreau
and several small marshmallows."

Merr smiled, and again, the puppy heart thumped. Evie
silently scolded herself.

"Sacrilege, Dr. Evie. Marshmallows do not belong on a
respectable hot chocolate."

For some reason she couldn't quite put a finger on, Evie
found herself unwilling to correct the moniker that Merr
seemed to have adopted and possibly worse, laughed despite
her reservations. "Were you a victim of the dreaded 'upper-lip-
marshmallow-burn'?"

"Not exactly. Just a quirk, I suppose." Again, Merr's words
were pleasantly and slowly measured.

Jerry returned with a bag and handed it to Merr. She pulled
out three team T-shirts and offered them to Evie.

"Thank you, but I really must decline. You..." *Correction.*
"Farmexal has done quite enough for today."

"Well, I hope we can do even better tomorrow." Merr pulled
a pen and small notepad from an inside jacket pocket and handed
it to her. "Would you mind jotting down your contact info? So we
can make sure we return your clothes?"

As Evie accepted the pad and pen, she noticed Kelly lurking
more closely. In seconds, she had sidled up to Merr.

"Mr. Chisley is wondering where you've gotten to." Her tone
was a mix of deferential and directive. It was heavier on the latter,

and Evie didn't miss the dismissive glance Merritt cast at her in response. She wondered if perhaps there was something going on between the two. Something beyond business. It seemed clear that at least Kelly wanted there to be. Evie chafed at the thought, set down her office address, and picked up the box of drinks.

"I'll be there shortly, Kelly. Please make sure Dr. O'Halloran's clothes are sent for cleaning?" Evie nearly smirked at the impersonal tone imbued in Merr's response. "They're in the bag in the bathroom." Her tone lightened as she addressed Jerry. "Would you be so kind as to accompany our friend to her seat?" Her attention then returned to Evie. "One more thing, if you don't mind." She took the box from her and handed it to Jerry, then took a smaller bag from inside the one containing the T-shirts. She pulled a green and white knitted scarf out and looped it around Evie's neck. "I arrived here plenty early today."

The surprisingly intimate gesture silenced Evie. She placed her palms on the scarf and felt another puppy thump. *Calm down. Enemy camp.*

Merr stepped back and smiled, dimples deepening. "It looks much better on you."

"I doubt that's true, but thanks." *Say good-bye before you make a fool of yourself.* Evie quickly wrote her building and room number at the university on the paper and handed it to Merr. "Perhaps we'll meet again some time."

"Perhaps sooner than you think." Merr smiled and touched Evie's forearm, squeezing it gently as she took the address. Then she headed toward the viewing end of the room.

As Evie walked through the mezzanine, Jerry at her heels carrying her box of drinks, she wondered about Farmexal's "new" employee. It seemed strange that she would have such authority over so many at the company as a mere…what was it she'd said? Bean counter? The dissonance was simply curious, harmless, certainly. But it was part of a larger conundrum their meeting had stirred in her. Merr was attractive. Plenty attractive. Had she been flirting? Or was she simply being a good corporate soldier?

A bit presumptuous. Annoyingly charming. Who was she really? Would Evie see her again? While wondering what Merr meant when she'd said "sooner than you think," Evie almost walked into the elevator before rerouting, Jerry still in tow, toward the stairs.

CHAPTER THREE

Merritt wasn't sure which scent had broken through to her half-asleep, somewhat-awake brain first. The mocha and caramel undertones of what she hoped was a French-roast coffee? The soft woodsy aftershave she'd finally convinced its wearer to apply at a level well below the advertiser's recommendations? Or perhaps the completely surprising yet intoxicating aroma that suggested apricot and almond? She heard the familiar thud of her large diner-style mug landing on her bedside table. One eye fluttered open. Dark roast, black. Check. Next, she felt her mattress depress and rise with increasing energy two, now three times.

Both eyes popped wide open, and the bouncing stopped. Brother Max. Check. "Not that I don't appreciate the service, but maybe knock next time? And God, what is that creation?" She could already feel the sugar coursing through her veins as she pried the plate of pastry from his hands. Breakfast. Check.

"It's a palmier. The classic. With a clear apricot glaze, just the way you like it. And don't make me laugh about intruding without knocking, as if you've got someone in here with you. Besides, it's Monday morning, and the bakery is closed so this is your only bedside service of the week. Our schedules haven't been crossing lately."

"That's because I am *not* a morning person, and you usually leave for work at three a.m."

Max was the baker and owner of the new local pastry shop, Boulangerie de la Régine. The name was a mixed-language tip-of-the-hat to both the queen and the city.

"The dough isn't going to knead itself, and in at least two ways, I knead dough. Ha-ha. *Knead* dough. *Need* dough. See what I did there?"

Merritt groaned. Like his wordplay with la Régine, her brother's sense of humor was similarly mixed. Customarily, it was an agonizing mishmash of knock-knock jokes, puns, and almost every bad dad joke. *Okay, all.* She knew from experience that her groan was a response to his self-satisfaction more than it was to his material. He was always his best audience.

"You know, Max, Uncle Joe's money would've gone a lot further if you hadn't insisted on attending the very best patisserie school and owning one of the nicest apartments in Regina."

"Yes, but it's in one of the worst parts of town." He laughed and bounced again. Simultaneously. *Pest.* "As for school, take a bite of that before judging my inheritance spending."

She knew his comment wasn't meant to remind her of what had happened to her share of their uncle's estate. She could never forget. Max was absolutely right, though, the palmier was sublime. Worth every penny.

"Speaking of dough," she said as she poked him, Pillsbury-style, in the stomach, "if I'm still in town, let's try to go for a ride next weekend. Before it gets too cold. Sunday afternoon once you've closed up the kitchen, right?"

"Yep. As it stands, we still close early on Sunday and are closed on Monday. That might not last. Business is picking up as people look to get out of the cold and into something warm and cozy. I'd like to meet demand."

"And you don't have a girlfriend."

"Obvs. For now. But I'm only thirty." he replied while

glancing around her room, his eyes landing on the empty side of her bed. "And clearly, singlehood runs in the family. What's your excuse, O great older-and-wiser?"

"Jerk." She smiled and rolled her eyes as she bit into the pastry, realizing that she'd come to rely on Max for more than empty calories since landing in Regina a month prior. He'd happily given her a key to his loft and had insisted that his "far older sister"—by a mere four years—stay with him until something else came along. He seemed to know better than to ask when that might be. She was just grateful that he knew her almost better than anyone.

"You did ask me to wake you up this morning, right? I have a bit of inventory to assess, so I'm off to work. And so are you, I imagine, to do whatever it is you do?"

"I told you. I'm doing a contract for Farmexal."

"Yes, you said. You're a 'compliance auditor.'" He air-quoted the last two words.

"I was wrong. You do 'listen' to me sometimes." She smiled, and poked him again.

"And so you came here to majestic Regina. All the way from Ottawa." His skeptical tone paired perfectly with his dubious expression. "Leaving your cushy government job to make a bit of extra cash. Do I have that right?"

"Well, I came to see my favorite brother."

"Only brother. But okay. I won't push you into telling me your secrets." He jumped off her bed with a bounce equal to his landing. "As long as you stay out of trouble."

"Naturally, bro, naturally."

With her history as a lead investigator with the enforcement team of the Ministry of Environmental Resources, he seemed to accept that there might be times she couldn't be completely honest. It wasn't that she didn't trust him. He was a vault. But she didn't want to put him in an awkward spot if things ever got dicey. They seldom did. But today might change that.

This afternoon, in an ill-conceived effort to reduce the

suspicions building in the community, Farmexal would be holding a public information meeting. Merritt had concerns about how the session might go. When CEO Chisley had reached out to the ministry to report the inventory losses they'd experienced, he'd accepted that an investigator would be sent to assess risk. As soon as Merritt had arrived, she'd observed the community concern over the apparent illegal dumping of the fertilizer and had suggested he make the company's response to the situation clear.

She had been thinking of something like an interview with a local reporter. As earnest as Chisley appeared to be, he did seem deeply affected by the rumors circulating about Farmexal and was letting his emotions get the best of him. He'd called for a public meeting. She'd tried to convince him otherwise because an open meeting meant protesters. In her experience, protesters could push the meeting's agenda in a far different direction. When she couldn't change his mind about a public meeting, she'd attempted to prepare him for how best to present an empathetic yet cogent message in such a potentially uncontrolled event. That was when he'd dug his heels in. Deep. He'd forcefully expressed his antipathy for what was quickly snowballing into a media frenzy, and he had little tolerance for the mounting protests.

"If they're mad, let them tell me why face-to-face," he'd said.

She feared where his bravado might lead and prepared for the aftermath, reminding herself to have a brief chat with the venue's security team. Protesters could be as passionate and obstinate as Chisley. She wondered if Dr. Evie was still planning on attending. *Of course she is. Passionate and obstinate. And lovely.* It was possible Merritt might not see her, depending on the crowd size, but it was more likely Dr. Evie would see her.

Merritt's preference was to stay out of the spotlight, but unless Chisley was miraculously able to rein in his emotions, she might be drawn into it. Which meant that Merritt could not let herself be distracted. But as her thoughts traveled back to the decidedly alluring Dr. Evelyn O'Halloran for the umpteenth time since Saturday's football game, she realized that was precisely where she was headed.

Focus on the job. Focus on Farmexal.

It took fortitude, but she replaced thoughts of Evie with the mantra and reflected on each member of the staff she'd spent time with thus far. How likely were they to be involved in the thefts? Chisley had invited scrutiny and was obviously in over his head. It was hard to imagine he would be capable of much beyond his current position. Of the two "boys," Mark Einerson was the quieter one. Maybe that impression was a matter of relativity, though, since he was usually with the oafish and constantly prattling Jerry Conroy. Conroy was, well, like Casper: transparent. The likelihood that he was involved was low, given his inability to stifle himself. Kelly Paxton was irritating but not hard to figure out, with behavior that stretched from flirty and friendly to petty and bitter, with a propensity for drama that stretched Merritt's patience. Fortunately, Merritt had worked these kinds of investigations before, and managing people's emotions were part of the skill set needed to get the job done.

Game time.

She looked at the clock. 7:20 a.m.

Get up and get at it.

She popped the last curl of flaky pastry into her mouth, chased it with the final, wonderfully chewy swig of coffee, and headed to the shower.

CHAPTER FOUR

The Hotel Saskatchewan was the oldest and certainly grandest of the historic hotels in town. Evie preferred its heritage aesthetic to the relatively impersonal modern high-rises that constituted most of Regina's offerings. She had stayed in many, but a few years ago had made the more contemporary casino hotel her touchstone because it was a shorter walk to her sister's house. And because she was a regular player, the pit boss always upgraded her to a suite. This weekend, however, the casino was fully booked with a poker tournament, and she couldn't have her usual. Lucky for her, Farmexal was holding its public meeting in one of the regal stone railway hotel's most elegant venues, the old library. She headed downstairs ten minutes early, hoping to meet Robby near the elevators so they could walk up to the mezzanine level together. As she descended to the first floor, she wondered if she might see the mysterious Merr Shepherd at today's assembly.

After plenty of thoughts about Farmexal's new hire since their encounter on Saturday, Evie had landed on the notion that Merr was tied more closely to the company's brass than she might have let on. Not that it mattered. Or did it? She was smart, well-spoken, and gracious. Who wouldn't hire her? But why be coy? Was she being coy? Was Evie being played? And if so, so what? Was it so bad to be the object of an attractive woman's interest? A younger, sexy woman? After all, if someone was going to occupy her mind, Merr was inarguably her type. If she had a type. There had been so much disconnect in Evie's personal life that lately, she wasn't sure.

The past few years, COVID had provided her with an additional excuse to keep her circle of contacts small: her sister and niece, two or three colleagues, and a couple of grad students she was supervising. But recently, she'd agreed to act as the faculty contact for the campus environmental group, Planet Change. Much of her work, outside of lectures once in-class sessions were deemed safe, was research-based and somewhat solitary, though intensely satisfying. And necessary.

She also adored her family and spent every other weekend and holidays with them, especially during football season. And of course, there was Walter. Maybe that was why, if she was honest, her pre-pandemic social circle hadn't been much bigger. Nor did it include anyone of a romantic nature. Nothing serious, at least. She had gone on a few dates before COVID, but nothing had clicked. They were nice enough, smart enough, but she didn't feel enough of anything to warrant a second date, let alone something sexual. Was this what middle-age felt like? Or was she truly in a rut? Now that things were back to the new normal, despite her elevator-induced, carpe-diem-esque epiphany, Evie couldn't imagine the circle widening in that direction. Merr's direction. Highly unlikely. Yet, here she was, imagining exactly that.

She distracted herself while waiting by appreciating the stunning sequence of segmental arches that lured her gaze upward to the magnificent vaulted ceiling. She looked a bit lower and noticed the blinking lights above the elevator doors. *Blinking lights on the inside, too.* Was that what she'd been staring at when she'd bolted through the doors to escape? Was that why she hadn't seen Merr until she'd almost crashed into her? *Not almost. Did. Ostensibly.* Yet there'd been no trace of spillage on Merr's clothes. How was that possible?

Before she could sort it out, Evie was enveloped by a hug

that squeezed every bit of air from her lungs. She gasped with delight. "Robby! Girl, you just about scared me into next week."

It amazed Evie every time she took in the sight of her slender niece just how lovely a person she'd grown into. Robby was wearing a T-shirt emblazoned with "Take the High," and its green color set off the emerald eyes that ran in the O'Halloran clan.

"Hey there, Auntie Evie."

"Love that you've evoked Michelle," Evie laughed, pointing at the slogan. "Hard to believe you're what? Thirty now?"

Robby laughed. "Ha. You wish. I'm almost forty, and yes, I'm expecting a big celebration, courtesy of my much older aunt."

The banter felt familiar and loving. Evie was only seven years older, so Robby felt more like a sister than a niece. As they walked up the stairs, they held hands and filled each other in on their lives since they'd last chatted. Which was almost every day.

"And how's your room? Swanky, I imagine?"

"It's gorgeous. I tried to stay at the casino hotel, but there was no room at the inn. Besides, it's cold out there, and I'm glad not to have to venture out again." She had seen thin waves of white powder billowing across the gray sidewalks on her stroll this morning and knew it wouldn't be long before the prairie winds blew inescapably colder from the northwest.

"Speaking of, where's Walter?"

Anyone who knew Walter also knew he never missed his morning walk. "His Highness barely dragged himself around the block this morning. I left him to sleep. He woke me up three times last night."

"Chewing on towels?"

"You guessed it." Evie shook her head in dismay. "Tell me, what possesses a five-year-old terrier to suddenly take a shine to towels? Correction, hotel towels. Apparently, the towels at home aren't good enough."

"Don't ask me. I think he's trying to tell you he needs more mom-time."

"Very funny." Evie elbowed her playfully. "We took a two-hour walk along Wascana Valley yesterday." She'd been taking both Robby and Walter on hikes along the well-used trail for years. Its gently rolling hills, meandering creek, and incredible vistas revitalized her. Usually. "He didn't even make it as far as the bridge. Insisted I carry him back."

Robby laughed. "You spoil that dog."

"I can't say you're wrong. But Cairns are a working breed. I'd hoped he'd be tougher."

"He is tough. He's also smart. Smarter than…"

"Don't say it, Robby, or I'll leave him to you in my will. And may God have mercy on your linens."

When they arrived on the mezzanine floor, Robby paused and looked down each massive hallway "Where are your Planet Change kids?"

"They texted me a while ago. They're already in the meeting room. Eager, the lot of them."

The library doors stood open, and the sound of raised voices filled the anteroom.

"I think it's great that you're helping stoke their activism. Speaking of eager, I'm pretty sure Kevin is also inside." Robbie looked at her phone, and Evie assumed she was looking for confirmation.

Kevin. *Great. Glad he found a parking spot.*

"Sounds like there's a good-sized crowd," Evie said, pleased that the community had shown up to express its concerns. Approaching the doors, she could see a glut of people damming the entryway, and she paused to consider their options. Surely, there would be speakers so that those unable to get in would at least be able to hear Farmexal's response to the tote disposal issue.

Before she could settle on a plan, Robby took her hand. "Come on, Auntie E, Kevin has our seats." Robby almost yanked her off her feet, excusing herself and Evie as they wove between the rack of bodies until they broke into the main room and plunked into seats just a few rows back from the podium.

The two men from Merr's odd entourage stood between the audience and the raised platform stage, their arms crossed and feet apart as if ready for battle. Kevin, as expected, was on his feet, jeering along with several other protesters as the Farmexal officials walked onto the stage.

Where did she find this guy? And when will she put him back? Evie scanned the filled rows behind. The turnout was impressive and beyond standing room only. She was struck by how tense the room had already become.

"Ladies and gentlemen. May I have your attention please?" A deep male voice filled the library, and the crowd hushed, heads turning to the dais at the front of the room. Evie started to settle until her eyes landed on a familiar figure standing near the side of the stage.

Merr Shepherd leaned against the wall, casually flipping through her phone. Every few seconds, she surveyed the crowd, then turned back to the screen. She might've been trying to look innocuous, but she looked captivating instead. Handsome, really. Makeup, just a touch. Enough to accentuate her dark eyes and highlight her classic cheekbones. Accessories, equally subdued but effective. Navy-blue pantsuit, pristine and fitted. Broad shoulders, muscled thighs. Gray pinstriped cotton shirt. Tailored. Nicely fitted. Block-heel suede ankle boots, tasteful. Surprising, Evie had to admit, but tasteful. Regardless of which side of the butch-femme spectrum Merr preferred, she appeared to float seamlessly between them. Today, Evie appreciated her style. It really fit. So did the strength and confidence that radiated as a result.

Process quality auditor, my ass. Who is she, really?

"What a bunch of privileged hacks," Kevin muttered loud enough to draw the attention of everyone in their row, the two rows ahead, and even Merr at the far end. His words had the same effect as lifting the lid on a simmering pot, and the anger steamed from beneath. The room filled with jeers again, and the crowd rumbled, increasingly impatient and vocal. Demanding. Her kids, as she regularly referred to her students, were seated closer to Merr's side of the room and near the front. They enthusiastically joined in the heckling, but their calls to action were more intelligently expressed than those on Team Kevin. Evie was proud of their commitment, and given the percolating tensions, she was equally relieved they were near an exit door. Hopefully, the mood would simmer. She turned toward Merr, seeking reassurance.

❖

Merritt caught Evie's eye. *There she is. And just as lovely.* An annoying acoustic squeal filled the room, silencing the rabble and causing most to wince at the high-pitched sound. Merritt turned to see James Chisley, Farmexal's chief, pulling the microphone unnecessarily close to his mouth, the electronic whine growing louder. His posture had become confrontational and borderline aggressive, revealing his frustration with the crowd's boisterousness. His face was red, his brows furrowed. Merritt looked toward Evie again with concern as Chisley continued to alienate the attendees.

"There's no point in me starting if you're not going to listen," he said with a growl.

Not off to a good start.

"Farmexal wouldn't do something like this," he shouted, responding to another reproach from someone near the back of the room. "We didn't do anything wrong."

Does he remember nothing from his coaching? Don't make it personal.

"I grew up here and so did my kids."

Obviously, he doesn't remember a word. She sighed deeply. He wasn't a dumb man, but no one would know it now. He hadn't come close to following the plan. First, hear them. Then, acknowledge that he'd heard before moving on to the action plan. It was a straightforward and proven approach: accept responsibility where possible and avoid conflict by presenting a reasonable solution. But he had gone rogue. Clearly.

Another shout from the back of the room rose above the others. "We want our kids to grow up, too, not die of some crazy disease. We're not your dumping ground!"

The chorus erupted again. "Not your dumping ground! Not your dumping ground!"

Chisley stepped back from the microphone as if it was the reason his message wasn't being heard. "You can't blame us. Anybody could've tossed those totes. And we don't even know what was in the twenty or so we found."

It was as if he'd thrown kerosene on a lit match. Everyone was out of their chairs; if they had torches and pitchforks, they'd be raised along with fists. To this point, only twelve recovered totes had been made public. Admitting that almost twice that had been found was bad enough. Suggesting that Farmexal hadn't identified the substance contained in those totes was worse. Chisley had stoked the crowd's fears. Merritt could only shake her head as they pummeled him with questions, not waiting for answers.

"What do you mean, twenty?"

"Is it twelve, or is it twenty?"

"You don't even know what's in them?"

"Why are you lying to us?"

"Where were they found?"

"Did they saturate the ground at the sites?"

At last, and to her credit, Kelly gently took Chisley's elbow and moved him farther from the podium before she took his place at the microphone. It surprised Merritt that she had the fortitude to attempt to deescalate the situation.

"You have every right to be concerned," she began, "and as your neighbor, Farmexal is doing everything it can to ensure safe usage and disposal of all fertilizers. We have systems, and these incidents fall well outside of protocol." She stared at the crowd and smiled a Dale Carnegie smile while modestly adjusting her blouse.

The crowd responded as Kelly had no doubt hoped. A few people took their seats. A woman standing against one of the many bookcases that circled the room stepped forward and spoke equably. "I found a tote at the creek near my water source. How do I know my water is safe, and that my land will be viable come spring?"

"You have my word that we will investigate how that came to be. Please see me after this meeting to provide the specific location. We are formally looking into all reports of illegal disposal, and I assure you that Farmexal does not, nor has it ever, encouraged—let alone practiced—unsafe disposal of materials in our community or in any community." She paused, letting her words sink in. So far, she was acting more like a leader than Chisley. And for a moment, Merritt couldn't help but be impressed. *For just a moment.*

"We have tested the water tables near every one of the reported-to-date sites, twenty in total, and thus far, there is no contamination detectable." Then Kelly looked directly at Merritt. Stared at her as if looking for reinforcement. As if she was the coach and Kelly was the quarterback. Merritt guessed that Chisley's discretion was as dependable as his professionalism, and that Kelly knew Merritt's true purpose at Farmexal. While the room rumbled again at the number of totes, Merritt pretended to check her phone, hoping that her lack of acknowledgment would scuttle any notion that she was connected to the totes and their contents. To the public, and Farmexal's employees, Merr Shepherd was just another of the usual oversight auditors making sure Farmexal's fertilizer was produced in a stable, safe facility.

"Twenty so far...plus that lady's one," shouted the same weaselly, redheaded young man who had made the privileged hack comment earlier. "How many more are out there? Is Farmexal trying to poison us all?"

Kelly retreated from the podium. Nothing she could say would matter now. The room was a tinderbox, the fire restoked.

Chisley moved toward the stage edge. "Absolutely not! We didn't put those totes out there. Anyone could've!" His face was beet red. Kelly pulled on his sleeve as if to rein him in.

"They're your totes," another protester countered. "Farmexal's name is on them."

Kelly couldn't hold Chisley back. He moved recklessly closer to the crowd. Conroy stepped in front of him, apparently trying to keep a protective distance around his boss.

"We're not polluters!" Chisley's voice boomed above the shouts.

Dial it back, big fella.

"And that's up to you to prove," added another angry voice from just over Merritt's left shoulder. People rose to their feet and began to surge forward.

Merritt forced herself to remain calm. Just as she'd feared, things had gotten ugly.

❖

Kevin's chair was the first to fall. Evie almost tripped over it, jostled violently as the people in the row behind either scrambled to escape from the escalating confrontation or hastened to join it. Like dominos, the metal seats around her fell and folded, clanking like something from a prison riot. She was shocked at how quickly the serene hotel library had become charged with anger and frustration. Her hope for a peaceful protest rushed out with the level-headed majority headed for the exits. With relief, she saw Planet Change kids leading the way out.

She watched in disbelief as James Chisley stepped down from the platform toe to toe with Kevin and another protester. *This is not going to end well.* Several panicky people had squeezed between the stage and the combatants, catching Merr in their flow as they tried to leave. They left a small path of destruction behind, including the long blue skirting that had once circled the stage. Evie tried to push through, powerless to get to Merr and stay upright in the blue fabric wave. The skirting tangled in upturned chair legs, the satin rope stage barriers, and their brass posts. The shouting increased, and Evie clenched her teeth, set her shoulders back, and shifted into a higher gear. *Survival mode.* She reached for Robby, who was trying to pull Kevin back from Chisley. She managed to grab a sleeve before a surge of people fell behind them and knocked them both to the ground.

"Auntie E! Are you okay?"

Evie scrambled quickly to her feet with a single thought on her mind. *Leave now.* "I'm good."

Unbelievably, Kevin and Chisley were still engaged, even as more chairs went down around them. *Idiots.* Evie grabbed Robby's arm, lifted her, and pushed toward the front, desperate to reach the exit. The onslaught of bodies to their right crested, tossing them toward the center of the fracas. Amid the crush, Evie hurriedly scanned the crowd and again caught sight of Merr only an arm's length away.

Get to her. Merr appeared to regain her footing until another wave hit, and she went down. *Too late!* Evie's stomach tightened, and she craned her neck, then crouched low in the hope of seeing past the tangle. A flash of gray suede. Merr's boot. She pulled Robby toward it, but it once again vanished.

Disoriented, she was now close enough to the idiot Kevin— still embroiled with the idiot Chisley—to take hold of his sleeve. "Kevin, knock it off. Now is not the time."

Her commanding voice seemed to catch the antagonists off guard, and they paused. But just as quickly, another body pushed into her from behind, causing her to fall forward and Kevin to stumble back. As he sought to regain his balance, Merr emerged from the other side of the huddle. The blue stage apron was tangled around her boot, and she lurched forward as if trying to separate her boss and Robby's boyfriend. But she and Kevin collided, his elbow making bone-crushing contact with her perfect mouth.

"No! Stop," Evie screamed.

Blood poured from Merr's upper lip. Evie's stomach flipped at the sight, and she felt the room tip. She shook her head to right it. "Merr, Kevin, stop!" She could barely hear herself above the bedlam. Across the crush, Merr reeled back. Evie tried again to reach her, but the crowd's momentum resurged. Their eyes met for an instant before Jerry swept in and gathered Merr's falling body into his arms.

Okay. She's okay. But Merr seemed disoriented as she pulled away from Jerry's hold. Another brusque shove knocked Evie aside, and Elevator Mark appeared, grabbed Kevin, and forced his arm into a hold behind his back. Kevin bucked, then winced and screamed. A smear of red decorated his elbow. Merr's blood.

Fuck you, Kevin.

Louder shouts filled the room again. *Police, thank God. Merr will be okay.*

"Robby. We need to leave. Now." Evie dragged her out and though the hotel and didn't let go until they were safe inside her hotel room. She didn't hesitate to bolt the door behind them. Even then, she had to force herself to draw a breath.

"Holy shit. That was crazy. Auntie E, sit down." Robby steered her to the couch and propped pillows around her. "Are you okay?"

"Absolutely," Evie lied. "Why?"

"You look a little, I dunno, off. Are you sure you're fine?"

"Yes. Perfectly." Her pulse was racing, but she attributed it to the adrenaline flood. "Nothing like a near riot to get the blood flowing."

To allay her concerns, Evie pulled out her phone and scanned through a couple of screens. "Thank goodness, my students are fine, too. They're on the bus and heading back to the Saskatoon campus." She sighed, tucked her hair back from her face. Her students were safe, and the police would have restored order down in the library. As she looked around, she noticed a different kind of chaos had taken up residence in her room. "Good God, what happened in here?"

Walter had curled himself into a nest of gnawed white towels. Surrounding his custom bedding were tatters of white fabric, including what looked like a duvet, if the feathers were any indication. True to form, he was indifferent to the scrutiny.

"The apple doesn't fall far from the tree, Auntie E. You know who he learned civil disobedience from," Robby said. "Remember that trip to Clayoquot Sound? It wasn't perfectly peaceful, was it?"

Evie took an easier breath and chuckled. She had just turned twenty when she'd convinced her older sister Bev to let Robby, barely a teen, join her in a massive logging protest on Vancouver Island. Though mostly peaceful, there had been many instances where the more radical activists had hijacked the mostly moderate agenda. Change had come, albeit in the wake of countless arrests. It was a miracle Bev still talked to her, given how mad she was after seeing them on the evening news, arms linked in a human chain across a logging road.

"Not perfectly, no, but keep in mind that eventually, public opinion shifted. The boycotts and everything good that came out of that pressure forced the corporations to respect the resource."

"True, and now the lands are back with the First Nations communities." Robby's phone chimed. "I have to take this. It's work."

While she tended to business, Evie considered the potential outcomes of today's meeting. No question, the protesters had made it clear that they were prepared to hold Farmexal accountable. And while considerably defensive, Farmexal seemed to be making an effort to address their concerns. What part Merr Shepherd had in that was still a mystery. One thing was for sure, though, Evie thought as she began picking up feathers, sometimes things needed to get a bit messy before they got better.

❖

Merritt sat on the edge of the stage and surveyed the room. The once orderly and charming library was now littered with fallen folding chairs. The information pamphlets Farmexal had handed out looked as though they'd exploded out of a cannon. Long, twisted blue fabric was woven amongst the debris. The room had been cleared by the police and hotel security, but Merritt had found her way back in to reflect on what had and hadn't been accomplished. Had Farmexal improved its standing in the public eye? No. Definitely not. Had the protesters furthered their agenda? In a way, perhaps. The incident would make the evening news, no doubt. But they had come in angry, and they'd left angrier.

She blotted her lip with a paper towel that a kind hotel employee had set beside her.

"Hey, sunshine. Making people happy today?"

Merritt looked up at the uniformed officer who stood in front of her, then smiled and sighed. "What are you doing here, Philly? Aren't there speeders you should be ticketing?"

Steph Phillips laughed and took a seat beside her. An RCMP sergeant had no official business here, but Merritt had texted to let her know what had gone down. If she was here, she must've known Merritt needed a friend.

"Yes," Steph said after several moments surveying her. "I do like this look. Not sure about your lipstick choice. Blood-red is not your color. But the hair is very Kristen Stewart—bad girl, natch—meets Ruby Rose, best one-season superhero ever. And is that an undercut? And lowlights? So much fancier than the usual. What's the occasion? Can't be a woman. Or can it?"

Merr summoned up an icy stare.

Steph smiled triumphantly. "Okay, okay. Let me see...ah, yes, the investigation. Looks like it's going great. Just like old times."

Merritt ignored the sarcasm. It was a skill she'd acquired since they'd met. They'd been rookies, Steph with the Flin Flon detachment of the RCMP and Merritt with the ministry's enforcement division. There had been a controversy surrounding the rerouting of a river for a hydroelectric project. Merritt had been on scene to make sure that the contractors weren't violating the court-specified boundaries. Steph had been posted to ensure that the protesters did not endanger themselves while objecting to the redevelopment of the area. During the hundreds of hours of surveillance, they'd developed a friendship that even the seventeen hundred miles between Regina and Merritt's home in Ottawa couldn't divide.

"Stewart and Rose, eh?" Merritt was impressed with the blend. "I'll take that as a compliment, Philly."

"Meant to be, Fish 'n Game."

Merritt didn't bristle at the nickname as much as she once had. The barb had come about when she'd tried to explain the duties of an environment ministry peace officer. "We're to the rivers, lakes, and forests what the Ministry of Fish and Game are to wildlife." Steph had picked up on the slight derisive tone she'd used to refer to the tag-checkers and from then on, Fish 'n Game had stuck.

"I hope the other guy looks worse." Steph swatted Merritt's hand away from her lip, then gently pulled back the paper towel. From the look on her face, the towel wasn't working.

"He does. But he didn't need a fat lip to make it so." She regretted the smile that followed and grabbed another towel from the roll, folded it neatly, and held it to her wound.

"What happened?"

Merritt had asked herself the same question over the past half hour. How exactly had she gotten hurt? "Things went as expected. Badly. The crowd felt provoked. They reacted. The first surge of people heading to the door took me off my feet. I tried to get to…" She wanted to say Chisley, who had stepped off the stage. But the only person on her mind at that moment was

Evie. Damn. She'd been there. She'd gone down. *Was she hurt? Is she okay?*

Merritt pinched her lip hard enough to make herself flinch. This was the problem. She'd been distracted. She hadn't done her job or protected herself because she'd wanted to get to Evie. A protester. She'd never live that down if Steph knew, and so she copped to a lesser humiliation. "I think I lost focus."

"No wonder, with that pop on the lip. Fist?"

"Elbow, as I recall." *Weaselly little shit.*

Steph looked around the littered room. "Was any of this worth it?" She knew about Merritt's assignment with Farmexal. As a friend who lived in Regina and knew exactly what Merritt's job with the ministry entailed, Steph would need no other information to connect the dots between the missing totes and Merritt's arrival in the city. Also, as a police officer, Steph anticipated the potential for RCMP involvement if the community was in imminent danger. Hopefully, it wouldn't come to that.

Merritt took a moment to calculate her response. "Yes. I've got my eyes on a guy named Mark Einerson. Something about him doesn't sit right. For a guy who works security, he took an awfully long time before stepping in to break up the fracas. Not sure how chaos might benefit him. Maybe he's just poorly trained. But he might be worth a deeper look."

"Any downsides, other than the obvious?" Steph grabbed another paper towel and handed it over.

"Well, I haven't done much to keep Farmexal from looking bad. I tried to prevent it. God knows, I tried. Not that it's my job, but they employ a lot of people, and I'd hate to see them put out of business. I'd like to get this one figured out so that doesn't happen. The other problem actually *is* my job." She went on to explain how Kelly's blunder at the meeting might have outed her real purpose for working with Farmexal.

"Do you think anyone noticed?" Steph asked.

Merritt might've imagined Evie's eyes on her when she'd reacted to Kelly's comment. But it was possible she'd hidden her frustration well enough as she'd turned casually away. But there was no question that Evie had been staring directly at her when she'd turned toward the crowd. The disappointment in those eyes had lasered into her from across the room.

"Not sure," she fudged. "It's not critical that I keep the investigation on the down-low, but it would make things easier if my true purpose wasn't made public. Folks are clearly on edge, and the public could easily misinterpret a government investigation, leap to conclusions, and vilify Farmexal. They don't need more of that right now, Philly."

"They sure don't. Listen, buddy, I can tell that your adrenaline is pumping because you're talking fast. Which means at almost normal human speed." Steph was smart enough to recoil before Merritt's punch landed playfully on her arm.

Merritt had been teased relentlessly about her slower than usual cadence by almost everyone in her life. Steph was the only one she'd tolerated it from. She smiled and again regretted it. She knew from the warm trickle down her chin that the paper towel wasn't helping.

"Come on." Steph helped her up. "Let's swing by the ER to get that lip patched up, and I'll drop you off at Regina's finest to give your witness statement. You must love paperwork."

Steph was right. She would be up to her eyeballs in reports for the next day or so. Reports to the ministry. Reports to Farmexal. At this point, she couldn't be certain what the impact or endgame was for the unaccounted fertilizer, but with over two thousand gallons of ammonium nitrate missing, there was significant cause for concern. That needed to be foremost in her mind, not the paperwork. Or protesters. Especially not Evie. Her throbbing lip would be her reminder.

CHAPTER FIVE

Evie liked the idea of Kevin being in jail. That was why she'd resisted when Robby had asked, begged, her to go to the precinct to post bail. Well, that and she didn't like him well enough to take on the responsibility of setting him free. Robby had explained that she had to finish some drawings, or she'd do it herself. She was an architect in a leading-edge firm, and she must've known that playing the work card would trump any of Evie's lame protests, not the least of which was ridding the hotel room of evidence of Walter's destructive rampage. Robby had also thrown in a dismissive "Kevin's an idiot" for good measure. Well played.

It turned out to be a surprisingly easy process. As much as Evie would have liked the idiot to rot where he sat, the desk officer at the Regina police department was someone she recognized from a recent tailgate party, and he'd been happy to help her sort through the paperwork. And there was little of that because according to him, the "biggity-wigs" from Farmexal had already shown up and had decided not to press charges. *Seriously?*

As he told her this, he threw a glance over his shoulder. There, gathered around a desk, stood Kelly-who-likes-it-rough and James Chisley himself. He looked tense and aggravated until Kelly tossed her hair, giggled, and put a hand on his bicep. He visibly thawed and eased toward her, revealing Merr behind him signing documents.

Thank God, she's okay. The last Evie had seen of Farmexal's so-called auditor, Merr's mouth had met Kevin's elbow, launching a spray of red. Evie had gasped as blood had saturated Merr's white and gray blouse, turning it crimson and black. Now, as Evie made out the spreading purple bruise and black sutures, she gasped again.

With horror, she realized how loud she'd been. Merr lifted her head, put the pen down, and nodded to her. Evie's pulse quickened, and she almost smiled back. *No.* She couldn't be cordial. Merr had not been honest. Or at least, not forthcoming. She wouldn't tolerate either.

Evie tried to play it cool, but as Merr drew closer, Evie could see the full extent of the cut above her lip and softened. It looked as though a large marble had been tucked between her lip and gums. A plum-colored band had risen beneath the injury, circling a terribly painful-looking contusion. Even so, her lips still looked impossibly perfect.

"Stitches?"

"And hello to you, too, Dr. Evie. Yes, two. They're hardly noticeable, right?" Merr began to smile, then winced.

"Hardly." It took effort not to smile back. *Stay cool.*

"I'm guessing you're here for Mr. Dyer. I should've guessed that he was one of yours."

One of mine? Evie scowled.

"He's being processed but will be released shortly. I just signed the papers. No charges."

Evie didn't care if her lingering disappointment showed. Having Kevin spend a little quality time behind bars might inspire humility, a trait he'd yet to develop. "Really? It was that easy?"

"Easy for the police. Not so easy to convince Mr. Chisley. He's..." Merr looked at him and Kelly, who were standing suggestively close to each other. "Was pretty angry." She then shook her head disapprovingly and looked back at her as if seeking agreement.

Evie hesitated, still miffed. "You undersold your powers, new kid on the block. Seems like you're not merely a bean counter but rather a notable part of Farmexal's cozy inner circle. I'm not sure I realized the kind of power a new auditor yields."

"I didn't want to show off." Merritt's smile was annoyingly charming. "I'm not going to school you, Doctor, on the inherent perils of judging books by their covers. However, situations often have many layers, each containing realities still to be revealed. Where's your friend?"

Evie paused. Layers was a fascinating term. In her work as a structural geologist, she knew a lot about the magic and mystery that time and pressure could create on a substructure. As much as she wanted to believe Merr, she had concerns about what her unusually-worded caution might be concealing. As for the "friend," she could only imagine that Merr must've seen her with Robby at the hotel. Before she could clarify, Kelly crept up behind Merr.

"Mary, we need to get back to the office."

Mary?

Was Merr a Mary? She certainly didn't seem like one. It seemed too ordinary a name for this extraordinary woman with the extraordinary lips. And dimples. It just didn't fit. Like a few things about her.

"Thanks to the melee today, we'll be working late," Kelly continued, moving around Merr and tossing another of her seemingly patented "bitch" looks at Evie as she bent to half whisper in Merr's ear. "It's my turn to buy. The usual?"

Evie wondered if the word smirk was a combination of the words "smile" and "irk." She decided that when it came to Kelly, she would always lean heavily on the "irk." Kelly was under her skin. Like a splinter.

Kelly returned to Chisley and began organizing some papers.

If the annoying pup was trying to mark her territory, Evie wasn't about to retreat. No matter how irritated she was with Merr's equivocation, she wouldn't let Kelly intimidate her. Far from it.

She turned and set a hand gently on Merr's. "Where were we? Ah, yes. My friend at the hotel. My niece, actually. And she's working. I think she's lost her appreciation for dumbass." Evie gestured toward the metal door she'd seen the detainees pass through.

"Ah, so today's rabble-rouser is not a student? Is he mythical-parking-spot Kevin?"

"One and the same."

"You must be proud."

"Ever so." Evie rolled her eyes.

"It's at the very least refreshing to know that your niece is engaged enough in her community to act on her social consciousness. And given that she might be considering kicking—dumbass, did you call him—to the curb, she's also smart enough to make good decisions about her alliances in pursuit of that objective."

Evie was struck by the grace and generosity of that comment. It echoed the kindness she'd seen at the football game. And it surprised her that someone so clearly hitched to the corporate wagon would be inclined to pull a bit against it.

A small trickle of blood pushed past Merr's suture and put Evie's reservations aside. *Kindness.* She reached into her pocket and pulled out a tissue. "I don't leave home without these now, since the hot chocolate. Sit here. Let me clean that up." She smiled, but Merr didn't have a corresponding grin. Instead, she seemed to be studying Evie. Sensing resistance, Evie leaned forward in her chair and lifted the tissue to Merr's mouth. Merr capitulated enough that she could gently blot the blood.

Was she imagining that Merr's breath was uneven? That her eyes had become more intense? Smoldering, even? Had she trembled beneath Evie's touch, or was it Evie's hand that was shaking? Unsure how to push through the mishmash of questions roaring through her mind, she removed the tissue, wondering if her observations were valid. Maybe her excessively pounding heart harkened back to the stuck-in-the-elevator pledge she'd made to live life more bravely. Less alone. She swallowed and calmed herself.

"Your lips are extraordinary enough already. There was really no need to add more allure."

Had she just flirted? She held her breath and was unexpectedly overcome by a wave of nausea. She swallowed again, hoping to shake it off. Merr must've noticed because she was reaching forward as if to steady her. Her chair felt strangely wobbly. What the hell was happening?

"So you're the reason we're still here." Kelly's accusatory tone cut through the blur of strange symptoms. Kelly had appeared beside Merr, a hand on her shoulder. "I thought you might be on the bus heading back to campus."

Evie blinked and forced herself upright. "What?"

"Yes, Dr. O'Halloran, I know who you are. I called the university about the bus full of students you dragged here just to make Farmexal look bad. Thank God none of them were hurt."

Evie bristled at the innuendo. The physical symptoms had passed, and whatever had caused her stomach to flip and the room to slant had been replaced with what her sister called her ancestors' fire. *Set phasers to stun.*

"They were not dragged. They are invested in their futures and make their own decisions. And of course none of them were hurt." Evie had seen them leaving the room before chaos had taken over. "Furthermore, it doesn't take a bus full of environmental activists to make Farmexal look bad. You're doing that all on your own. How dare you"—she turned to Merr, who was still holding the tissue to her bloody lip—"and you hold us responsible for what happened in that room today?"

"Hang on. I didn't say—" Merr began.

Evie was not about to let her finish. She jumped to her feet, and her metal chair slid into the desk behind it with a resounding clang. She ignored the turned faces of the others. "Your company's response to its malfeasance is unforgiveable, and your boss is a loose cannon." She turned from Merr to Kelly. "My students did not cause that brawl. Far from it." She then looked to Chisley, who stood at the end of the room. *Chicken.* She raised her voice above the room's din, which had gotten a lot quieter, and directed her comment at him. "Your negligence and refusal to be honest and hold yourselves accountable are what started the ball rolling. All of what happened today was avoidable." She glared at Kelly, then focused on Merr. "Sorry if it means you have to work late, *Mary.*"

Merr ignored her comment, instead moving quickly between Evie and Chisley as if predicting her next move. "Don't do this, Dr. Evie—"

"It's Dr. O'Halloran." Her tone dropped twenty degrees, but it felt like fire was shooting out of her ears. She clenched her teeth. "And he," she added, pointing at Kevin, who stood by the door, "is most definitely *not* 'one of mine.'"

Chapter Six

From the time Merritt had first disclosed that she was from Maymont, a small town a half day's drive from Regina, Steph had taunted her with almost every joke there was about Saskatchewan. How boring it was to drive through. How flat. How square. And innumerable taunts about the unique place-names.

Merr's favorite was the one about the couple from Ontario driving through the province: The husband stopped to ask a passing farmer where they were. The farmer said, "Saskatoon, Saskatchewan," and when the husband got back to the car and his wife asked what the farmer said, he replied, "I don't know. He didn't speak English."

Merritt loved the province despite its quirks. Probably because of them. She'd lived in Ottawa for almost six years but still missed the fields of canola that bloomed in yellows so vibrant they could blind a person to almost everything else. There was nothing comparable to how the blue prairie sky arched unendingly until night, revealing a sky so dark that it was impossible not to see a zillion stars stitched into its unearthly black quilt.

After the chaos yesterday, it felt good to be back in the heartland. She airplane-winged her arm out the window of her Cadillac CT4 Sport. Not her usual ride. A too-flashy rental, courtesy of the ministry. The highway between Regina and the exit at Lumsden was four-lane for the most part. Much of the traffic on a fall Tuesday, aside from commuters and transports, would be farm vehicles. It was mid-September, and the canola harvest was in full swing. No harvest was bigger in Saskatchewan, and nowhere else in the world came close to the province's production of the oil-producing plant. Merritt had anticipated the increase in farm vehicles and had left as early as she could manage. She'd finished off the reports from the previous day and had emailed them to her supervisor at two a.m. after spending several hours with Kelly, helping to put together a press release. Honestly, the latter task had been the most grueling, and she'd worked as quickly and efficiently as possible to escape Kelly's distractingly relentless flirtation.

Speaking of distractions, how unpredictable was Evie O'Halloran? One minute, she'd been gently tending to Merritt's wound. The next, Evie was at verbal war with Farmexal, and by association, Merr. *I didn't see that coming.*

Merritt hated to admit it, but these impassioned sides of Evie—the tender and the outraged—were downright sexy. As arousing as Evie's intellect. Yet, in between the two discordant minutes, Merritt had witnessed a tipping point, and for the life of her, she could not quite comprehend what had caused that shift. She'd even worried that Evie might faint. She'd certainly seemed to have recovered when she'd lobbed her last verbal assault and had marched out of the station with the weaselly agitator in her wake.

This was exactly why Merr had to stop thinking about Evie. Unless the totes stopped showing up in fields, Evie and her band of protesters would continue to be a distraction. *Especially Evie.* "Keep driving," Merritt said aloud. *Foot on gas, eyes on road. Hands on the steering wheel and nowhere else.*

Before long, she arrived at the address provided by the woman at yesterday's meeting, the site of the most recent tote. Carm Augustyn's farm was well-managed and in full operation.

Several pickups were parked near a large grain bin, suggesting a somewhat larger-than-family business. Large cutters and combines were actively working the surrounding acreage.

"Hop in," the farmer said, nodding toward Merritt's CT4. "No need to mess up that pretty little Caddy."

She buckled into Augustyn's Chevy truck. The canola producer was much calmer and friendlier than many of the other farmers she'd met recently. Augustyn drove along a narrow creek and entered an adjacent acreage, edging the crop line before gearing down and pulling up into a corner of the field. The tote literally went against the grain. It was obvious that no attempt had been made to conceal it. The uncut canola was only steps away. Why not nestle it below the seedpods, where even swathing might not reveal it until spring?

"That's exactly as we found it. I didn't want any of my workers touchin' that thing. Not knowin' what was—or still is—in it."

Totes were a familiar vessel for distributing chemical supplements in agriculture. Merritt had seen the bigger, hundred-gallon version of these plastic, cube-like boxes most of her lifetime, in the back of pickups, on flatbeds, and sometimes stored in metal cages that made them sturdier for transport. The smaller totes held twenty gallons; two people, or one with mechanical assistance, could manage them on and off a flatbed with ease.

Merritt wondered how many hadn't yet been found. She took several pictures before gathering soil samples. Once collected, she rode back with Augustyn and promised that a crew would be by later in the day to clean up the site. Tomorrow, the samples would go to the analysis lab at the university in Saskatoon, and with any luck, they'd show only light traces of residue. Even if those were the results, the discovery of yet another tote would still fuel the protests and leave two questions Merritt needed answers to before Farmexal's luck ran out: Who was stealing the totes in the first place? And why?

❖

Evie stretched out naked beneath the cotton comforter, wondering why hotel beds held such appeal. Was it the pristine white sheets or the quicksand-like properties of a mattress designed to give someone little option but to surrender and order room service? She considered the many beds she'd been subjected to in her travels. The hot, humid jungles of Mexico and the bitterly cold wilds of the Scottish Highlands were not luxury locations. And no bed had even come close to this one. Extending her stay in Regina an extra day wasn't a hardship.

Her sister used to insist that Evie stay at her house. It was plenty big, and back when Evie's student loans were eating into her discretionary spending, she'd been happy to accept the offer. But that was when Bev had been married to Alan. Once Lonnie was on the scene, the hotel was Evie's preferred base. Lonnie hated dogs, and frankly, she and Walter weren't so fond of him, either. She laughed and rubbed Walter's head as her phone beeped.

Speak of the devil. Bev: *Hey, sis. Can't do lunch today. Lonnie's in town and needs a few things.*

Familiar story. Lonnie's needs trumped all.

Evie typed *dumbass*, then backspaced, replacing it with a more congenial *Gotcha. Next time, okay?*

Today, Evie couldn't let herself get dragged down by worry for her sister. Not only had she experienced enough disappointment in the past twenty-four hours, but she couldn't stomach a lunch where Bev pretended that nothing was amiss in her domestic life while lecturing Evie about the importance of finding love.

Evie found it curious that her sister still believed in happily-ever-after in light of her own fraught relationship. Residual from her late husband, perhaps. Alan had been happily-ever-after worthy. Kind. Loving. Attentive. Everything Lonnie was not. Maybe Bev's behavior was vicarious. Maybe she wanted Evie to find what she didn't have. Maybe she'd read one too many romance novels. Or watched too many episodes of *The Bachelorette*. Whatever the reason, Evie now had to find another reason to escape to the tender embrace of her pillow-topped suitor.

She texted Robby. *Lunch today?*

Can't, came the immediate response. *Have to work.* Her work was deadline driven, and she was strident. *But next weekend, let's check out that new patisserie, k?*

The bakery did sound interesting. Robby had mentioned that the owner was trained in France or from France. It would be odd if he was, in fact, from France. Outside of a strong Métis community, there weren't many European French in Regina. Inexplicably, a number of classic old-world patisseries had nonetheless sprung up in the city.

For sure. Heading home soon. To Saskatoon, but only because it was close to campus. Otherwise, she'd have chosen to live closer to her family in Regina.

Robby replied, *See you next weekend*, followed by a heart-eyed emoji.

Evie sent a hug emoji back and flipped to her weather app. She could see what looked like blue sky through a small crack in the heavy brocade draperies that covered one whole side of her room. Sweater weather. A bit warmer than expected, especially given that snow had flurried earlier in the week.

Good for the farmers, she thought. Good for football, too. The season-ending Grey Cup would take place in a few weeks, and there was a tradition of playing in the snow. But with most of the league's stadiums—including Saskatchewan's—being outdoors, Evie didn't mind if the real snow didn't make an appearance until after the big game.

"Walter, it looks like it's just you and me."

He barely raised one of his fuzzy brows. She knew what he was thinking. Until she pulled the covers off and her feet hit the floor, he would stay put.

Not wanting to admit that he was right about her tendency to procrastinate, Evie flipped to her calendar. This afternoon, she had a lecture. Before leaving campus, she'd stop at the analysis building to look at some samples just in from Mexico. Her calendar was embarrassingly light for a professor, but that was the privilege of tenure. She'd also just wrapped up three years as interim dean and wouldn't apologize for the reduced schedule she'd been rewarded with as a result.

For the next two years, she'd secured a mid-week course schedule and few advisory duties. It was a nice perk, but she found the extra personal time a challenge. Evenings and weekends were usually spent buried in research when she wasn't in Regina. Her area of expertise in the structural integrity of cenotes—underground limestone caverns prevalent throughout the Yucatan Peninsula—kept her in constant contact with her Mexican colleagues, and while it had been twenty years since she'd been back, just thinking about the water-filled sinkholes made her heart drop and sense of dread rise. Not like they had back then. But still. Just like in the elevator. Or any small space. *Ever since.*

Just as quickly as she'd slipped in time, Evie rebounded with thoughts of Merr. *Just doesn't seem like a Mary. Not a name common for her age.* Regardless, after making herself clear about what she thought of Farmexal, its CEO, and its minions, there was no point fantasizing about future run-ins with Merr.

"I guess I shredded my own towels yesterday, Walter." She slipped from under the covers and into her slippers.

Walter jumped to attention.

"That's right, lil' bit, I'm lookin' at you. We have time for a walk before we head home. At least I have you to keep me young."

As she headed to the shower, Walter at her heels, she noticed the green and white scarf slung over the back of the chair. She hadn't said anything at the police station that she didn't mean, but she regretted that she'd lost her cool. Merr, Mary, whatever her name, hadn't simply been in the line of fire. She was part of a company that made decisions based solely on the bottom line. It didn't take much to find example after example of human-caused environmental disasters that could have been avoided if factors other than profit had been respected. Evie hadn't been looking for a fight, but if it meant that Farmexal would start finding a way to clean up their messes, then she would drop her gloves anytime. Mary or no Mary.

Merr.

She shrugged and looked at Walter, who seemed confused by her change of pace and was circling her feet.

"All right, Walter, let's go see if there are any other exciting things to discover in Regina."

CHAPTER SEVEN

By the time the week was half-over, Merritt had gathered samples from sites and reviewed numbers from Farmexal's CFO to better assess current inventory losses. Her guess of two thousand gallons wasn't far off, but she was still at a loss as to how the liquid was leaving the manufacturing plant. She decided she needed a tour of the facilities and reluctantly accepted Kelly's numerous offers to show her around. As expected, the company's multitasker seemed thrilled to show off her knowledge.

"These are the pallets." Kelly's voice was singsong, and she waved Vanna White–style at a standard wooden slat base loaded with totes.

Merritt held back a response as she noted there were three columns per side, stacked four rows high. "I thought they'd be larger," she said. "The pallets, I mean. Could they not support more totes?"

"Physically, yes. But we try to consider the end user. Keeping the stacks short allows one person to manage the unloading without mechanical help."

"Makes sense." Merritt managed to sound impressed as she mentally calculated the number of totes per pallet. "So, there are thirty-six totes per pallet..."

"Not on those pallets, no," Kelly interjected.

"My math skills are bad, Kelly, but four rows with nine totes per layer adds up to…"

"Not nine. Just eight. The center stack, which we can't see from the outside, is empty. So there are only thirty-two totes containing product per pallet."

Odd. "Why empty?"

"Coring."

Merritt wondered if Kelly was baiting her to ask more questions. But she needed to know, so she bit the hook. "And coring is?"

"Okay, so Farmexal serves a lot of different markets, foreign and domestic. Receivers and customs officials in foreign countries, typically very big orders, want to be able to lay eyes on each tote's contents before signing off on quantities. Domestic customers are another story. Since the center core isn't visible—"

It was Merritt's turn to interrupt. "They would be forced to unwrap each pallet and disassemble the stack to confirm quantity."

"Exactly. And you know that's not going to happen. People are just plain lazy," Kelly explained, then pointed at a large scale across the dock as a forklift lifted a pallet and loaded it into a waiting transport truck in the bay. "Anyway, the empty core also keeps the total pallet weight under three thousand pounds, a threshold that gives the company a break on shipping costs."

It seemed strange to Merritt that they'd ship empty totes around the world. "Then why put the empties there at all? Why not leave the center stack out altogether?"

"Stability. We shrink-wrap the pallet so it doesn't shift during transport, and the core keeps the other totes from moving during delivery."

Merritt committed the shipping process to memory before turning toward the inbound dock on the other side of the bay. There, several relatively untidy stacks of empty totes sat on partial pallets. "Are those the empties that complete the pallet?"

Kelly shook her head and waved toward a neat row of totes on the shipping side of the warehouse. "Just the ones here. Totes are refundable, but the ones customers return need to be washed before they're used. Those over there need to go out for a wash first, then come back here for either refilling or coring."

"Washed?" She was lost and noticed that Kelly was entering the "how did this idiot get her job?" zone. To prevent another eye roll and deep sigh, Merritt forced an apologetic smile and flashed her eyes as if amazed by Kelly's pool of knowledge. She would only admit to herself that the pool was unexpectedly deep.

Kelly smiled back, seemingly unaware of any artifice. "These pallets are loaded and shipped to international markets. As you can see, this is all liquid. We also manufacture solid fertilizer for the domestic market." Kelly took a beat as Merritt caught up. "And before you ask, the packaging for the solids is vastly different. Different weights, different containers, different plant."

"So domestic customers don't get liquid?"

"Correct. By law. Banned in 2008. We manufacture it but only because we follow the strictest government protocols. At least, we thought we did."

Merr read disappointment on her face. She cared. For Farmexal or the bedraggled Chisley? It didn't really matter. "I gather that, when the liquid form is used, absorption into the ground is faster than with the pellets?"

"Yep, pellets usually take a couple of days to dissolve, longer if we're having a dry spell."

Merritt had a good idea what the fallout of that legislation might be. Weather conditions during an already short growing season were unpredictable and critical for farmers. If she was in their shoes, the liquid would be preferable. But to be sure, she asked, "And how do domestic customers feel about that?"

"Not happy, especially at first. It costs money to modify or replace their spreading equipment. Farmexal offered domestic customers rebates, which helped a bit. They didn't have to do that." Kelly paused.

Last week's events at the hotel and at the police station were taking their toll on many of the employees. They were standing in a very harsh spotlight, Kelly included, so she'd obviously found an example that spoke to Farmexal's generosity and needed to make sure Merritt understood that. She did.

"Like every government restriction, people get used to it," Kelly continued. "Besides, high density prill is safer to store and transport. And we don't want another Toronto situation, right?"

A while ago, police in Toronto had interrupted a plot to kill thousands of people using explosives made of liquid nitrate. "Absolutely." She did a quick look around the shipping area, noting two cameras positioned toward the shipping door. She checked across the large room at the recycling side but couldn't locate similar surveillance. "So only liquid product is shipped from here to international markets. Understood. And washing?"

"We don't have the space here, so Farmexal set up a separate washhouse near the breweries."

Merritt knew the area because it was just across the tracks from Germantown, not too far from Max's apartment at the north edge of the heritage district and very close to his patisserie. Worth a look-see.

"Maybe you can take me to lunch, and I can fill you in on more?" Kelly chirped.

Lunch? Already?

She pulled out her phone and checked the time. "Kelly, I am so sorry. I have a meeting in Saskatoon, and I'm going to be late." It was the truth, but she could sense Kelly's chagrin and felt badly. Thanks to today's tour, Merritt had a number of items for follow-up. "Rain check?" She smiled, genuinely this time.

Kelly winked and nodded. "Sure thing. But I'll pick the spot. It'll cost you."

I just bet it will.

❖

Merritt slid behind the wheel, then took a breath and a moment to reflect. It wasn't just being around Kelly that was so exhausting; it was also trying to absorb a vast amount of logistical information and then determine how and if it fit with the investigation. As she headed north toward Saskatoon, she contemplated what she had learned this morning and tried to sort out where in the chain the missing inventory might be redirected. Farmexal manufactured liquid fertilizer and shipped it only to international customers. The empty core Kelly described had Merritt's Spidey senses tingling. But pallets were weighed before leaving the shipping dock, so there was no way the core was being secretly filled and then siphoned off somewhere along the route between the warehouse and the customer. Still. Tingling.

Merritt decided to give her observations time to mellow, reminding herself to follow up with a visit to the washhouse as another good next step toward piecing things together.

"Siri, call Max."

"Hey. sis, we missed you last night."

Merritt expected his cajoling. She knew better than to make promises, even to family, when her schedule wasn't her own, but even so, she felt bad that she'd missed the family dinner. "Sorry, brother. Hopefully, next time." Not a promise.

"Mom and Dad worry when you don't show. You've all made such progress in the past few years, and they don't want to lose you again. And there are no excuses now that you live in the province, just a half day's drive from good ol' Maymont."

"They didn't lose me. I was just…"

"Embarrassed? Humiliated?" *At least.* "Yeah, I know, Merr, but that was a long time ago, and it wasn't your fault…as much as you tell yourself otherwise."

"I should've seen it coming, and we all know it."

"The only person who could've seen it coming was Natalie. If they can forgive you for calling them tree killers, you know they can get past all that money stuff. And I'm telling you, they have."

She cringed, happy that he couldn't see her. He was right. She'd put her parents through the wringer when she was younger. That was undeniable. First there was her fierce opposition to her parents' publishing business, which she'd once declared "ate forests for breakfast, lunch, and dinner."

"In my defense, I'd just spent a whole summer in the sweltering British Columbia heat planting saplings." It maddened her that her family benefitted from the senseless harvesting of acres of lumber already stressed by natural events like wildfire. Especially when there were options.

She was eighteen, and the consequences of greed and global warming had demanded action. *Protest.* So she'd reacted to her parents' resistance to going digital at Shepherd Press with the delicate diplomacy of a stampede. Feathers had flown from one end of Maymont to the other. The dissidence was followed by Merr's self-imposed exile to a university in Ontario to study Environmental Management. Then a handful of years later, there was Natalie. Yet despite the laundry list of defiance and bad judgment, her parents loved her.

Merritt winced at the memories and looked out at the fields speeding by, hoping to distract herself from the guilt she still carried. She knew Max's heart was in the right place, but she hated reminders of what had happened. It made her feel like a victim, which she was, but she despised feeling that way. "I'll do what I can to catch up with them later today," she almost-promised.

"Fine."

The one-word response meant that he was on to her but was willing to let it drop for now.

She seized her moment. "I have a business dinner tonight, so I'll be home late."

"No problem. You know that you're welcome to stay at the loft as long as you want. I'm sorry I'm not around much, but that seems to be working both ways at the moment."

She appreciated him more than he probably knew. She hoped

that his efforts at the bakery paid off so he could work in some time for a personal life. Maybe a girlfriend. Like she could talk.

Once she hung up, she rolled the windows down and glanced across the fields. Bronze ribbons striped the landscape as far as the eye could see. A thin plastic dry-cleaning bag labelled "Dr. O'Halloran" was rippling with the flow of air in the back seat. *Dry cleaning always reminded her of Natalie.* Maybe she should've guessed earlier that Natalie wasn't the poor student she'd claimed to be by the way she'd insisted on getting her clothes professionally cleaned. Merritt had thought it cute at first. Quirky. Only in retrospect, it had been a sign. And as many times as Max had urged her to put the responsibility for the loss of a small family fortune on Natalie's shoulders, she couldn't help but bear the brunt of it. Because she had missed that sign. Many signs.

"Damn," she muttered as the main highway exit for the University of Saskatchewan showed up in her rearview.

Now she had missed another.

CHAPTER EIGHT

The signs directing Merritt to the Thorvaldson Building made it easy to find the Saskatchewan Structural Sciences Centre. Once at the reception desk, she signed over the samples taken at the Augustyn farm and provided a brief explanation of the situation. She didn't want to provide too much information to the technician so the results couldn't be accidentally swayed.

Turning to her second task, she headed toward the exit. She wondered if it might seem strange that she was personally delivering the geologist's cleaned garments. *No. Not strange at all.* Merritt was at the centre for legitimate reason, and from what she could tell from the campus map, Dr. O'Halloran's office was in the adjacent building. The personal gesture might even change Evie's mind about how seriously Farmexal was taking things. Merritt hoped it might be grand enough to reset Evie's opinion of her. She reached into her satchel for her keys, and when she raised her eyes, there stood Evie O'Halloran. And it appeared she was just as surprised as Merritt was.

"What are you..." Evie began. "I mean, why—"

Merritt raised a hand to allay any fears of stalking before noticing Evie didn't seem bothered by her sudden presence. Rather, she was smiling. No hard feelings, apparently. Just sparkling eyes that granted Merritt an extra moment to find the right words.

"Good afternoon, Dr. O'Halloran." Merritt doubted she'd ever be welcome to call her Evie again. "I am here on official business. Dropping off some soil samples from the latest dump site."

"Are you now?" Another unexpected sparkle. "That seems like quite a range of responsibilities for a compliance auditor."

Merritt was back on her heels, realizing that at some level, her presence at the university might be less about dropping off soil samples and more to do with seeing Evie. Might as well own it. "Well, in this instance, I wanted to be personally involved. And as an added bonus to Farmexal's bottom line, I've also taken out two birds with one stone, if you'll pardon the unkind imagery. You'd given Kelly your address here at the university, so I am also delivering your dry cleaning."

"You're quite the corporate soldier, though I see no evidence of dry cleaning," Evie waved around them as if magically divining the delivery.

"Fear not, your clean clothes are hanging in my car. I was just on my way to get them."

"I was about to head out myself. Do you mind swinging by my office for a moment so I can pick up a few things, and then we can walk together?"

Merritt was relieved by the unexpected détente, and on the way to Evie's office, she took the opportunity to ask about her field of study.

"My academic focus is on structural sciences as it relates to physical geography. This is my building here," she said, pulling open a heavy glass door near the corner of a building not far from the center.

"As in rock layers? And tectonics?" Merritt knew just enough from reading *Nat Geo* to draw an impressed nod and smile.

"Those are definitely aspects of the science. In fact, I spent most of my initial research years studying layering and pressure variations in the Earth's crust. Now, I direct several graduate studies in a variety of fields and applications, but they're all structurally based."

Evie turned down a corridor. "My office is just up one flight," she said, nodding to a set of stairs across the main entrance. A large arched window lit the red-bricked lobby. The stairs were old-school floating slabs of polished granite, speckled with black, gray, white, and rose, and were made more impressive by the high ceiling of the grand entrance. The stairs were worn by a hundred years of foot traffic. It was clear by Evie's steady pace that she'd run these steps regularly, and she was on the landing several steps ahead before Merritt caught up.

"Here we are. One of the benefits of tenure is having a pick of office space," she said, keying open the door nearest the stairs.

She ushered Merritt inside an office that looked quintessentially academic. Shelves from floor to ceiling, packed with books and stacks of worn paper. The walls were covered with maps, several framed teaching awards, multiple photographs of buttes and cenotes, images of buckling bridges, earthquake destruction, and rock-lined riverbanks. Pinned to a bulletin board amongst fifty or so others was a photo of Evie and a small group of women, all wearing square, pink knit hats with the US Capitol Building in the background. A large rock with a fossil embedded in it sat like a giant paperweight on an overfilled filing cabinet. The entire room was confetti'd with sticky notes, a rainbow of handwritten memos that varied as much in content as they did in colors:

Watch for slippage.
Oblique.
Tsunami.
San Andreas = Strike-slip.
Scotland = Reverse thrust.
Fault.

Taking in the kaleidoscope, Merritt was drawn to the chair behind the large desk. She was convinced she'd seen it move, even though neither she nor Evie was close to it.

"His Highness has arisen," Evie announced with a hint of pageantry. "Walter," she said, appearing to address the chair, "I'd like you to meet Merr."

A dog swaggered out from behind the desk, and Merritt took a knee to be closer to him. "Well, hello there, fella." She turned her palm up and let him sniff her fingers. "My gosh, he has the face of an Ewok. Is he a Yorkie?"

"Close. A Cairn. Similar, but Cairns consider themselves infinitely superior. And not just to Yorkshire terriers. To all terriers." Evie shook her head defeatedly, and sweetness spread across her face. "No," she added, "to all dogs. And *Star Wars* creatures."

Walter moved his face against Merritt's hand, and she scratched him gently below the ear. He moved closer, rubbing his whole head against her knee.

"Let me know if he's bothering you. He can be very demanding of affection."

"I see nothing wrong with his strategy." She wondered if her words sounded as awkward as the sentiment sometimes felt. In truth, she knew at a very core level that returning the affection of a dog was so much simpler than managing the depth of feeling that came with human relationships. *TMI.* "So, Walter, how did you get your name?"

Evie waited a beat, causing Merritt to wonder if Walter was going to answer. "You're likely too young to be familiar with the reference, but a while back, there was a movie called *On Golden Pond.*"

Merritt laid claim to Walter's belly. "Walter was the name of the fish. The one that Henry Fonda and the young boy were trying to catch." She looked up, smiling in response to Evie's bewildered expression.

Evie crossed her arms and nodded. "You are the first person to have ever guessed correctly."

"Well, I have some skills. And I'm not that young. Also, I'm a big Katharine Hepburn fan. Truly, name one lesbian who isn't. The woman could rock a pantsuit."

Evie smiled and continued to pack an overstuffed saddleback briefcase while Merritt glanced again around the room. "How did you get into this? Your field, I mean."

"The way most kids do, I imagine. Dinosaurs. Dad used to take me down to the Big Muddy and Swift Current. Heck, even the Qu'Appelle Valley has terraces where mammoth remains have been found. Eventually, I became fascinated with what the rock itself was able to do, rather than the dinosaurs. One thing led to the next, and here I am."

"What rock is able to do?"

"Yes, geologically speaking. See this picture?" She pulled a small, slightly faded framed photo from one of the shelves. It showed her as a young woman, crouched in front of a rock face. The rock face itself was split horizontally, as if stacked. The top portion was a dark gray that looked like coal, save for the plants growing from its jagged crevices. The bottom was a mottled brown and looked like sand or limestone. Young Evie's hand spanned the two dramatically different layers of rock. Her smile was wondrous. She looked extraordinarily happy.

"You look as if you just made an important discovery."

Evie laughed and nodded. "Well, someone did. I only wish it was me. But that discovery was over a hundred years before this picture was taken at the very spot a critical geological controversy erupted. This is usually when most of my students begin to nod off, so I'll understand if you'd rather skip the story."

Merritt enjoyed the self-deprecation but couldn't imagine who could possibly check out with Evie at the front of a lecture hall. "Please, I'd be disappointed if you didn't explain what put that smile on your face."

Evie blushed. "This is a place called Knockan Crag, in the Scottish Highlands. My hand is spanning, quite literally, millions and millions of years. That wouldn't be astonishing in any sense, really, were it not for the fact that the dark metamorphic formation at the top is older, much much older, than the younger sedimentary layer below. You mentioned tectonics?"

Merritt nodded noncommittally. "Don't test me, but I think it refers to the movement of the Earth's crust, right?"

"Correct. Most people think of earthquake zones like the San Andreas Fault. Before this thrust was discovered at Knockan Crag in the 1880s, no one had considered that kind of lateral movement was possible."

"That seems so recent, relatively speaking."

"Yes. Contentious as well." Evie was obviously in her element. "But eventually, the science bore out the theory, and advances in mapping and predictability were possible. Okay, you've indulged me long enough. I could go on for hours. Suffice to say that, for a geo nerd, this moment was astonishingly special. It whispered in my ear."

Merritt loved the turn of phrase. "And what did it say?"

Evie looked fondly at the photo, rubbing a bit of dust off the frame with her thumb before replying. "That so many of our ideas about time and age have yet to be discovered."

Merritt fought the urge to say "fascinating," thinking it might sound patronizing or sycophantic. She was impressed by Evie's intellect. *No question.* But the word didn't adequately capture her meaning, so she kept it to herself while Evie grabbed a waxy, plaid-lined Barbour coat and pulled her satchel strap over her head. Walter stuck close to Merritt's heels as they exited the office and headed in the direction of the analysis building's parking lot.

"My car is this way, Doctor."

"I think I'd prefer that you call me Evie. Now that you've seen my office and met my dog, I'm willing to set aside formality. And perhaps apologize for speaking to you so aggressively last week. Don't get me wrong, I stand by what I said, just not how I said it. Farmexal, bean counters included, needs to step up."

"I'm really more of a pencil pusher, but I hear what you're saying." The truce lowered Merritt's shoulders.

"I'm surprised Walter has the energy to walk," Evie said, her eyes keenly on him as he ambled adroitly down the path toward the lot. "We had a long walk at Wascana before leaving Regina earlier in the week. He's been recuperating since."

"The trail or the centre?" Getting to the head of the Wascana Trail required a short drive out of Regina, while the in-city park known as the centre was located on over two thousand acres of First Nations and Métis original lands. Both had a lot to offer a dog. And a beautiful woman.

"The centre. It's a nice walk from the hotel, and we'd been out to the trail on the weekend. Walter appreciates the variety."

Merritt noted the hotel reference, curious as to why Evie didn't stay with the family she had in town, then decided, based on her own family dynamic, not to pursue it.

"Voilà," Merritt said, handing the crinkling bag to Evie, who hooked the hanger on her finger and slung it casually over her shoulder.

Evie nodded in approval. "Such personal service."

"The best kind." She wished "personal" was more firmly in the cards.

"I expect Farmexal is hoping to mend fences one person at a time?"

"They want truth," Merritt said genuinely. "They're not faceless. The people there will take responsibility, if need be, but Chisley shouldn't if it's not his to hold." She cut short her defense when she noticed the pendant on Evie's necklace. Set in a swirled silver design, the stone was perfectly teardrop shaped with shimmers of blue. It looked like black ice that might've been pulled from an arctic lake. It was striking, and it provided a safe diversion. "May I ask about your pendant?"

Evie glanced down and took up the stone, rubbing it between her fingers. "This? It's larvikite. A pretty good sample, too.

There's a lot of blue feldspar suspended in the black. The worry stone, some people call it."

"Why? Where does it come from?"

"Some people believe it relieves anxiety. Many Norwegians feel it's a talisman that helps people adapt to change. I'm not sure there's any good science to back that up, but there's none to the contrary either. I found it while collecting samples at a greenstone belt near Flin Flon."

Merritt loved that Evie had upwardly inflected the "Flon," inviting a query in case Merritt didn't know what or where Flin Flon was. As it happened, the small town straddling the provincial border between Saskatchewan and Manitoba was a place she knew well. "I'm familiar with the place. I had a job up there a few years ago." And by "up," she really meant north. *Far up north.* As a very cold crow would fly. Flin Flon was over six hundred miles slightly northwest from Grand Forks, North Dakota.

"Counting beans for 'big potash'?" Evie's guess seemed educated since much of the industry in the northern part of the province centered on harvesting the salty mineral crucial to the manufacture of fertilizer. "I imagine there are a lot of companies requiring your skill set." It was clear by her tone that she wasn't a fan.

"Not potash. I was pushing paper for, um, a dog food company," Merritt lied. Badly. It was stupid, given that she said "dog food" while looking at Walter. But for some reason, she wanted Evie to like her. And being employed by an industry Evie considered a greed-centered, environmentally irresponsible band of heartless corporate pillagers, true or not, made her feel deeply unlikeable.

"Is that right?" Evie spoke as though she'd caught on but was going to let Merritt run with scissors.

Cornered by her own lie, Merritt mentally ran, trying hard to keep from tripping. "You might be surprised how many companies, like people, need to account for themselves."

"That may be true. You seem to have no trouble with the

bottom line, especially ones involving the truth of what you do at Farmexal."

Ah. There it was. Evie might be letting her off the hook about the dog food snafu, but she had her snagged in another regrettable lie. Deception, she rationalized. After all, she was working to make Farmexal accountable, if that was where the facts landed. But she was posing, and Evie had seemingly sensed it. *A tangled web indeed.*

As much as she wanted to be honest, she preferred to keep the ministry investigation confidential. For now. "Ouch," she managed. "That's fair. The truth is, I wasn't thinking about my job when we met. It's been very hard for me to get that image of you out of my head."

"The one with me covered in hot chocolate? That's not very flattering for an apology, if that's what this is."

"*Tsk tsk,* Dr. Evie. Remember what I said about rushing to judgment? In truth, I'd been thinking about that classic line about getting out of wet clothes and into a dry martini."

"I'm not sure whether to be shocked, amused, or intrigued."

Merritt couldn't quite read Evie's reaction, distracted as she was by the mysterious smile. She guessed playful. "Just be you. I'm old-fashioned, really. Under different circumstances, I would've asked you out to dinner." Even imagining a date with her made Merritt's heart warm.

"Circumstances, you say? So if they had been different, and I had accepted, where might we have gone for this dinner?"

Playful it is.

What followed was a debate about where to find the best pasta in town and who poured the best martini, followed by why sushi was never a good idea in a landlocked province. The friendly culinary discussion wrapped where it had started, with hot chocolate. They agreed that the prominent orange flavor of Cointreau was the perfect accompanying liqueur but still held opposing views on the inclusion of marshmallows.

Evie apologized again for rushing blindly out of the elevator.

"Just to be clear, I was driven more by my claustrophobia than by negligence. I'm sure that if the drinks and doughnuts hadn't landed on me, they would've landed on you."

"My reflexes are pretty quick. I'd have survived."

"That's not what the data suggests." Evie lightly touched the bruise around Merritt's split lip. "It looks like you might end up with a bit of a scar, but it's healing very well." She seemed as if she had more to say, and Merritt waited out the silence. She hoped Evie might volunteer more about her claustrophobia but instead, she pulled her coat more closely around her. Merritt glanced at her phone. Late afternoon? Already? The Farmexal execs were meeting over dinner, and she was expected to provide them with her findings. *Crap. Late again.*

"All part of my master plan to look suitably tough." She opened the car door. "Speaking of, I have to get back to Regina for a meeting."

Evie laughed and picked up Walter, who had been roaming between their feet until finally nestling on Merritt's toes.

"We're off, too," she said, "Clearly, you know where to find me. In case there are more mini-doughnuts that require launching. Or if ever those *circumstances* should change." Evie set Walter on his feet before turning and heading toward her vehicle, Walter walking at a clipped pace behind her.

Merritt slipped behind the wheel and cranked up the heat, her cold toes missing Walter, and her mind hoping that change would come. Soon.

❖

Merritt spent most of the drive back to Regina chastising herself. Why had she lied about working for a dog food manufacturer? Had she seriously thought such a lame deception would slide past Evie O'Halloran? That it wouldn't give the intelligent, capable woman pause to wonder? Against her better judgment, she'd allowed the conversation with Evie to become far too personal. That was where she'd really tripped up. What possessed her to comment on the pendant? Much as the stone complemented the sparkling in Evie's eyes. *There you go again.* Evie was smart. Eventually, she would guess the truth of Merritt's work with the fertilizer manufacturer. Any serious breach would not only make her investigation more difficult, but given Evie's politics, it could also devolve into a messy public relations fiasco.

If there was one value Merritt held to, honed after Natalie, it was honesty. Lying for a greater good she could tolerate. Otherwise, it was a deal breaker. And that deal went both ways. Did the fact that Evie had withheld details about her claustrophobia constitute lying? No. By omission? Maybe. How could she really know? Merritt couldn't shake the feeling that there was much more to Evie's story than a fear of small places. And maybe that was plenty reason to keep extra distance. After all, she'd been fooled in the past when her attraction to Natalie had obscured the lies. Love might be blind, but now she was so attuned to deceit that she saw lies everywhere. That was the terrible takeaway from a million-dollar lesson that she couldn't afford to forget.

CHAPTER NINE

Merritt was biased. She knew it. Even so, the coffee Max served at his bakery was inarguably above and beyond any fare in Regina. He'd sourced the beans from Café Femenino coffee collectives he'd visited personally, donating back to fund their growth. He'd contracted a local roaster and had ground each little brown bean in an unimaginably expensive grinder suited to the specific texture required by the offering, just like an artist with colors. Coarse for French press. Fine for drip. Extra fine for the almost molasses-like consistency of his current customer favorite, the high-octane espresso.

Merritt's morning cried out for the latter. The previous evening's dinner with the Farmexal senior staff had gone way too late and had been far from productive. Exhausting. The questions still outweighed the answers they were so desperate to find. Coffee was an answer. A salvation for her, at least. She spooned the fine caramel-colored foam from the top of the tiny cup and indulged, letting the cinnamon sit for an extra second on her upper lip as a test of her wound's recovery.

Recently, she'd been struggling to sleep. She knew her restlessness was a result of the duplicity she was enmeshed in. During her preparation for the investigation, her colleagues at the ministry had warned her that the deceit inevitably weighed you down, and that the best practice was to keep the lies to a minimum. Doing so made it easier to keep track. Not to stumble. *Easier said than done. Dog food. Really?* When she'd awakened from the moments of sleep she'd had, she couldn't bring herself to bike to the bakery, deciding to walk instead. For the first several blocks, she'd reflected on why she hadn't yet reached out to her parents, despite her promise to Max. It wasn't that she didn't appreciate her family, but her commitment to Shepherd Press had been more about what her parents wanted than what she did. They'd long hoped that despite the ideological differences, she'd grow to understand that plenty of readers still enjoyed the feeling of a bound book over an electronic device. While that might well have been the case, her heart wasn't set on finding out. In fact, she realized that if anything positive had come from the Natalie incident, it was that it had provided the impetus she needed to fly from the nest and discover her own wings. Today, her feet were dragging, as if those wings were almost too heavy. Lies, she imagined, did that.

By the time she took her usual spot at the corner table near the back of Max's bakery, she'd managed to walk off most of her angst. Maybe people with dogs had it all figured out and that walking was like yoga. But less boring. The coffee was perfectly thick and rich, and Merritt sensed the caffeine pushing her into another gear. Her contemplations shifted from sluggish but fluid to rapid and disjointed. *It would be nice to have a dog but a small one. Like Walter. An antidote for what ails you. Maybe I need a larvikite talisman. But why not get a dog? Just a small one that would fit in my backpack. Right beside my firearm. Maybe not a good idea.*

Merritt didn't like to carry a weapon. Even as a peace officer, it was unusual to be granted a permit to carry in Canada. But after several physical encounters on more than a few investigations, and with Steph's encouragement, she'd relented. The money involved in the illegal trades and practices that fell to the Ministry of Environmental Resources to enforce had skyrocketed. With the stakes higher, the dangers of her job had correspondingly escalated. Now the sidearm was considered protocol. Heavy, awkward protocol.

So no dog. Or maybe one for Max. That he would share.

"I'd offer you a penny for your thoughts, but I can tell from that look on your face that they wouldn't be worth even that."

"That would be funnier if we still used pennies in Canada," she retorted, dogs and guns now pushed to the back of her mind.

Steph laughed as she took a seat across from her and tossed a brick-sized, newspaper-wrapped bundle toward her. Merritt snapped to attention and caught it. Before she could ask, Steph said, "It's from Angela. It's cheese."

Angela was Steph's longtime partner in life, and her recent pursuit after having spent time at a Trappist monastery in neighboring Manitoba was cheese making. After several attempts, it had become clear to everyone who loved her that she might need to spend more time with the monks. But no one had the heart to say so. Angela was more a saint than a cheese maker.

Merritt's face must've reflected that she'd been recounting the last batch—a blue-veined furry cream that had perfumed her refrigerator and everything in it until Angela herself had texted the next day to suggest Merritt dispose of it for health reasons—because Steph rushed to reassure her. "Honestly, Merr, this one is really good. Nothing funky about it. I think she washed it with pinot."

"I don't know what that means, but if she washed it, then maybe it won't smell like the last wedge, which had an unquestionably fetid quality."

Steph pushed the bundle farther across the table and sat back. "Don't be unkind. Pinot is cheese talk for boozy. I promise, you'll like it. What's the news?"

Merritt knew that anything she said to Steph about her investigation would stay between them. Better yet, sharing her findings was an effective way to brainstorm with someone who knew how to investigate, had reasonable expectations about the time it took to be diligent, and understood discretion. Unlike the Farmexal folks. *Some people can be trusted.*

"The soil samples have shown barely trace amounts of nitrates. There's nothing to suggest the totes are being emptied on site."

"So if it's not going into the ground, where is it going?"

"Good question. The CFO claims that inventory levels are still off, which suggests that the increased scrutiny—if it has been noticed—hasn't changed the behavior."

"Meaning you're not on the perp's radar. That's good. But I'm not sure I get it. Why make a show of disposing of the empties? Why not bury them somewhere?"

Merritt shrugged and finished her espresso. "Maybe it's personal. Maybe it's a red herring. Maybe we're not dealing with a genius. Or geniuses. Maybe they feel invincible. Invisible. Maybe they're hiding in plain sight."

Max came by and found room on the table for a small plate of cream-filled éclairs, a large Americano, and a refill for Merritt, and then he greeted Steph with a kiss on the cheek and a brief shoulder rub. "No time for fun with my fave gals. Less daylight means more coffee to grind." He hustled back to the counter to assist his staff in what was becoming a regular rush of Saturday morning customers.

Merritt peeled the chocolate off the top of her pastry and set it to the side. She then used her spoon to rake the cream from the middle and set it beside the chocolate. Only then did she pick up the perfectly baked, crispy pâte à choux and dip it into her de-crema'd espresso before taking her first bite. Max was a genius. Steph was glaring but seemed to know better than to comment on Merritt's exacting approach to eating.

Merritt wished it was as easy to pick apart the situation at Farmexal. Her cup rattled as she picked it up from the saucer. *Time to switch to decaf.* She'd hoped to have more to share by now, and the dark cloud of responsibility floated over her again.

Steph must've sensed it because she put a hand on hers and gently squeezed it to stop the shaking. "Don't worry, you're doing everything right. Use your resources. Trust your instincts."

Merritt wondered about trust. To be honest, she was amazed at the notion. Who and what to believe incessantly dogged her. The cloud grew darker. She did trust her instincts, but doing so seemed to take so much effort. It was always so hard now.

"Is any of this about Natalie?" Steph asked. "Because you know, if we had even a sniff of her, I'd let you know. My guy in international owes me a favor, and this is how I've called it in. If he or anyone south of the equator lays eyes on her, I'm *his* first call, and you're *my* first call. Got it?"

"I think we know the reality of it, Philly. I wasn't Natalie's first mark. She wasn't working independently. She couldn't have been able to disappear without so much as a breadcrumb in what, eight years now? She's deep, and I know we're not going to find her."

"Okay, no bullshit. If you're right, can you make peace with that? Let it go?"

"No bullshit? I don't know. Because idiot that I am, I had feelings for her. So when it all went down, I didn't just lose a small fortune..." Merritt couldn't push the words out past the python of emotion that constricted her throat.

"You lost your heart. I know. And I'm so sorry, baby."

Steph was the only one outside of her family who knew the full story about Natalie. The countless hours of surveillance they'd done together had eventually whittled down her resistance, and they'd shared every embarrassing bit of their young lives. Steph had used her formidable RCMP resources only to discover that organized schemes that bilked unwitting victims of billions of dollars worldwide, a seven-figure fraction of that Merritt's share of an inheritance from her bachelor uncle, were complicated webs. A few years after defrauding Merritt, Natalie—whoever she truly was—had used that same name in a forging scheme in São Paulo. Investigators had followed up, but again, she'd vanished. Since then, nothing.

Merritt had swallowed the shame when it had all happened and had graduated. She'd refocused with laser intensity on her career path and had secured a position with the ministry. Eventually, that path had led to Ottawa and a self-imposed relationship hiatus.

"Hey, there. Who are you, little fella?"

Merritt was ripped from her recollection by Steph's strange question. She had called Merr many things over the years, but "little fella" wasn't one of them. Her surprise did not abate when she looked at the furry visitor weaving around her feet. "Walter? What are you doing here?"

"Walter?" Steph exclaimed, extracting her foot from the twists of leash that had followed his figure eight around the table.

"Walter! Get your furry little butt over here this instant."

Evie approached the table and carefully placed two ventis down before reaching and extracting Walter and his leash. "I'm so sorry. He is so pushy around pastries."

Steph laughed. "Aren't we all?"

Merritt was happy to be distracted and happier to see who was doing the distracting. "Hi."

Evie stood, Walter bundled in her arms, her face flushed. "Hi back."

The pause that followed could not have been more than a couple of seconds, but during that moment, it seemed to Merritt that the hustle of the coffee shop slowed, and the chatter dropped several decibels. Even the light in the room had changed, softening and radiating around Evie's face.

"What my rude friend here is trying to say is, 'Walter's mom, let me introduce you to my bestie, Steph Phillips.'"

Merritt watched mutely as Evie reached across the table, smiled, and shook Steph's hand.

"Very pleased to meet you, Steph. I'm Evie O'Halloran.

And, yes, you've already met Walter. Sorry if he caused any trouble."

"Call me Philly, please. Would you two care to join us?"

Merritt's instinct was to kick Steph beneath the table, but the end of Walter's leash was now tangled around her ankles. Instead, she leaned down to unravel the tether and handed it to Evie, who acknowledged her with a smile before turning back to Steph.

"Thank you, but I'm here with my niece. It was nice meeting you, Steph...Philly. Nice seeing you again, Merr. I'll leave you to enjoy what's left of your goodies."

Merritt followed Evie's eyes to the plate that was now scattered with shards of chocolate and expunged pastry filling. Evidence of Merritt's ritual elicited a quizzical look, then another smile as Evie gently put Walter's feet back on the ground, gathered up the coffees, and made her way to a table near the front window where Robby had already settled.

"Wow. I'm going to have to amend your nickname to Fish 'n because, girl, you got no game." Steph snorted, almost choking on her Americano.

Merritt nodded a greeting toward Robby before turning to Steph. "No game, Philly. Dr. O'Halloran is just someone I met. Ran into, actually. On Farmexal's time. Speaking of which..."

"Very good. You almost made that change of topic sound casual." Steph looked back over her shoulder at Evie, then nodded. "I see Kate Winslet with a solid touch of Christina Hendricks."

"*Easttown* Kate, I hope. Please not *Titanic*."

"Yes, *Easttown*. In the way she carries herself. But more femme. Easy to imagine her in a blazer, silk shirt, and pencil skirt. I can tell she has nice legs under the skinny jeans. Very Hendricks. And the eyes. Wow."

Merritt was finding it hard not to share Steph's observations. She imagined that a silk shirt would absolutely be something that Evie would look nice in—snug against those ample breasts—and she had to admit to herself, if not to Steph, that she'd already noticed the toned and contoured legs. Still... "I doubt it's acceptable to objectify women this way. And I'm sure your wife wouldn't appreciate you imagining what's under another woman's jeans."

"I'm sure you're right. But you should crawl out from under that rock and have a look at women sometime. Especially the beautiful ones."

True, Evie O'Halloran was quite beautiful. Blond wavy hair. A touch of strawberry. Femme for sure. Not that Evie was waifish. Or overly delicate. Steph was right. Evie carried herself with a certain gravitas. She flashed back to the press conference and how Evie had wrestled the crowd to get to Kevin. Powerful. More substantive. Soft curves. Sensual.

"Anything you want to tell me about her?"

Merritt rushed to answer, then checked herself. Best to sound dismissive. Admitting even the smallest bit of attraction would unleash Steph's inner matchmaker. It might also force her to consider feelings for Evie that were best guarded. "She's a protester. A career protester, as far as I can tell." She leveled her tone and avoided Steph's eyes. *Keep it cool.* "She organizes the university's environmental club. Planet Change."

"Weren't you in a group like that back in uni days?"

Merritt flashed a *shut up if you know what's good for you* look. "Philly, after what you and I have seen of protests and protesters, are you really going to take her side?"

"No sides, buddy, just a pretty lady. Okay, I'm going to let this one go for now, but we'll come back to it. I'm on a schedule. Tell me more about the investigation."

The reprieve loosened the tightness in Merritt's chest, and she finished relaying the details with Steph. A half hour and a third espresso later, they had developed an expansive list of follow-up items. Steph pulled on her coat and gave Merr a thud on the back.

"Gotta get back. Angela's got a list of chores a mile long for me."

"Please thank her for the cheese...unless it kills me, in which case, well, don't."

"Will do. Seriously, though, promise me you'll watch your back on this, Merritt. I'm not kidding around. Where there's money, there's desperation."

"Always. All points."

As Steph made her way out, Merritt snuck another peek at Evie. The hush and the radiant light again fell softly on the room. A comforting sensation wrapped around her shoulders like a favorite blanket, and the warmth moved lower in her body. Much lower. *This is not helping. Definitely not cool.* She shrugged and pushed her espresso cup across the table. *No more caffeine for you, Shepherd.* If only it was that simple.

❖

As much as Evie tried to give Robby her full attention, it was drawn repeatedly across the room toward Merr and her friend. Though Steph had introduced herself as Merr's bestie, they had clearly been holding hands when she'd first arrived. Which could mean nothing. Or something. Was this the "circumstance" Merr had alluded to? After all, they were both young and attractive. Both undeniably butch, which meant nothing. Obviously, they were comfortable with each other. Maybe their relationship was more open than most. That could explain, even possibly excuse, the heavy flirtation that had taken place in the parking lot earlier in the week. Sure. It could.

"Hey, you still with me?"

"Absolutely," Evie fibbed. "I'm just lost in this brioche. It's divine. For the sake of my thighs, I must forget this place exists."

"Come on, Auntie E, you put most near-fifty-year-olds to shame! I'm hoping it's genetic, but I suspect Walter is your personal trainer."

Evie laughed and was caught by the sight of Steph leaving. She mirrored her "bestie's" good-bye smile and nod as she maneuvered through the patrons and left. Once again, Evie's attention bounced to Merr, who was handing one of the bakery workers a small package. Odd. *But really, Evie, none of your business. Family is business this morning.*

Robby had sounded unsettled last night. Evie reeled back her focus and took a guess at what might be on her mind. "First of all, as you well know, I'm nearer to my mid-forties than fifties. For several more months. Secondly, how's your mom? Really?"

Evie knew how her sister was. Anxious. Fearful. Feeling every reasonable and rational emotion that a woman in an abusive relationship typically would. But Evie was asking because even with her perspective, Robby's feelings about Bev's situation needed a place to be heard. And Evie was that place.

"Lonnie is a jerk. Plain and simple. I have been trying for years to get Mom to believe that she deserves better, but she just isn't hearing me."

Evie shared her frustration. She'd started trying to get her sister to listen from the first sign that Lonnie was trouble. He'd insisted Bev quit the curling league, claiming it was because he couldn't attend all her games. But if she wanted to switch from her mixed team to the women's league, that would be fine by him. His fuse was short, and flare-ups over the smallest misstep regardless of fault usually ended sending emotional shrapnel Bev's way. Evie had heard a handful of backhanded references to gay agendas, "fairies," and "dykes," enough to know to keep her private life from his radar. Not that she was plugged in to her community, but nonetheless, he felt dangerous. And after seeing him throw a rock at a neighborhood cat, she'd also kept Walter a healthy distance away. Why Bev tolerated his meanness was a mystery, but scolding her for her decisions wasn't supportive. Evie was working on a different tack. "Robby, it could be that she is hearing you, but for her own reasons, she can't manage whatever change would be in her best interests."

"I hear you. But I swear, if I find out he's raised one finger against her, I'll lose my fucking mind."

"Let's hope it doesn't come to that." The words were barely out of Evie's mouth when a plate of pastries appeared on the table between them. "We didn't order…"

"No, you did not." The words floated down, landing just as softly as the sweets. *Merr.* "And no, I am not stalking you," she continued. "My brother owns the place, and I get a pretty generous discount."

The whole time she spoke, Evie basked in the evenly measured cadence of her speech.

"You must be Robby. It's nice to meet you. I've heard nice things from your aunt. I trust Kevin made his way home safely? I hope his brief detainment didn't traumatize him. He seems"—she paused and looked at Evie as if seeking her approval—"delicate."

Evie fought to stifle a guffaw, succeeding only because of the detached expression that had come across Robby's face.

"I wouldn't know. He's no longer my responsibility." Robby's response was directed toward Evie, and her announcement was weighted with finality. Evie felt relief but also knew that, even though Kevin was a first-class dope, Robby hadn't come to the decision to break up with him easily. Before she could formulate a suitably condoling response, Robby had turned her attention from all things Kevin.

"I'm sure Farmexal knows little about responsibility, though, right?" Her words were directed at Merr and filled with provocation. Evie could tell they'd hit the mark only by the way Merr's knuckles whitened. Otherwise, she maintained absolute composure, her posture visibly relaxed before she responded. She leaned down and placed both palms on the table, smoothing the lace doily beneath their pastry plate gently with her long, nimble fingers.

"They have good people there who are continuing to look into it, and Robby"—she paused, no doubt for impact—"I am certain that this situation is their number-one priority." Then Merr smiled. *Who wouldn't believe her?*

Evie shifted in her seat, hoping the skip in her breath hadn't been noticed. Merr's words could've been interpreted as "the company line" coming from any mouth but this beautiful one. Instead, they settled on the table like cozy blankets. Before she could abandon dignity and curl up in them, a man remarkably resembling Merr approached the table.

"Hi, I'm Max Shepherd. Welcome to Boulangerie de la Régine. I trust you're enjoying my pastries, if not my sister's company." He nodded at Merr and smiled a deep and similarly delicious smile. At Robby. And she smiled back.

Evie knew at that instant where things were going to end up between Robby and this particular Shepherd. If only she could be equally intuitive about the possibilities that might exist with the other.

❖

The sun was still shining as they stepped onto the sidewalk, and Evie squinted in a way that showed a pleasing array of fine laugh lines at the sides of her eyes and mouth and a positively cute furrow on her brow. Merritt was struck by how little she knew about their source but accepted that she shouldn't ask. *Keep it light.*

"Thank you so much for rescuing me." Evie smiled, sliding on a pair of sporty sunglasses. Merritt missed the eyes, but the intense autumn sunlight demanded that she follow suit. She slipped on the classic aviator Ray-Bans Max had given her for her thirty-fourth birthday.

"It seems that I'm fine-tuning that skill where you're concerned. But honestly, it was my pleasure. That"—she gestured over her shoulder toward the shop—"was painfully, almost embarrassingly uncomfortable."

"Wasn't it? I felt like a third, wholly unnecessary wheel." Evie laughed.

"And I was the fourth."

"I'm sorry. You must think my niece is flaky. The ink is barely dry on her breakup, and she's already flirting with your brother."

"He was all in on flirting back. And he is charming."

"Runs in the family, I suspect."

Merritt blushed and was unfamiliarly at a loss for words.

"My niece is actually a pretty serious young woman. Kevin wasn't serious material."

"He didn't appear to be, though in fairness, I didn't know him."

"Trust me," Evie laughed again, "you experienced most of what he had to offer."

They walked toward the train tracks that ran east to west through the city. The railway had deep roots throughout the country, and Merritt remembered learning in high school how many of Canada's major cities and towns were built around the over twenty thousand miles of track laid by the national railway companies. She marveled at remembering anything from high school, caught up as she'd been with athletics. And girls. And women.

"I hope you don't mind that I used your dog's need for a hydrant as an excuse to get out of there."

"Not at all. I'm pretty sure the pheromones floating between your brother and Robby were making Walter uncomfortable, too. Besides, he loves to walk. On his own terms. He can be profoundly lazy but also a bit of a busybody."

"He's a good boy, and I appreciate his lack of focus. I myself have had several espressos too many. I'm also sorry I interrupted your conversation with Robby when I brought over your pastries. Was it as intense as it looked?" Again, Merritt chastised herself for furthering a personal connection during an investigation. "My timing has never been great." *To say the least.*

"Not at all. It was fine. We'd been talking about her mom. Well, more about her mom's live-in, Lonnie. He's a piece of work. Makes Kevin look good. Really good." She gave Walter a dark flaky wafer, which he didn't take the time to chew before gulping down. "I confess, we'd actually come for the pastries, which live up to their reputation."

"I'll let Max know, though I suspect the expanding waistlines of the locals testify to that. But he'll be pleased that Robby thinks so."

"I'm sure. I don't get to walk much on this side of the tracks. I usually stay on the casino side. It has been so gentrified here over the years. Hard to believe it had such a notorious past."

"Did it? How so?"

Evie looked at Merritt as if assessing her interest. "During Prohibition, trains were used to move liquor from town to town. Al Capone's organization was said to have built and utilized underground tunnels extending out from the train yard in Moose Jaw to rum run."

Merritt loved listening to her. Her interests were exceptionally idiosyncratic. "As far north as Moose Jaw? That's almost unbelievable."

"And yet, it is truth. Prepare yourself, Merr, there's more. Did you know Regina has its own tunnel system?"

"I'd heard rumors."

"I can absolutely confirm that they exist, though most of them have collapsed or have been sealed off. Unlike Moose Jaw, Regina's tunnels weren't infamous. They were constructed as a warmer way to move between main governmental and other key historic buildings like hotels and bars in the winter."

Idiosyncratic on steroids. "For real? I thought they were just local folklore. Like the ghost train up near Prince Albert. Or the flying saucers at Waterhen Lake."

"Well, I can't say for sure how valid those comparisons are. Yes, I'm older than you, but people have been reporting seeing the lights on the tracks up there since the 1920s, and I'm not so old to possess firsthand knowledge of the ghost train." She winked, the fine lines dancing around her eyes. If she was older, it couldn't be by much. Even if she was, did it matter? "As for

UFOs, well, I think I'll keep my mind open on that one. Just in case." She looked up, slowly scanning the blue sky.

Merritt threw her head back and laughed. "Seriously? A doctor and a scholar believing in aliens? I may have misjudged you. And I doubt you're that much older than me." She had noticed Evie's brisk pace and more than once had to quicken hers in order to keep up. "How does Walter keep up with you?"

"You'd be shocked by how much he eats. As for the paranormal, life is full of surprises and quaint little mysteries."

"Well, you can keep your little mysteries, Dr. Evie, because I prefer to trust only what I can see." Merritt realized she was delving into personal disclosures again and brought it back to the tunnels. "Tell me about the tunnels. What's down there?"

"I can't say for certain what's left of them. It's been several years since our department included them as part of an undergrad research study, but they were a useful way to show students the geological striations beneath the city."

"You don't do that anymore?"

"I never did. Not personally. Too..." Like her response, Evie almost came to a dead stop. She adjusted her sunglasses before continuing, but Merritt could tell it was a ruse. *There's more to that story.* "They're too decrepit to make real use of, and the faculty made a decision last year to stop the field trips. Our students can learn just as much about the passage of time from the layered rock along the river. Lakes as well. Pretty much any body of water has a story to tell."

Again, the narrative ended abruptly, as if she was self-editing. More to the story was right, Merritt thought disappointedly. *What is it she's not telling me?* She dodged her self-analysis—after all, wasn't she a bit of a hypocrite, given the secrets she was keeping—and was about to ask Evie to continue, but as they turned the corner on the street running parallel to the tracks, a low warehouse building with Farmexal signage caught her eye.

This might be the washhouse Kelly had mentioned during the manufacturing and shipping tour. It was a Saturday, so it didn't surprise her to see that the employee lot was empty. What did surprise her was the red pickup parked at the side entrance. The files she'd been given hadn't even listed a security guard for this facility. So whose truck was it? And where were they?

She needed to investigate. But how could she without bending the truth? *You need to get in there. And she can't come with you.* It tore Merritt up, but the only choice was to bend it. Hard. With that thought, she knew that Evie's equivocation would pale by comparison to what she had to say. She would need to shoulder the guilt and regret because now, it was her turn to edit the story.

❖

"I won't be long. Five minutes? If you want, I can meet you back at Max's shop." Merritt had made up an excuse about needing to sign some papers left for her at the washhouse. When Evie had asked, she'd said the authorizations *could* wait until Monday, but it would save time if she could just pop in and do it while here. "Pencil pushing waits for no one."

Lies upon lies. This was her job, and as much as she hated lying and wanted to be unedited with Evie, she had to put the work first. Graciously, Evie had insisted she'd be happy to wait outside the washhouse with Walter on such a lovely day.

As Merritt approached the entrance, she studied the truck while trying not to draw Evie's attention. Like Einerson's, this truck was red and appeared to have what Conroy had described as the "sweet chrome package." A small yellow smudge stained the trailer hitch. Dings and dents always seemed to happen in those first few weeks of vehicle ownership, and if it actually was Einerson's truck, he'd have been pissed. He must've saved like crazy to be able to afford it and all the bells and whistles.

The employee entrance door had been propped just enough to prevent it from closing. She stepped inside, opening it as little as she could. She leaned against the framing wall to let her eyes adjust to the relative darkness and removed her backpack. She quietly opened the main compartment and removed her harnessed Wesson Commander Classic. Like most ministry-issued weapons, the Bobtail had never been fired off-range. She had no reason to believe she would need it, but she slipped the harness over her shoulder before putting her jacket back on. Desperation did change people. She swallowed her fear and moved through the gray light slowly, breath even and eyes keen.

Her vision adjusted, she stepped into the loading area. Pallets of empty totes were lined up in rows. Those nearest the shipping docks were neatly stacked. Clean. The others sat next to what appeared to be an industrial-size washer and contained a pale-yellow residue, yet to be processed. She took only a few steps in before metallic bumping noises came from a basement stairwell, then got louder. Closer.

Retreating behind a corner near the shipping doors and a stack of heavy-duty caution-yellow dollies, she clenched her teeth and willed her heart to stop hammering. She wasn't concerned about encountering Einerson, if that was his truck, but there was no Farmexal reason for her to be there. Out of the corner of her eye, Merritt caught movement near the door and froze.

❖

Evie had stepped out of the sunshine and into the wedge of light cast on the floor of what appeared to be a storage facility of some kind. It had been longer than five minutes, and she'd promised Bev she'd stop by for a visit. Merr was likely in an office somewhere inside. Pushing paper.

Evie scooped Walter into her enormous leather sling bag and took a few steps forward. She was just about to call out for Merr when the door closed behind her, and the room went dark. Panic began to swell in her belly. *Stay calm. You're okay.* She took a few tentative steps, and an arm wrapped around her torso, pinning her arms and Walter and using her bag to immobilize her. The panic buckled and heaved. *Nowhere to go.*

Another hand forcefully covered her mouth, pulling her into an even darker corner of the room. *Fuck no.* Her attacker spun her against a wall and bent one of her hands behind her back as if she was a rag doll, her mouth uncovered for only an instant. She curled her other arm around Walter and tried to scream, but a hand pressed over her mouth again. The words were bouncing around in her brain like cake-fueled children in a birthday bouncy castle. Incessant. Loud. *Get out!* She tried another cry when her attacker pulled her phone from her pocket.

The screen lit up. Merr. Merr was her attacker? What was happening? Confused, she squirmed, her fear turning into anger. Merr flicked the phone into silent mode and clicked the screen to black. The darkness frayed Evie, and she began to unravel. Her chest seized as if under a truck. She squirmed, kept Walter in his bag, and latched on to her larvikite pendant, twisting the chain around her finger, unable to draw the breath to try to yell. The space around them was shrinking, terribly, awfully smaller.

Her heart raced. She swallowed bile, and her knees began to wobble. The hand on her mouth slowly pulled away, but a single finger replaced it. Warm breath against her ear whispered, "Shush." For a second, she thought she might be able to breathe, lulled by the soothing cadence of the softly spoken word. But even the unexpected intimacy couldn't stem the roiling panic that pushed up from a deeper place, seeking release.

Air. I need air. Evie wanted to scream, but her sight had adjusted enough to see Merr's eyes. Wide, they stared as if warning against the smallest utterance.

Fighting the overwhelming urge to bolt, Evie drew as deep a breath as she could. Her head filled with the tarry notes of leather, a sweet hint of cinnamon. The odd combination calmed her. She released the pendant, and her shoulders relaxed.

Merr eased her enough to allow her hands to move more.

She placed them along the sides of Merr's suede jacket and felt a cold, hard lump. No. Couldn't be. Was it a gun? She gasped, and Merr's hand was on her mouth. She struggled, but Merr pinned her again. Harder this time.

Evie's ears rang, panic deafening her. Merr pressed something into her palm. Leather. Metal? Her fingers scrambled across the surface. A badge. Confusion replaced her panic. Merr had a badge? What was happening? Slowly, understanding replaced confusion. Farmexal. The missing totes. The screams in her head were replaced by the sound of footsteps coming closer. She froze. Merr didn't release her until the footsteps subsided, and a wedge of light burst across the epoxied cement floor, then disappeared.

❖

Merritt waited another five minutes before leading Evie outside. As Einerson's truck left the lot, she processed what had happened. No, that certainly wasn't the ideal way to reveal who she really was. Grabbing Evie so forcefully and holding her and Walter captive to keep from being discovered wasn't part of the plan either. But plans changed, and foremost in her mind was ensuring that the investigation wouldn't be compromised. Despite what was clearly a terrifying event for Evie, she calmly calculated her next move.

"I have no right to ask," Merritt began carefully, "but—"

"No need to ask, Merr. I am adept at filling in blanks." Her voice was icy. "You lied to me. Not that I hadn't guessed you were no ordinary auditor. But no matter. If you're a cop, it seems that ultimately, discretion would be the best course of action."

"Not a cop. I'm a peace officer with the Ministry of Environmental Resources. Enforcement team."

Evie's hands were trembling. She gently took the unfazed, tail-wagging dog from the carry bag, setting him at their feet. Silence took up most of the space as they headed in the direction of the bakery. Merritt didn't trust herself to unbend the truth, but she needed to say something. "I appreciate that you're willing to keep this between us. I hope Robby's not worrying about you."

No response, no eye contact.

They walked for half a block until Merritt decided to disrupt the unbearable lull, eager to get a truer sense of where Evie might have landed emotionally. She'd been nothing short of terrified in the washhouse. Merritt wanted to take away the fear that had followed them down the street. "I can't believe Walter stayed so quiet. Has he done undercover before?"

Evie stopped walking and gave Walter another treat. "He never barks. I'm not sure he's able, or maybe he's never had a reason. Regardless, it's not a quality I'm going to ask the vet to resolve."

Merritt was pleased that Evie's tone had thawed, and her sense of levity had returned, especially given how extreme her reaction to the tight quarters had been. Maybe panic had been the expected reaction for someone claustrophobic? Maybe not. *Don't act like it doesn't matter.* "Are you sure you're okay?"

Evie met Merr's gaze for the first time since the washhouse. "No."

She nodded and put a hand gently on Evie's shoulder. "I'm sorry I had to deceive you. Truly, I am."

More silence. Merritt's stomach was in knots, but Evie hadn't pulled away. So that was progress. Evie held out her hand, palm up. "Give me your phone."

Merritt immediately obliged. Seconds later, after several finger taps, she accepted it back.

"There's my number. I'm here until early afternoon tomorrow, then heading back to Saskatoon. I like blackjack, and I allow myself one night a month at the casino. Tonight is that night if you'd like to join me. No pressure. No questions asked."

❖

While Merr disappeared behind la Régine 's almost-empty rack of bread behind the cash register, Evie took the same spot at the table she'd occupied an hour ago and hooked Walter's leash to the leg of her chair. Robby was still clearly delighted with Max's company, and given the goo-goo eyes and smiles zipping across the café table, it appeared mutual. Evie was contemplating third-wheeling herself back to the hotel when Merr reappeared at her side with a brown-paper-wrapped bundle in one hand and her knapsack in the other. The large bulge beneath her jacket was no longer discernable, but it appeared that she carried the knapsack with additional caution.

"Cheese," she said to her brother.

"Angela's?" he replied.

"It is. Lucky for you, I plan to take you down with me." She turned from Max to Evie as she spoke, so Evie wasn't sure why someone would be going down or where exactly that was. It felt like some covert sibling code. Merr must've seen Evie's perplexed expression because she promptly directed her next comment toward her. "Dinner at Max's loft at seven thirty? I'll text you the address."

Evie wondered if she'd lost her mind. Had Merr just asked her to dinner? Had she agreed to go? A gentle squeeze of her hand drew her to Merr's eyes. And smile.

"I'll keep it light so there'll be time to make your blackjack date." Merr turned to Max and Robby. "You are both welcome to join us if you'd like. You, too, Walter." She waved good-bye and headed out the door without waiting for a response.

As Evie watched her leave, she wondered at Merr's presumptuousness. She was certainly confident. Quite the opposite of how Evie must've appeared at that building. In the confines of their hiding spot, she'd felt close to passing out. Now, she realized that even if she had, she'd been held so tightly against Merr that she wouldn't have fallen. It mystified her that rather than the fear and panic she'd felt in the moment, her most vivid recollection was the rapid pulse of a strong heartbeat in her ears as she stood pinned against the leather jacket. The smell of a cappuccino at a nearby table carried her back to the strangely enticing restraint of her captor. She traced the area around her mouth where Merr's fingers had pressed. Demanding submission. Captivating. Captivated.

Evie wondered whether she could trust this newly revealed Merr Shepherd. Whether she should. Government investigator? Enforcement, no less. Still, ultimately, a civil servant contributing her findings to the inexcusably slow-moving cogs of environmental policy development. Evie would normally rail at the ludicrous approach of lawmakers who had been trying for years to stop a flood with an empty glass, but for whatever mindboggling reason, she'd apparently accepted a dinner invitation. Maybe it would give her some insight into the mystery totes. Reassurance, possibly, that an environmental catastrophe was not as imminent as it appeared. Even so, at least two unanswered questions remained: could she believe anything Merr Shepherd told her? And what was so dangerous in the building that it required a government agent to carry a weapon? There was only one way to find out. She gathered up Walter, waved good-bye to Robby, and headed to the door, slowing only to indulge in the tempting fragrance of coffee and cinnamon.

CHAPTER TEN

A s Merritt drove home, she reflected on what had happened, curtailing her impulse to daydream about where the night might lead. Seeing Einerson at the washhouse didn't implicate him in any wrongdoing, and rather than resolve anything, it left many questions unanswered. What was he doing there? Given that the washhouse only handled empty totes, it wasn't the likeliest fail point in the distribution chain. Still, she couldn't imagine what business Einerson might have at that location on a Saturday. She'd have to check the duty rosters to see if he was working a security shift.

It had certainly been a close call. If she'd been discovered, she wasn't sure how she'd have explained being there. As an auditor, she could've made something credible up on the spot, but she'd listened to her gut and hidden. But when Evie had appeared, the situation had rocketed from could-have-gone-bad to could-have-gone-worse. What if Einerson had found them? What if things had escalated? What if Evie had gotten hurt? Her gut clenched. This was the reason for distance.

Distance, she thought with a laugh. There'd been zero distance between her and Evie when they'd hidden in the washhouse. Their bodies could not have been closer. She thought about how she'd physically controlled Evie. Held her. Pinned her. Felt her fear. Her panic. Worse, she recognized her own response to the close contact. Her need. Desire. Feelings she'd tamped down for years. To stay safe. But now, she sighed. This woman. Evie. This warm, soft body that just hours ago had molded against her.

Shut it down. Hindsight was unequivocal. This was exactly the reason for distance. Physical distance. Emotional distance. And psychological distance. Her mouth went dry. Where was hindsight when she'd invited Evie for dinner?

Merritt unpacked the lasagna ingredients onto Max's butcher-block island. She started the pasta water and searched her mind for what she could share with Evie. She owed her an explanation, but how far could she go? Should she go? What might be wise to withhold? For the sake of the investigation, the answer to the latter was easy: as much as possible. For everyone's safety, including her own.

Merritt had finished most of the dishes and was about to grate the parmesan when Evie buzzed up. Her stomach in knots, she stood near the front door, listening to Evie's heels on the stairs. Heels? She glanced at her reflection in the hall mirror and tucked back the strand of hair that habitually fell over her right eye. Not terrible. Once the lasagna was in the oven, she'd had just enough time to shower, jump into a pair of faded black khakis, and finish with a black V-neck tee beneath a blue collared shirt. No heels on her combat boots, but she thought she looked pretty good. Until she opened the door. *I am way underdressed.*

Evie stood in the doorway. Breathtaking. As predicted, and as hoped, she looked elegant and splendid in an open-neck, collared white shirt, gray pencil skirt, and black heels. Pearls surrounded her neck. Very stately. Her hair, which Merr had only seen held back, cascaded over her shoulders. The soft curls moved like a field of August wheat in a gentle breeze. Steph was right. Hendricks and Winslet, check. She licked her lips against the dryness, then realized that Evie was watching her. Heat blazed across her cheeks, and she struggled to stem her embarrassment as Evie walked to the couch and put her bag down.

"I think I should change," Merritt almost stammered as she wiped her palms on her T-shirt.

"Don't be silly. I think you look perfect."

During the pause that followed, Merritt wondered if the awkwardness was as obvious as it felt. The fire from her cheeks flashed across her whole body, the heat so radiant that it was impossible for Evie not to have noticed. *So not cool.*

"Let me explain," Evie added, snagging a piece of parmesan. "This weekend, I only brought dog-walking clothes, a pair of dress slacks and a button-down, and this outfit. The dress slacks and button-down met the universal fate of lunchtime's kimchi mayo, which jumped from banh mi to shirt and slacks before I even took a bite. And so here I am in this."

"Remind me to send a thank you note to the banh mi." *Smooth, Shepherd, really smooth.* Steph was right again. She had no game.

Evie smiled and brushed across her skirt as if pressing out imaginary wrinkles. "The suit was originally intended for my Tuesday department meeting. To be honest, it's not a bad strategy."

"I'm sorry, what isn't?" Had Evie just caught her staring at the string of pearls, wondering how it felt to touch that flawless skin? "I mean, why isn't it bad?"

"The clothes. When I was learning to play years ago, I read a book that suggested women playing blackjack tend to win more because the pit crew is often chauvinistic. Obviously, the theory is sexist, and I'm sure the only evidence they had was anecdotal, but it stuck with me. The truth is, dressing up makes the player feel like a winner." Now it was Evie's turn to blush. "At the casino, that is."

"You make it sound like the casino has ultimate control over who wins and who loses," Merritt said, trying to push down the almost visceral memory of Evie restrained between her and the wall. It took every bit of control not to bury herself in Evie's sweater as she neatly hung it in the closet.

"You're not so naive as to think a casino operates entirely aboveboard," Evie said, flipping her hair back over her shoulder and tucking it behind an ear.

"Of course not. But I'd like to say I'm hopeful." Merritt thought about what she was really hoping for in that moment, and it had nothing to do with the house odds. She led Evie to a seat at the kitchen island.

"Me, too. I don't think the law of attraction applies to clothing per se, but the whole 'feel like a winner, be a winner' probably has some merit." Evie pulled a bottle of red wine from her bag and set it on the island. "I'm not ready to create a dream board, but given the casino's long-run advantage, I can't afford to leave everything to chance."

While the lasagna baked, they debated New Thought philosophy, agreeing that the notion of manifesting one's dreams was fascinating but perhaps not objectively supportable. As Merritt finished her glass of chianti, she began to relax. Evie was so attractive and not only by attire. She was smart, witty, and had excellent taste in wine.

"In case you were worried, I don't just come to Regina on weekends to gamble."

"I am curious about that, but we can talk about your perplexing weekend-destination choice another time." Merritt laughed, moving to refill Evie's glass. "Suffice to say, I'm glad you packed light because you look like a winner to me." She surveyed Evie again. This time, she let her eyes drift down the shapely legs to the dark navy, ankle-strap stilettos. Not too high. Sensible but stylish. She sensed Evie watching her. "As you could probably tell from my tumble at the press conference, I'm don't pull off heels very well. Even low ones."

"Not true. I happen to think you looked very captivating that day. Alluring in spite of the tumble." She linked her baby finger with Merritt's and drew her even closer. "You still do."

Words jumbled in Merritt's head, rushing for her lips, then retreating with equal haste. There was no mistaking the energy between them. Even without touch, it felt like their bodies were magnetized, the invisible pull of attraction strong and indisputable.

How, exactly, is this distance?

❖

It wasn't fair. That was all Evie could think. It was clear that her desire for Merr was reciprocated. She could tell by the way her eyes stayed on hers, sparking and smoldering like coals on a windy day. And of course, there was also evidence galore in Merr's sudden and uncharacteristic loss for words. But along with undeniable temptation came a sense of disquiet from knowing that Peace Officer Shepherd had been sent to do a job. Public service.

As much as she disagreed with the tactic, Evie couldn't add to the weightiness of that load, so she switched her attention to another elephant in the room. Aside from the obvious contention that existed around protest versus policy, there was also the age difference. Fifteen years? Those elephants alone were difficult to see past, especially with Merr so close. The political issue might shift a bit if someone was willing to relent, but thus far, no one had blinked. She had to set her feelings aside. It really wasn't fair.

"This place is a winner, too." Evie pushed back, spinning slowly on her stool as she surveyed the loft. "It's very dynamic. Great lines and flow, given the enormous open spaces. Modern but with an old soul."

Merr was quietly slicing a fresh figs and setting the pieces like dominos around a large, unusual piece of cheese. No doubt it was the cheese that she and Max had been quipping about at the patisserie. Since the silence had become awkward, Evie took the first step at addressing another of the immovable beasts between them. This one was taking up more room than even Max's enormous loft could accommodate: the incident at the

Farmexal building earlier in the day. *The gun. The badge. The truth.* "Are the closets in this loft bigger than the place we visited this morning? I realize I didn't get the full tour, but I promised my sister I'd have lunch with her while Lonnie was out of town. Thanks to your detainment, I ran a bit late." Though it had been terrifying at the time, she was able to see the humor in it now, but Merr seemed to be taking in more seriously than ever.

Merr put the knife down slowly. Evie recognized her thoughtful expression and gave her time to choose her words. When she at last made eye contact, Merr said, "I know this situation is a bit uncomfortable, and I really am sorry. You have every right to ask about this morning's...surprise. I promise, I'll answer any questions I can, but Max and Robby are going to show up any minute now. May I ask for your continued patience until we have some alone time?"

Evie's first thought was how sweetly forthright Merr was. Her second was how she'd rather spend time alone with Merr now. Much rather. But she'd come to terms with the fact that the odds were stacked against them. Someone just needed to convince her unbridled hormones of that. Hopefully, Merr would fill in some of the blanks regarding what had happened and put her mind at rest. "Absolutely. Can I help with the salad?"

"Yes, thank you." Merr pulled open a drawer and fished out an apron. She walked behind Evie and slipped it over her head, gently tying up the strings on her lower back. "I wouldn't want you to get dirty."

My thoughts already are. She could feel the dampness between her legs, and she tensed. *Damn.*

❖

Since Max and Robby could show up anytime, Merr repressed the urge to lift Evie onto the counter and do what they were both no doubt imagining. Their chat was still enjoyable.

Merritt seized the opportunity to learn more about her guest-turned-sous-chef, who whisked a dressing for the salad.

"I hope you don't mind my asking, but I've always been curious about claustrophobia. When did you begin feeling symptoms?"

"I'm not quite sure I noticed at first. It took time, years, to equate the sensations with the condition."

"Years?" Merritt was surprised. The severity of Evie's symptoms couldn't have been easy to manage for a short period, let alone years.

"It's a long story. Remember when we met on campus? At the SA Centre?"

"Structural Analysis...yes."

"I was there because of an ongoing project I'm spearheading. It has to do with testing soil and stone samples for stability and salinity levels in cenotes. Do you know what they are?"

"I do if you are talking about those amazing underground, water-filled caverns in Mexico." She'd swam in one on a trip when she was young. A beam of sunshine had cast a magical column of light deep into the pool's azure waters, and a repeat of the experience was near the top of her bucket list.

"Primarily in Mexico, yes. A couple of other countries have them, or at least similar karst features...I'm sorry, I tend to ramble. The short story is, I try to predict weakness in the structures of cenotes. And collapse."

"You're not rambling." Merritt said. "I'd never considered cenotes dangerous."

Evie took a noticeably large sip of wine. "They can be. For a few reasons. Many people don't realize there's vegetation growing in spite of the darkness, and it's capable of entangling feet and arms. Or diving equipment. There's also the occasional algae bloom that can disorient even the most experienced divers. But, yes, cenotes are also subject to substrate collapse."

A pained look passed across her face, and her typically

twinkling eyes lost their luster. Merritt knew there was more to the story. She was about to ask when the loud metallic clank of the loft door signaled the end of the opportunity. Seconds later, Max and Robby lunged into the room, jostling as if they'd been best friends for years. Drunk with love. Merritt caught a quick glance from Evie, who was likely on the same page. They were sweet but annoying.

Max set a loaf of crusty bread and a white-corded bakery box on the counter and winked at Merritt before giving her a hug.

"Did I hear someone say cenotes?" Robby said as she claimed the stool next to Evie. "You must be as good a listener as you are a talker, Merr, because Auntie E doesn't usually talk about what happened."

Merritt ignored Robby's light-hearted jab. Instead, her ears perked and her mind churned. *What does she mean?*

Evie cast a look at Robby that seemed to say, "not now." She gently placed a hand on Robby's and shook her head. "It's okay. I was just saying how dangerous cenotes could be. What I hadn't quite gotten to yet is the unfortunate incident that happened years ago during my studies. A fellow grad student…" She paused. "A friend was exploring a cenote cave when a portion of it collapsed."

"Oh my God, that's terrible. Was she okay?" Max asked.

"Unfortunately, she eventually succumbed to her injuries."

Merritt sensed an inordinate depth in Evie's pain. *More to the story indeed.* As much as she wanted to reach across and take away the agony in the words, Merritt respected Evie's need to tell the story. She topped up Evie's glass before setting others in front of Max and Robby.

"She, this colleague…friend…had been told of the risk but went ahead in spite of it. I'm sorry, it's such a terrible story. Hardly dinner party conversation." Evie took a sip of wine, and Robby put an arm around her. "It stuck with me over the years, though, and I'm reminded of it whenever the walls get too close."

"You're claustrophobic?" Max asked.

"A bit, yes. Your sister can back me up on that." She appeared to appreciate the opportunity to ease the conversation, and the sparkle slowly returned to her eyes.

Merr dog-eared Evie's story, though, for what it told her about Evie and for the details missing. There was more to learn, but this was not the time.

As Evie told the stadium elevator story, Merritt set the lasagna on the island next to a bowl of parmesan and an earthenware jug filled with steaming marinara. Max set the loaf of calabrese on a cutting board and cut several thick pieces before passing it around. Evie finished the story, which she'd told self-effacingly and with humor, then tossed the salad and sent it after the bread.

The rest of the dinner was light. Banter and laughter came easily, and Merritt enjoyed the familiarity between Evie and Robby. Max and Robby were notably more inclusive with their interaction than they had been at the bakery, perhaps having reached a more sustainable orbit after their explosive launch earlier in the day. Still, there was a syrupy sweetness to the way they looked at each other, touched, and listened as if every word told a whole story. Merritt was forced by the honest adoration to set aside her typical cynicism.

"I have never had the sauce served separately," Evie said while pouring the marinara onto her lasagna. "Is that a family tradition?"

Max smiled. Merritt read his mind and saw that he was ready to throw a "weirdo" comment her way, no doubt followed by a long list of her food peculiarities. It wouldn't be the first time. She managed to shut him down with a quick series of eye daggers, though his silence likely had more to do with Robby's presence. Best behavior and all.

Merritt tried her best to sound casual as she poured sauce to the side of her cheesy stack of pasta. "I'm not sure. I must've seen it in a blog." *A blog?* She despised blogs, another lie. What was it about Evie O'Halloran that caused her to jump to evasion, distortion, or even plain old fabrication with disturbing ease?

She was an investigator, dammit. Didn't falsehoods go with the territory? Merritt shrugged, hoping to shed the guilt and knowing that when it came to Evie, the answers were not so simple.

By the end of the meal, the synergy between Max and Robby had reignited, and they excused themselves, claiming they were off to a brewpub. Max explained that they had live music on Saturdays, and a local band that both he and Robby liked was playing.

"Auntie E, I'll stop by your hotel on the way and take Walter for a short walk. Are you in the same suite? At the Saskatchewan?"

"No. I'm back at the casino hotel." Evie reached into her bag and handed Robby a pass card. "Take my key and leave it at the desk on your way out? And thank you."

"No problem. See you at Mom's on Sunday." Robby hooked arms with Max, and they headed for the door.

"I've left your order on the counter, sis. Enjoy."

As soon as the door closed behind them, Merritt turned to Evie, and they both let out an exasperated sigh. "I hope I was never that sappy," Evie said.

Merritt had been. Once. And it had been one-sided. "Exactly. There's not enough insulin in the world to counteract that much sweet."

Evie laughed, a big round laugh that suited her to a T. It made Merritt so happy that she didn't want it to end, but the sooner she settled things with Evie, the better. She owed her the truth. If not the whole truth, then at least what she could afford to pay.

"I'm very sorry that I surprised you today. Scared you, actually."

"Don't forget hurt me," Evie said while rubbing her forearm.

"I am so sorry. Really, I am. I hope you know I didn't have a choice at the time. Here's what I can tell you, most of which you already know." She poured coffee as she organized her thoughts. "I am a peace officer with the Ministry of Environmental Resources, in their enforcement branch. I'm usually stationed in Ottawa. I'm working at Farmexal, at their request, I might add, investigating some inventory loss." She hadn't revealed anything that a reasonable person, let alone an intuitive person like Evie, wouldn't already have figured out.

"The totes. Yes. Should you be telling me this?"

"I suspect I'm only confirming things." She more than suspected. "And I had a friend check you out. Your record is virtually spotless. Protester, yes. Peaceful, mostly. Maybe someday, I'll learn more about a small crop you and your high school friends were growing in your neighbor's cornfield."

"I'm not sure I like that you know that. Privacy is still a privilege we enjoy in this country. But it was a long time ago, Peace Officer Shepherd, if that is your real name. And as far as I know, another privilege we enjoy is the right to protest, and I won't ever lose sight of that."

"I would never presume to ask. And, yes, Shepherd is my real surname. Merritt is my first."

Evie seemed gratified. "So not Mary?"

"Never by choice. But if you don't mind, please keep it to Merr. Not to change the subject, but was that you trying to pull Kevin off Chisley in the library last week?"

"I'm sorry my effort didn't go according to plan. And I hope you managed to get the blood out of your suit. Blue is your color, by the way. I'm not the only one who thought so."

Merritt acknowledged the compliment with a nod. "Who else noticed?" It didn't really matter. Evie had noticed.

"Blond. Well, blond-ish. Perky. Your age-ish. Thirties."

Merritt paused. Kelly? She was certain that Evie knew her name. Was Evie jealous and just pretending she couldn't bother to remember the name? She rolled her eyes, hoping it expressed her complete disinterest. "Oh. Yes. Kelly. She is quite something, that is for sure."

"Quite a young something."

That was definitely jealousy. *Or hoping?* Regardless, Merr waited for the flutter in her gut to pass as she crafted a response. "Youth doesn't always prevail. Or so that picture in your office suggests, right? Knockan Crag? The older thrusting over the younger plate." She didn't mean it to sound so oddly evocative.

Evie smiled and shook her head, eyes sparkling. Merritt smiled inwardly, pleased that her comment had landed in the spirit she'd intended. She took two plates from one of the pale green cabinets and gently placed matching pastries on each. Wow. Max had truly outdone himself.

❖

"I have never seen such a beautiful pastry. Honestly, Merritt...Merr...it's like a work of art." Evie picked up her fork but couldn't bring herself to ruin the stunning desserts. Each of the layers was spectacularly evident, the precise cuts revealing orange, white, and dark brown cakes and mousses. She didn't know what each was, but the aroma of chocolate and orange filled her senses.

"Max has a flair. When I floated the concept by him last week, I had no idea he would create something so irresistible."

Not the only irresistible thing in the room, Evie thought as she touched each layer with her fork and tasted what she picked out. But dessert was what was being served, and it was equally compelling. "Pencil pusher by day, entremets inventor by night? Impressive. And where did you get the inspiration for this masterpiece?"

"I think you can guess. I'm not one hundred percent sure what each layer is, but my brother kindly wrote them on the bottom of the box." Merritt pointed to each as she read. "From top to bottom, we have a vanilla genoise, milk chocolate mousse, orange curd, praline feuilletine—not sure exactly what that is—more vanilla genoise soaked in Cointreau syrup, followed by a toasted marshmallow mousse, another syrupy genoise, all topped with a dark chocolate mirror glaze decorated with cacao nibs that have been robed in toasted marshmallow."

"It's a deconstructed hot chocolate. Reimagined exquisitely.

Bravo!" Evie speared her fork through the layers and teased out a corner. As it passed her lips, she noticed Merritt staring. "All you need to know about the feuilletine is that it is as delicious as every layer of this dessert." She moaned, self-consciousness run out of town by pure indulgence. She knew the moment of Merritt's inspiration now, amazed that she'd remembered Evie's comment about how the hot chocolate should have been enhanced. She lifted her gaze to Merritt, who had a tiny bit of marshmallow on her lip. Evie did her best not to stare. Or at least, not to look like a moony teenager. "I thought you didn't like marshmallows?"

"I don't like them on my hot chocolate. This," she said, pointing at the stack of deliciousness, "is not hiding anything." She picked up the pastry and took a bite, then slowly licked a larger sugary smear off her lip. Evie was anchored, breathless. Merritt shifted. Had she made her uncomfortable? "Evie, I can't tell you how long things with Farmexal will need to stay on the down-low. I honestly don't know how I can thank you."

Evie was dumbstruck by an avalanche of ideas she would never have the courage to propose. Not that they could be acted on anyway, given that things had to remain platonic. Didn't they? She took another bite. After another carefree moan, she took a sip of coffee. "You don't have to negotiate my silence, but if you did, Peace Officer Shepherd, this dessert would've sealed the deal." She licked her lips and noticed Merritt's eyes drawn to them. They settled there. Evie felt her pulse pounding. She reached for her talisman pendant, suddenly very self-conscious. *Say something.* "How is your lip?" *Not that.*

Merritt put her finger to the spot where Kevin's elbow had left a purplish circle centered by a small red slash. "Tender." Her gaze hadn't shifted from Evie's lips.

Evie closed her eyes, hoping to break the spell, but she could feel Merritt's warm breath moving across her cheek. Pearls rolled across her neck. Then, lips as inviting as the morning sun brushed hers, and she welcomed them.

"Tender," Evie breathed. *And tasty.*

They kissed again, and Evie felt herself absorbed into Merritt's arms. She didn't feel the urge to retreat, even as her personal space was shrinking. Fear usually reeled her back, even during rare intimate moments, since that day in Mexico. Was it possible she'd at last moved past the issue? Had Merr moved her past it? She hoped so. Merritt was sexy, and her desire was palpable. Or was it the elevator pledge? Evie was still sitting on the stool, but Merritt had somehow stepped between her legs. Her tight skirt slid up her thighs just enough that Merritt's hips almost pressed against her wetness. The heat in the space between them flashed. *No, it was definitely Merr.*

Evie closed her eyes, her heart thumping wildly. She heard a muffled gasp of delight, felt warm breath on her ear. A hand on her chest. Evie opened her eyes as Merritt slowly and gently stepped back. Her head had lowered, but her fingers still rested gently on Evie's collarbone, her thumb stroking the pearls.

"Things..." Merr muttered, shaking her head.

Evie was confused. She trembled with desire, hoping to find the warmth her body had just bathed in. "Things?"

"They've changed. Things. Circumstances. Things have changed."

Evie cleared the cobwebs of lust that had entangled her mind and revived the parking lot conversation from the previous week. The imaginary date. Had it not been for "things," it would've been an actual date. Yes. Things. Now she understood what those things involved. An investigation. Ongoing. A home in Ottawa, three thousand miles away. Reluctantly, she pulled back and let her still trembling hands fall from Merritt's hips. "This probably isn't a good idea."

"Of course it's not. It's a terrible idea." Even as she said the words, Merr moved her hand from Evie's chest, slid it beneath her hair, and cupped her head and stroked behind her ear with a thumb. "Which makes this a really, really terrible idea."

Merritt kissed her again, and Evie fought back her reservations until a disturbing thought crossed her mind, and she pushed back. "Could this be more serious than we think? This situation with the chemicals? It would be devastating if the undiluted ammonium nitrate penetrated too deeply into the soil. Is that what's happening?"

"Hard to tell. We really don't know exactly what we're up against. What the objective may be. Fertilizer, properly manufactured and distributed, does a world of good for crops. But until we can figure out why the totes are showing up where they're not supposed to, there's no way to know for certain what has happened to the contents."

Merritt's gaze drifted down her chest to where her hand had been moments earlier. As much as Evie wanted to go back in time. Someone had to defuse things before they escalated. She could hear the irony in those thoughts. Things had definitely changed. She'd never wanted a woman the way she wanted Merritt. But she knew from experience what could happen if she didn't exercise caution. If she ignored the warning, walls collapsed. She also understood what could happen if concentrated fertilizer found its way into a tract of land, or worse, into a water table. If there was even an outside chance of either, Merritt's investigation needed a quick, unimpeded resolve.

Evie took a deep breath, gently pulled Merritt's hand from behind her head and held it. "Then, as much as I like that 'things have changed,' maybe it would be best to keep your focus on your job." As the words came out, she wanted to pull them back. But if she'd learned anything from Mexico, it was to account for all possibilities.

Merritt shook her head and made as if to kiss Evie again but stopped. "I hate that you're right." She tucked a piece of Evie's hair behind her ear and took a step back. "This?" She placed a hand between them as if feeling the heated air. "Whatever this is, would be risky."

Evie could sense Merr's dejection as she watched her retreat behind the island. Distance. Ottawa. So much distance. But that wasn't Merr's fault. It was her job. Eager to lighten the mood, Evie straightened and shifted gears.

"Speaking of risk, let's go to the casino." She reached across the granite and left her hand there until Merr covered it. "I ride-shared here, so you're driving. Come on," Evie said, grabbing her bag and tugging Merritt toward the door. "I can't waste this outfit, and I feel lucky."

❖

It was hard for Merritt to keep her eyes on the road. The kisses in the kitchen had flooded her like a triple espresso. And now that they were in the car, she was enveloped with the scent of Evie. Lilac. Cotton. She glanced over and noticed how the cut of her blouse showed off her glorious cleavage. It made complete sense how an outfit like Evie's could distract other players at a card table. Likely dealers, as well.

Definitely me. Small talk. Make small talk.

"Tell me," Merritt began, trying to distract herself from the embers ignited in the kitchen that still smoldered inside. "How did Robby get her name? It's unusual. Is it short for Robin?"

Merritt caught Evie biting back a smile. Her attempt at dialing down the sexual tension had not only been artless but obvious. Graciously, Evie went along with it. "Roberta, actually. My sister named her after Joni Mitchell."

"The folk singer? Her name was Roberta?"

"Roberta Joan Mitchell. Yes. Bev is a big fan. You know she started her singing career in Saskatchewan, right?"

"I did not. And Bev's not alone. 'A Case of You' is a constant on my playlist. How is your sister?" Merritt was interested in Bev's well-being more because of the guy Evie had described as a "piece of work," Lonnie. Steph had shared countless numbers of domestic abuse cases, and while Merr had no specific reason to believe he was trouble, he was now on her radar.

Again, it was as if Evie could see beneath the pretense of her question. "Bev has made better choices than Lonnie. He doesn't hold a candle to her first husband, Alan. She was in her mid-forties when he died of an aneurysm. Robby was off at university, and I think she was afraid to be alone."

"Grief can lead to bad decisions." Merritt had done enough soul-searching to know that the pain she'd experienced when Uncle Joe had died had led her to make plenty of them. *Natalie.*

Evie seemed surprised. "It can do a lot of things. But Bev knows what needs to happen. She needs to end it before he realizes she's thinking about it."

Evie had avoided stating the obvious. Lonnie was abusive. Physically? Psychologically? It didn't matter. It hurt just the same.

"Is she being extra careful? Guys like him have inexplicably accurate radar when their victim is looking for an exit." Merritt was doing her best to contain her mounting concern. "Also, if you'd like, I'll happily give you the name and number of a friend in social services who helps women, very discreetly, who are in Bev's circumstances."

"Thank you, Merri…thank you, Merr. For everything."

Fortunately for Merritt's still-raging libido, the drive to the casino was short. It was well within walking distance from the loft if the weather was decent. But she'd recalled something Conroy had said about Einerson having an extra job doing security at the casino, and since she was in the neighborhood, she might as well see if his truck was parked nearby.

She hoped Evie hadn't noticed the empty parking spots she'd driven by as she descended into the underground levels of the parking garage. If she had, she'd not let it be known. On the lowest level, she spotted his Ford truck. She reminded herself that nothing, including seeing his truck here, had thus far implicated Einerson in anything. In truth, the bit of surveillance she'd invested tonight could as easily exclude him from the suspect pool. But ultimately, since it meant additional time in the car with Evie O'Halloran, every minute felt worth it.

CHAPTER ELEVEN

By the end of the evening, the air had turned colder. Evie was thankful for the sweater she'd stuffed into her bag before heading to the loft and wrapped herself in it as they walked out of the casino. She had insisted on accompanying Merritt to her car, even though the lot was one of the closer ones. "Just in case you run into any elbows," she'd teased. She was aware that she would've walked anywhere, in any temperature, sweater or not, to spend more time with Merritt. Even if it was as friends.

The agreement they'd made at the loft had an unexpected result. Evie had been able to tune out their sexual attraction, or at least turn the volume down, and had made it one of the most enjoyable evenings she had spent in a long time. The first hour or so, she'd taught Merritt the basic strategies of the games and the customs of the casino. Merritt had eased into it like a pro, dropping her usual cautious formality, and soon, they were both putting money down. Evie was donating more than winning, but it didn't matter. It was fun to be in the company of a sexy young woman. Who also happened to be an outstanding kisser.

"I'm aware that I haven't explained much about the investigation." Merritt hooked her arm in Evie's. Touching had seemingly proven too hard to resist, so Evie accepted the concession. "I appreciate your not pressing the issue."

Evie had decided to show faith in her judgment. "I trust you'll tell me what you can, when you can. I am curious about one thing, though. Are you in any danger?"

"No. At least, none of which I'm aware. I haven't gotten close enough to make anyone uncomfortable, so that's good."

"Have there been more totes found?"

"You didn't hear it from me," Merritt said carefully.

"How many more?"

"I can't say."

The circumspect responses reminded Evie that they were in very different camps on the topic. But it was important. She wanted reassurance, something the meeting last week did nothing to provide. "Do I...do *we* need to worry that the quantities are sufficient enough to cause irreversible damage?"

"Please, Evie. Let's not get ahead of ourselves. We have no evidence of anything at this point." She spoke more quickly than usual. Evie's reaction must've shown on her face because Merritt returned to her usual, unhurried pace. "Yes, there is an inconsistency in the supply chain. Inventory shortages. Measurable and not attributable to normal manufacturing losses. If I can figure out 'where' in the chain, we'll be that much closer to figuring out the 'how' and 'why.' The likelihood is that someone is trying to buy liquid because it is otherwise unavailable in Canada."

Evie let the assurances sink in. Everyone in a farming community knew farmers had resisted when the pellet form of fertilizer was given the green light. Most of their equipment was designed for liquid, and the cost to change was on their dime. But the dangers that liquid posed when used or stored incorrectly—not to mention intentional misuse—outweighed cost and convenience. She continued to mull things over, and by the time they reached the car, she was willing to let it go. Not the concern. Just the topic.

"It was nice of you to come, Merr. I know gambling isn't your thing, but it certainly worked in your favor tonight."

"I could easily make it my thing. Tonight, I just got lucky." Her dark eyes flashed. "Well, almost."

They both laughed, and Evie was happy that the seriousness surrounding the investigation wasn't detracting from the sweetness of the evening. "So did I. I may have to look more deeply into your gambling history. Something tells me that wasn't your first time at the blackjack table."

"I think you distracted the dealer with that blouse, and she kept giving me aces meant for you."

"Not likely. I think I'm just underestimating you, again." She paused and waited for Merritt's gorgeous smile, which came almost instantly and made her heart thud. "I'd hoped that switching to the roulette wheel would help me recoup my losses, but I should know better than to play roulette in North America."

"Are there different rules elsewhere?"

"The odds are just slightly better on a French wheel. Long story. The odds are always in the casino's favor. Wager accordingly."

"Which is no more than we can afford to lose."

Evie laughed. That was the first lesson she'd shared when they'd arrived. Merr had learned quickly. "Precisely."

"Well, I enjoyed watching you have fun."

Indeed, the attention had followed Evie throughout the evening, and despite the crowds, it made her feel like the only one in the room. "I trust you're more subtle on the job."

"Maybe tonight, I didn't mind being caught looking."

"Maybe I didn't mind you looking." Evie stood with her back to the Cadillac, palms pressed against the hood behind her back.

Merritt pressed her hips into Evie's, pinning her gently against the car. "Maybe I have other, more practical skills," she murmured.

The kiss was proof positive of those skills. Evie's resistance flaked apart like feuilletine, and she doubled down. "Maybe you should come up to my room?"

"Better odds there?"

"If you keep kissing me like that, I'm willing to bet it won't be long before we both get lucky, one way or the other."

"I'm very curious about 'the other.'" Merritt stepped back, her eyes dark with desire. She blinked, closed her eyes, and slowly shook her head. "You are so sexy, Evie. Please don't think I'm not interested, very interested, in you." Her eyes opened. "I just…"

"I know." And she hated that she knew. She stepped back and touched Merritt's pouty lip. "You are much too responsible, you know that? And far too hot. Triple-flaming-sevens hot." Merr smiled, and Evie's shoulders relaxed with resignation. "But I do understand. Now, go before I put you in a position where you are forced to use your peace officer powers on me."

"You make that sound fun."

"It would be."

Merritt leaned in for another kiss, but Evie put a finger on her chin.

"Remember lesson two? Good gamblers respect the limits." She smiled and nodded toward the casino. "I should probably go make sure Walter hasn't eaten the towels. Again."

They laughed, the sound tinged with disappointment and exasperated sighs.

"Thank you again for dinner. Dessert was exquisite. Sweet. Like you." *So sweet.* "Good night, Peace Officer Shepherd."

"Good night, Dr. Evie O'Halloran."

❖

Merritt watched Evie walk back up the ramp, hopelessly drawn to her curves, the fine feminine musculature of her calves, the sway of her hips. She'd truly enjoyed the evening, surprised at the nuances of casinos and gambling. And Evie. At one point, returning from a trip to the bar for martinis, Merritt had watched unobserved as Evie had played roulette. She'd appeared in her element. Confident. Hot. Men had flocked around her. Even the female croupier had been paying extra attention. She'd looked flirty and fun, much more casual than when they'd played blackjack. Then, Evie had been keen. Focused. The cards hadn't fallen in her favor, but she was nonetheless generous, teaching Merritt the basics.

Her kisses had been generous, too. Full and warm, accepting. They'd affected Merritt much more than she'd wanted to admit; it was out of character to reveal so much about the investigation. Was it because she found herself trusting Evie? *Trusting an activist? What was not to trust?* The strange behavior she'd witnessed at the police station and in close spaces was explainable. Passion. Claustrophobia. Ultimately, Evie had an unflappable quality and Merritt was convinced that anything she shared would remain between them. Only them. Which was good. Certainly good. Yet their relationship had to remain platonic.

Merritt put the Caddy into gear and swung by the spot where Einerson's truck had been parked earlier. Without his vehicle obstructing the wall, she had a view of a large door, its etched iron greened with age. It reminded her of an old freezer door, the kind they had in hotel kitchens or banks back in the day. Maybe it was decorative? Max had cottoned on to the upcycling trend in the process of designing his loft, and he'd taken Merritt on a couple of "treasure hunts" to find remnants from defunct industrial manufacturing plants that could be turned into objects d'art. "Creative reuse," he'd called it. If it was a functional door, Merritt couldn't imagine what it led to. It also had a large not-so-vintage chain and padlock. A storage room, maybe?

The thought of a small dark room behind an old cement wall reminded her of the small corner of the washhouse where she'd secreted Evie and Walter. And their walk, when Evie had mentioned tunnels. Most had been sealed off or had caved in. Was it possible some were still intact? Possibly, the investigation might be headed down a new, old path.

❖

Walter might've been trying his best to appear disappointed that Evie had chosen to spend the evening without him, but he betrayed his true feelings by wagging his tail and circling incessantly until she scooped him into her arms. Thanks to Robby, he wasn't in a hurry to go out and waited patiently for her to change into sweatpants and a hoodie. She'd explained to him before leaving that she was going to Merritt's, and perhaps as a gesture of approval, he'd not chewed a single towel. He seemed to like her. They had that in common.

As they walked around the block, Evie detailed the evening's events for his pleasure. There was nothing better than a good listener. Especially one who completely withheld judgment. She wrapped up by explaining that, no, she and Merritt hadn't made future plans. And that was okay. It had to be. For now. Maybe once the investigation was over, Merritt would call.

"Of course she will, Walter." There was no possible way Evie had misinterpreted the reciprocity that had supercharged their kisses. Or the suggestive repartee. Or the light touches on the lower back as she stood at the roulette table. Hopefully, the case would wrap up quickly for many reasons. Missing fertilizer foremost.

Once back in her suite, Evie contemplated how she'd been more assertive than usual that night. Merritt made her feel that way. Sexy. Bold. And ultimately comfortable in Merritt's presence. If things didn't go forward, as sad as she might feel, Evie had made huge gains. She would take those lessons with her and find a partner who made her as happy. Who would that be? Someone older but young at heart? Someone who lived closer? Her heart sank a bit as she set aside hope and considered a future without Merritt. She sat on the couch and pulled Walter up with her, snuggling him until her phone vibrated against the coffee table. She'd not reset it since that day in the loading dock corner, preferring to be in charge of when she'd check messages instead of feeling the rush to silence the dings. In case it was family, she picked it up.

It was Merritt texting: *Hi. I enjoyed our evening.*

My pleasure. It had been. *Me, too.* Also true. Evie held her breath, wondering what would follow the bouncing dots.

Would you mind passing this contact info along to Bev? Chantal is a friend and the liaison for the RCMP's Relationship Violence Victims' Services.

She exhaled, disappointed but not sure what she'd been hoping for. She inhaled all feelings except for gratitude. Merr's thoughtfulness could make a difference for her sister. *Of course. Thanks.*

Anytime. Sleep well.

Her heart fluttered as she imagined Merritt's slow, strangely seductive voice in the texted words.

Good night. With that, Evie gathered up Walter and headed to bed. She might be alone tonight, but there was a chance that her luck would soon change. *What were the odds?*

CHAPTER TWELVE

It had been a grueling and frustrating week, and even though Friday didn't have the same end-of-work appeal for Merritt, she was glad it was over. Almost a dozen more totes had been found. And she'd just spent another two hours with the Farmexal executives, trying to convince them to stay the course and give her more time. They'd agreed but only because their choices were limited.

She'd had a few encounters with Einerson. He was quiet and almost always with Conroy, who verbally overshadowed any exchange, so she'd come no closer to finding out why he had been at the washhouse last weekend. She tinkered with the other pieces of the puzzle. There was still no real evidence of how the fertilizer was leaving Farmexal's plant, but maybe it was safe to assume the empty totes had been used to transport it. To where? Unknown. Why? Unknown. How? Also unknown.

Given all the unanswered questions, she would work the best lead she had first: Einerson. Fortunately, most Farmexal employees were out of the office that afternoon to take advantage of the Thanksgiving weekend except for Kelly, Conroy, and her best lead. Kelly had been trying all day to rally the sparse troops for drinks after work, and when Merritt stopped by her office to accept, she lit up. Ruling out Kelly as a suspect might be premature. Maybe drinks with "the gang" would reveal something useful. If she could get past Kelly's persistent, and at times cheesy, attempts at seduction. It made everything so much more awkward. In truth, being around a flirtatious beautiful woman only made her think about Evie.

How can I miss her? I'm not sure I know her. They had texted a few times throughout the week but had kept things light. Evie was going to be in Regina on Saturday until past Thanksgiving Monday. If the polite and circumspect nature of their texts was any indication, they'd come to terms with their new hands-off policy. Begrudgingly. Regardless, it was hard to resist driving to Saskatoon to see her. Merritt was negotiating the pros and cons on her way back to her office, but as she passed the break room, she noticed Einerson filling his coffee cup.

"Hey, Mark." She tried to land somewhere between charming and mildly seductive. "We're heading out to the Buzzpub if you'd like to join us."

"Can't tonight. I've been working doubles. Heading home to bed." After adding an obscenely unhealthy amount of sugar to his cup, he paused for a moment and looked her up and down as if reconsidering. Merritt could tell he was reading much too much into her invitation. From the way he adjusted his body, pulling his shoulders back and sucking in his gut, she half expected him to say something inappropriate. But the expected, "if you want to join me…" wasn't proffered. Instead, he smiled and raised his mug to her. "Another time?"

"Absolutely, Mark." *In your dreams.*

❖

After several hours spent writing field updates for her ministry supervisor, and a weekly report for Chisley, Merritt could almost taste the chocolate oatmeal stout she planned to order at the brewpub. It would help dull more of Jerry's empty chatter. But just as she was getting in her car, she read an email from the Structural Analysis folks. So far, the soil samples taken from the area around the discovered totes showed only trace amounts of liquid. They had been emptied somewhere else before dumping. Merritt sighed, relieved, but there was much more to do. If nothing else, the good news would make the stout taste even sweeter. She set off to the bar.

Kelly was already halfway through a pink-bottomed umbrella drink and smiled broadly when Merritt joined her. No Conroy. Kelly explained that he had backed out of drinks, too. "So," she crooned, "it's just the two of us." She licked the tip of her straw, evoking every bad seduction scene Merritt had ever witnessed. Extra cheesy.

By the time the stout arrived, Kelly's brand of endless chatter had Merritt longing for a classic Conroy football story. *Gawd.* Kelly was replete with unfounded-bordering-on-ridiculous gossip from Farmexal, excruciating detail of the latest episode of *The Kardashians*, and as Merritt had feared, unwelcome innuendo. If Kelly was involved in anything requiring secrecy, well, what was it Ben Franklin had said? "Three may keep a secret, if two of them are dead." Merritt laughed at the truth of it.

She wondered if she was experiencing another half-lucky day because during Kelly's meandering explanation of why Jennifer Lopez would never show her true age, Conroy joined them. Kelly declared it was keto, then turned to him. "I thought you were heading to the casino?"

He pulled out a chair and signaled to the bartender, who apparently understood and began tapping an ale. "Nah. Figured I'd hang out with two pretty ladies."

Merritt and Kelly rolled their eyes at each other, breaking a bit of the tension. It was a relief for Merritt. Kelly appeared annoyed, probably at losing Merritt's complete attention, which made her chuckle because she'd mostly checked out of the conversation five minutes into it.

"Besides," Conroy added, "there's another poker tournament there tonight, and I didn't want to hunt around for a parking spot.

I was hoping Mark would give me his, but he's working the night shift."

Merritt's ears pricked. Einerson had said he was going home. Which of the two wasn't being truthful? Lies, even innocuous ones, said a lot about a person's credibility, and if she'd learned anything from Natalie, it was "where there's one rat, there's fifty."

She decided to drive by the casino on her way home. Maybe circle the floor in case Evie had arrived in town earlier than expected. Not likely. She'd texted something about submitting midterm marks before the weekend. Probably best. Along with making two advances in the case—learning that the totes were empty and that Mark had been caught in what seemed to be deception—came an urge to share that progress with someone. Max was on a date with Robby, and she still couldn't be completely up-front with her brother, despite his suspicions. Steph was at a family dinner; besides, they had plans to meet in the morning. It was Evie she wanted to tell. It was Evie she was thinking about. It was Evie who mattered.

CHAPTER THIRTEEN

Boulangerie de la Régine was jam-packed on Saturday morning, with patrons lining up out the door for Max's delights. On days like this, family privilege was as sweet as the pastries. Max had set aside a table far enough from the others to allow Merritt and Steph to talk in relative privacy.

"Einerson's truck was parked at the casino again last night. So why lie about going home? And what was he doing at the washhouse last week? The best thing to come out of that shit show was getting close to Evie. Uncomfortably close, as far as she was concerned. Scared her senseless." *Why did I say that? Damn.* Steph pounced.

"It's about time you thought about something, someone, other than work. I like this shade of pink you're wearing on your cheeks."

"I'm glad you're enjoying yourself, but she knows about my assignment at Farmexal. I had no choice but to bring her in at least partway."

"It sounds like she already knew. She's a smart woman. A beautiful, smart woman who, for reasons I can't fathom, seems to keep showing up on your radar. Now, why is that?"

Her cheeks betrayed her again. Steph knew. Might as well spare herself the inquisition. "We kissed."

The resounding fist that hit the table almost knocked

Merritt's coffee off its saucer. The patrons at the nearby tables gawked disapprovingly. Steph couldn't care less, it seemed. "I knew it! And?"

"And it was wrong. For a million reasons, Philly. The investigation. The fact that I don't live here. For God's sake, she's actively protesting the company I'm trying to vindicate." That wasn't quite a million. Far from.

Steph beamed. "But it was good, right? Like, really good? When are you seeing her next?"

Wish I knew. "Not sure that's going to happen. Besides, did it ever occur to you what could happen if ammonium nitrate—"

"Blah blah blah. Seriously, Fish 'n Game. You like the doctor. Written all up and down your pretty butch face."

"You're a pain in my ass."

"On the subject of ass, how do you eat whatever Max serves without packing on the pounds?"

"First of all, stop checking out my ass. Secondly, you know I can't resist raisins. Besides, Max left a note this morning telling me what the daily special was, so I worked out extra hard." The whole truth was that she'd worked out extra hard to distract herself from a libido that had kept her up half the night. "Have a piece. It's spiced-rum pound cake."

"And what did you make him serve on the side this time?"

"Raisin crème anglaise." Merritt dipped a piece of cake into the sauce.

"Did you ever consider it might be insulting to a food artiste like your brother to have his creative pairings separated?" Steph asked, dipping into the bowl.

"He likes to spoil me."

"Speaking of spoiling, I can't stay." Steph pulled back from the table and gathered her coat and phone. "I wanted to see you, of course, and it's been a delight hearing about your girlfriend. God, Angela will freak right out when I tell her." She playfully punched Merritt's arm. "But I can't go home without Thanksgiving goodies for the kids."

Merritt didn't begrudge the errand. Since she and Angela adopted their two sons, Steph had blossomed. "How are the boys?"

"They're teens, so…bratty. Pasted to their gadgets. But fortunately, I can still buy their affection with butter tarts."

"I don't believe that. They love you two to death. Tell them I say heya."

"Say the same to Evie." Steph pronounced the last word with three syllables and topped it with a kissy-face.

As Steph exited the still-jammed bakery doors, Merritt hoped that Evie would walk in. She took a moment to think about what it would be like to have kids. Did Evie like kids? Was it possible that she had kids but didn't talk about them? No. That didn't sound like her.

Merritt scolded herself. She shouldn't be thinking about Evie having kids or about how her kids might look or how they might have her sense of humor, intelligence, and curiosity. Gorgeous hair. And eyes. Certainly, her smile. And laugh.

Merritt looked at the half slice of cake that remained and had an inexplicable, irresistible urge to pour the sauce on top.

❖

Evie wasn't a big fan of driving to Regina on Saturdays. The traffic was always just that bit heavier, doubly so on any long weekend. This year, Thanksgiving dinner had been shifted to Monday to accommodate Max's bakery schedule. The change was as much about keeping Robby happy as Max attending, and Bev hadn't so much as blinked when asked. When Max had offered to bring some freshly baked butter rolls and dessert, he'd only sealed the deal.

The delayed departure for Evie wasn't ideal. She was happy to have her midterm marks submitted and even happier to have had the distraction of finalizing them over the past week. But she also had to return to Saskatoon first thing Tuesday morning to invigilate an exam, which meant the weekend was shorter for her than usual.

Maybe less time in Regina wasn't such a bad thing. It was clear that staying away from Merritt was like staying away from carbs. She wanted to, but, well, carbs. If her kisses were that amazing, what would it be like to be truly touched by her? Held in her muscled arms. Moved beneath her. Licked.

Fuck. The lane departure beeps alerted her that the car was drifting, and she overcompensated to her original lane. Her mother's china, carefully situated into the back of her Outback, rattled. She held her breath, admonishing herself to pay less attention to what might only lead to disaster—fantasies involving Merritt Shepherd—and more attention to the road.

Evie loved Thanksgiving dinners. The menu had morphed over the years as food trends emerged, but Bev's maple-brined turkey was a tradition set in stone. Evie found the phrase funny. After all, stone itself was not unyielding, so neither was anything set in it. Stone compressed, shifted, eroded and transformed. It moved along plates, crested fault lines, and fell into seas. It had since the planet was formed, and it would long after humans carved into it. With any luck.

But there was increasingly disturbing data that she wished people like Merr and her policy-making bosses in Ottawa would better understand. With the increased rainfalls created by global warming came alarming stresses on the aquifers. Deforestation by wildfire or timber companies had a direct impact on erosion. Cenotes were like the canary in the coal mine. And Evie's research suggested that its wings were rapidly fluttering. How Merr could ever think that legislating their way out of irreversible damage was possible, she couldn't imagine. Her heart was breaking.

A horn sounded behind her, and she bolted to anger until she noticed her speed had dropped considerably. *Dammit, Evie, focus.*

She made good time in spite of her distracted drive. As she was pulling into Bev's driveway, she saw Lonnie throwing a rucksack in the back of his truck. She put her vehicle in park, silently congratulating herself for choosing to do so despite her feelings about Bev's partner. Only then did she release a restless Walter from his safety harness. He jumped on her lap, stared out the window, and growled, the closest he ever came to barking and only when Lonnie was in sight. Dogs were intuitive, no question.

She stepped out, securing Walter in her arms. Lonnie rolled down his window as he drove past, sneering his usual greeting. "I'm outta here. Back midweek. Tell your dog not to even think about pissin' on my lawn. Tell your sister to set aside some turkey for me. No dark meat."

He made Evie want to growl, too. She pretended she hadn't heard and laughed. *The lawn is all yours, Walter.*

More often, she and Bev would meet for lunch or dinner when Lonnie was away. Even when Lonnie wasn't home, though, Evie felt uncomfortable in the house. It had become sterile and unwelcoming, likely because Bev had become afraid of having anything out of place. Fortunately, Lonnie's job at a potash mine up north meant that he was usually gone for anywhere between a day and week at a time, so Bev had a break from his constant scrutiny. Evie couldn't imagine being in a relationship where she could only truly breathe when her partner was away.

But she knew what it was like to be away from Merritt. Physically, at least. Despite the realities that made a sexual relationship with her impossible, she ached in a way that surprised her. If only it could be different. Evie was three years from retirement. An early one, thanks to a life of few vices. But there were plenty of distances between her and Merritt. Age, maybe a dozen years. Politics. Maybe she'd been a bit tough on her at the police station. Friendly fire, but still. And if they needed more distance, there was Ottawa. Two whole provinces away. Wow, talk about getting ahead of herself. They'd shared a few kisses. Spectacular kisses. Memorable kisses. U-Hauls had been rented for less. But soon, the memory of those kisses would be as far away as their lives.

For now, Evie was consoled by stalking Merritt virtually. Twice a day, at least, she'd checked the Farmexal site for public updates on the company's investigation. Wondering if Merritt had contributed to them. To their credit, Farmexal was being more transparent than many corporate offenders. Or at least, it seemed that way. Who really knew what the truth was? Merritt, likely. And once the investigation wrapped up, she'd head back to Ottawa. Pushing paper. Evie had to prepare herself for that inevitability. Other than Max, would there be any reason for Merritt to stay in Regina? In Saskatchewan? In Evie's life? She'd already started delaying her text responses, hoping to create more space, even though it was heartbreaking. It would make it easier. Feeling adrift, she hugged the box of china like an anchor as she pulled open the screen door with her pinkie.

Bev stood at the sink watching Lonnie's truck roar down the road. Evie's shoulders dropped incrementally.

"A little help here?" She was balancing the box on her hip and holding the door open for Walter with her foot.

"Here." Bev rushed over. "Let me help you with that."

Once the box was on the table, they faced each other. Evie wondered who would be the first to break. Their last disagreement had been a doozy, and it had ended with two weeks of cold silence. Maybe she had overstepped with her concerns regarding Lonnie, and Bev just wouldn't admit she needed out. But Evie was scared. Even now.

Bev must've noticed the concern because she pulled Evie into her arms and gave her a big squeeze. "What's this I hear about Max's sister? She's quite something, is she?"

Evie helped herself to coffee as she struggled to formulate a response. Yes, Merritt was something. Unavailable. "Um, I'm not sure what Robby told you, but nice…" She hesitated. "As pleasant as Merritt is, our politics don't exactly line up." That was the easiest way out of the conversation. She didn't want to feel how it tore into her when Merritt's name was mentioned.

"Speaking of which…" She dug into her back pocket and handed over the folded piece of paper Merritt had asked her to pass on.

Bev took a moment to read it, then tucked it into her cleavage. She stood back and inventoried Evie from bottom to top. "You look different."

"Thanks?"

"Don't thank me. It wasn't me that put this little glow on your edges. Invite her for Monday's dinner," she said flatly.

"I'll do no such thing. I don't even know her. And what I do know, I don't exactly favor." Seeing Merritt would completely uproot the garden of forget-about-her she'd been tilling over the past week.

"You seem to know enough to have decided on her politics."

"And she decided on mine. We disagree. Fundamentally."

"Maybe you should consider stepping down from your high horse just this once? Surely, there's more to her than what I can only assume is a different perspective on how to save the planet? Tell me she's not running oil tankers aground. Or hiding recyclables in her garbage bags."

Evie clenched her teeth and tried not to growl. "Would you ever ask Robby to set aside *her* values in order to please a *man*?" Around the edges of her words were thoughts she'd intended, for the sake of their truce, to tamp down. Thoughts about how much Bev was sacrificing and suffering to be with the likes of Lonnie. The room grew eerily quiet. *Tamp, dammit.* Bev began opening the cardboard box and emptying its contents.

Evie pivoted and spoke more softly. "I can't ignore the data, Bev. With global warming comes higher temperatures. Drought. Fires. And with the loss of our forests comes erosion. Floods." *Collapse.* "Businesses and governments are unbearably slow to react. We are running out of time."

"And do you really think this Merritt is responsible for all of that?"

She rolled her eyes. "Of course not. That is not the issue."

"It's not only *your* job to save the planet. Or me, for that matter."

Evie sat at the table and turned her palms toward the ceiling. "I can't do nothing."

"Okay, then," Bev said gently, taking a seat and placing her hands on Evie's. "Do this. Invite her for dinner."

Nothing was making sense anymore. She pulled back and squeezed her hair, holding her head up by the tangled waves, elbows on the table. "It's complicated."

Bev laughed and shook her head. "It always is with you. So serious. Ever since you were a little kid, you shouldered the world and everyone on it. More so after Mexico."

Evie winced.

"Do you remember Alan's pet name for you?"

Evie wiped tears. "Dr. Even. Robby still calls me that now and again."

"Do you know why? Because you once declared that the world needed to be more like a football field. Level. Fair. With rules that everyone followed. Baby, has it ever occurred to you that there's more to life than making things even? And that maybe people are allowed to play by different rules, and that alone doesn't make them unworthy. Or disposable."

Was Bev talking about Merritt or herself? Before she could ask, Bev elaborated. "Only you can figure out who you'd like to play with, or that field is going to be even but empty. I wish you'd do that before you're an old lady like me."

"Bev, you're only in your mid-sixties. That's hardly—"

Bev waved her off. "If you're interested in this woman..." She squeezed Evie's hand until she looked in her eyes. "And I think you are, then asking her to dinner will probably be the easiest part of whatever comes of it."

"She'll say no. And she should, really. She's busy with more important things."

"Well, then, I dare you to ask. She's an adult. She can decide how busy she is."

Evie sat back in her chair and muttered "I hate you."

Bev smiled. "I know. I hate you, too."

❖

Merritt rubbed her belly and moaned.

"Serves you right," Max chided. "You ate more turkey than the rest of the family combined. Where do you put it all?" He reached over to the driver's seat and poked her in the side.

"I have a high metabolism. And I love turkey. A lot. The way Cartman loves his Cheesy Poofs." Merritt knew he'd appreciate the *South Park* reference.

"A pop-culture reference? I'm impressed."

They both laughed, their moods light. It had been a surprisingly good dinner at Susan's, their sister. Their folks had just returned from what they'd described as an exotic holiday in Iceland, so most of the conversation had revolved around adventures that included hot springs, spectacular auroras, and unrelenting winds. Susan, her partner Bruce, their kids, and Max had filled in the rest of the evening's chatter.

Merritt had happily escaped without having to field the usual embarrassing questions about who she was seeing, if she had ascended the civil servant ladder, and if there was any word on Natalie. The latter two would have grated. The relationship query might've felt different this time around. Even though she was not convinced that things with Evie would lead to something, there was still...potential, maybe? Or was it optimism? Did it matter? It was as though she was sitting in sunshine just thinking about the possibilities.

"Hey, sis, thanks again for the ride home," Max said. "I would've gone back with Robby, but she got a call from a contractor and had to go early this morning to sort out some blueprint issue."

"Really? You sure it's not your material?"

"Not a chance. She has a thing for dad jokes and still thinks

I'm the bomb. Oh, and don't pretend you didn't get that text about dinner tomorrow at Bev's. It's kinda rude that you didn't RSVP. I know. Work. Work. Well, maybe you can ignore Evie, but I promised Robby I'd drag your sorry, workaholic ass there come heaven or high water."

Merritt didn't correct him. It was rude that she hadn't responded. But she hadn't been ignoring Evie, really. It wasn't possible. The truth was that outside of the casino outing last weekend and dinner tonight, she was drowning in work. The text from Evie earlier today inviting her had felt like a life raft, but she couldn't bring herself to take hold. She wanted to, but she also had a sense that Evie needed distance. Merritt had picked up on the dwindling number of texts, the steadily longer lags between each, and the conspicuous unresponsiveness to some. She didn't feel ghosted, exactly, but it was quite possible that Evie had come to prefer someone less committed to their job. Especially a job she could not, apparently, stand.

"Did you two have a fight?"

"No, not really. We just see the world in different ways." Merritt didn't want to disclose too much. The investigation was coming to an end soon, she could feel it, and she couldn't risk tipping her hand, even to her brother.

"It seems unbelievably coincidental that you accepted a job at a company currently embroiled in an environmental scandal that the ministry you used to work for"—he air quoted—"would be in charge of investigating. Don't you agree?" If he had been playing a villain in a Bond movie, he'd be tapping his fingertips together.

Merritt drew upon her recent experience at the casino. *Control your tell.* "I would say so. Quite a coincidence." Max's eyes were on her. Don't look.

He folded first and nodded. "Okay, then, let's not talk about it. Back to Evie. Not my business, but if you're at all hesitant about her because of the age thing, remember, Evie is different. She's got substance. And she's not..." She knew he was about to say Natalie but had the good sense to rein himself in. "Anyway, I have a good feeling about you two, if that counts for anything."

"It does." Funny that he'd brought up the age difference. Not that she hadn't noticed it, but she'd never considered it a deal-breaker. There were already enough of those.

"So I will see you tomorrow." His words sounded more like a statement than a question.

"I didn't say that."

"But you didn't say no. Your agreement to attend will be considered in lieu of this month's rent."

"That's hardly fair. You're fairly compensated by my wit and charm."

"I made pumpkin cheesecake."

Merritt almost took her foot off the gas. "With caramel cream? And spiced pecans?"

"On the side, as you like."

She was tempted. And not just by the cheesecake. Seeing Evie would be sweeter. Before she could talk herself in or out of it, Max weighed in again. "Evie is solid. It'll be all right."

She took a moment to consider his point. "If only I could believe that."

He pulled on his seat belt and turned in his seat. "You can take that chip off your shoulder anytime, sis. That was then, this is now. Remember what Dad has always said about Sundays?"

Reluctantly, she recited the adage. "Don't ruin them by thinking about Monday."

As she tossed and turned that night, doing nothing but, she realized that her feelings for Evie, regardless of the age difference, the volatile investigation, and even her own fragile heart, were impossible to ignore.

CHAPTER FOURTEEN

Any concerns Merritt might've had about spending Thanksgiving Monday with the O'Hallorans faded almost instantly upon entering the modest home. The franticness of Susan's kitchen yesterday was replaced by Bev's calm, easygoing rhythm. The conversation played out just as easily, true in most events where everyone had little history and a lot to learn about one another. Fewer ghosts. And no Lonnie. Based on what Evie had shared about him, Merritt felt sure that his absence explained a lot about the relaxed demeanor.

Evie gave no indication that she was anything but delighted to have Merritt there. Beyond expectations, Evie had even kissed her on the cheek, then lightly touched her hand as she'd accepted the autumn bouquet and wine Merritt had brought. It was too crowded for a private conversation, so Merritt satisfied herself by belly-rubbing Walter while Evie garnished serving platters and bowls in the kitchen. Competently, she delegated tasks to family and friends alike and set the food on matching vintage flow blue platters. Every now and then, she'd wipe her hands on her apron—the one proclaiming "Your opinion wasn't in the recipe"—tuck her hair behind an ear, and catch Merritt looking.

Merritt didn't want to look away. She liked how Evie looked. And she liked the way Evie looked at her.

They took their seats, and as Max circulated with a basket

of freshly baked yeast rolls, the conversation turned to Robby's line of work. Max had mentioned she was an architect, but her specialty was one Merritt was keen to learn more about.

"Most people know it as green design," Robby explained as she passed the turkey. "I design a lot of energy efficient and off-grid projects and work with contractors to create energy retrofits."

Evie's fingers brush Merritt's as the rolls came her way. She definitely did not imagine that touch but wasn't sure she could explain it. After all, nothing had happened to change the fact that they butted heads on some core issues, and their commitment was intractable. Did that mean, though, that they couldn't manage civility? No. Friendliness? No. Beyond that, perhaps not. But she'd given a lot of thought to what Max had said about what could be lost by thinking too far ahead. The investigation would come to an end eventually, and she could think about what was next. For now, she wasn't going to spoil the moment. She wondered if Evie had come to the same conclusion.

The room quieted.

"You going to keep that?" Max asked.

All eyes were on her, one pair more beautiful than the rest, and she blushed, realizing that she was still holding the breadbasket. She sent it on its way and jumped into the conversation. "I've seen several large homes with living roofs. And solar panels. Is that part of the approach?" She was genuinely interested in Robby's perspective, and it was nice to have a less polarizing conversation than the one they'd had at the bakery.

"Sort of. But the vision is not necessarily about 'large.' In fact, one core goal is to reduce the overall square footage of buildings in order to use the land for other more community-fostering and sustainable spaces."

"I've seen that in Europe and Central America," Evie said. She elbowed Merritt playfully. "The trend is to create more adaptable spaces that are not just economically beneficial but environmentally beneficial as well."

Everyone had something to contribute to the discussion

and how green design wasn't limited to architectural design. It was also extended to policies, manufacturing processes, and agriculture.

Merritt thought Robby summed it up nicely. "I like to think we'll eventually make big changes with smaller spaces that are also aesthetically pleasing."

Max bookended the meal by putting the dessert he'd promised Merritt on the table. It was outstanding as usual, and the room fell silent short of the chorus of moans.

"Max, is the bakery a family business?" Bev asked.

"No, it's not. The Shepherd family owns a publishing empire," he said, smiling, amused no doubt by the embellishment. "That is in our sister Susan's capable hands now that Mom and Dad have retired. Merr had been the heir apparent, but both she and I went in other, quite different, directions."

Merritt gave him a look, hoping he'd change the subject. It was important not to get too close to the truth or the deceit. Bev and Robby didn't deserve to be misled about her role at Farmexal, nor did they need to know the whole truth. Evie must've picked up on her discomfort because she tossed her hair back, tucking it behind her ears, and began clearing the dishes.

Merritt happily took the opportunity to abandon the table and join her. At one point, while stacking the plates and attempting to balance the cutlery, their hands tangled. A sleeve of goose bumps formed on Merritt's arm. She pulled away but not before Bev, busy packing the leftovers, winked at her. Merritt met it with a tilted shrug and diffident grin.

Don't think about Monday.

Once the cleanup was done, Robby and Max announced an early evening and headed out. Bev apologized for being a poor hostess before starting upstairs, explaining that she'd been up since dawn preparing for dinner. She stopped on the third step and looked back at Merritt and Evie.

"And I'm keeping Walter for the night. He's already upstairs sleeping off the turkey he was treated to under the table. As if I didn't notice." She looked accusingly at Merritt, then at Evie. "You can pick him up tomorrow before you head back. Morning would be best. I have a big day." With no further explanation, she carried on upstairs.

Just as Merritt debated whether she'd be considered a terrible guest if she stayed a bit longer, Evie went to the fridge and pulled out a bottle of wine. She handed her two glasses and took her by the hand to the swing on the front porch. Merritt sat and stifled a moan. Two big dinners in two nights. She calculated the miles it would take to bike off the festive fare as Evie took the spot beside her and set the tulip glasses on the table. Merritt gave up as the prosecco bubbles raced to the crystal rims.

"It's a gorgeous night," Evie said. "Do you think it's true what they say about Canadians? That we talk about the weather more than most?"

"Absolutely."

She turned, casually twirling a strand of hair that had strayed. "It sounds as if you've given that some thought."

Merritt smiled, caught up in how happy she was in the moment. A warm October evening. A full moon. Cold sparkling wine. And a beautiful woman who seemed—no, was—interested in her. Or at least, her theories about the weather. The less contentious ones. *Take what you can get.* "I think Canada is one of the most diverse countries in the world. Not only in terms of geography, but also people. People who were here. Are here. And people who came here."

Evie nodded. "And the weather?"

"I think it's human nature for people to look for a common denominator when developing social relationships. What is more ubiquitous than the weather?"

"And has that worked for you before? Finding relationships through weather chat?" She grinned mischievously, and Merritt shook her head. She'd grown tired over the years of feeling the way she did whenever someone tried to talk about her past. Awkward. Embarrassed. Foolish. Was it possible she was giving the memories power by withholding them? She filled her lungs, hoping to inhale courage. Maybe it was time to talk.

"I can't say it has, at least not good relationships. Plenty of bad." With the door open a tiny bit, Merritt felt extraordinarily vulnerable. She took a healthy sip of bubbly and hoped Evie would walk through. Instead, she sat quietly, her foot pushing against the railing enough to fuel the swing. Maybe Evie didn't really want to know her, after all. Maybe she thought she already did. Merritt's bubbling need for reassurance competed with the prosecco.

"Max mentioned something about your family's business," Evie said tentatively, "Is that the 'bad' you're referring to?"

Door open.

"Not really. I mean, we've had our struggles as all families do, but we've worked through it. And continue to." Merritt quickly considered her options. Shut the door now, or open it all the way? She found the courage the moment Evie's hand settled on her thigh.

"I was involved, romantically, during my grad year in university. It turned out that she wasn't in love with me at all. She didn't need to be. She just needed me to believe she was." Shame blanketed her, but she pushed through. "The fact that I loved her so deeply made her ultimate goal that much easier. Her name was Natalie."

She told Evie the details of how she'd met Natalie while on a trip to Peru soon after she was gifted with a substantial inheritance from her uncle. "She'd claimed she was attending university there but was planning to move to Ottawa. She said she had an uncle in Toronto who was sponsoring her immigration. I can see how she played me now. She knew my uncle's death had left a hole in my life, in my heart, and she filled it. We bonded over our dismay about the pillaging of the rain forest. The drug cartels had their fingers in everything, including the timber mafia."

"Timber mafia?"

"Organized and very illegal logging. On a massive scale. Natalie claimed her town was owned by gangs, and she and her fellow students had tried to protest, but it had become dangerous to do so. She felt threatened and like an outsider in her own country. And in my grief, I also felt like an outsider. She led me to feel as though I was pursuing her."

Evie squeezed her thigh. "She wanted you to feel a sense of control."

"I was young. She spoke about an international student scholarship she'd been granted for her education and never asked me for a penny."

She paused and refilled Evie's glass, then her own. She was further into recounting the story than she'd ever been. Even when she'd had to face her family and confess that she'd been victimized. Then, she'd taken the brunt of responsibility. As if the money had been stolen not because of Natalie's deception, but because she'd been naive. Irresponsible. Blind. Telling it now, with Evie, it all felt different. Maybe it was the prosecco.

"Six months in, she'd groomed me well enough that when she proposed a joint bank account to help with her permanent residency application, I didn't blink. And I didn't read the papers she had me sign 'for the bank.' By that point, I was so entranced that I would've given her my inheritance if she had asked. But she didn't. She just took it. All of it." Merritt took a deep breath and felt Evie's hand again tighten on her leg. "And then she disappeared."

"Merritt, I'm so sorry. That must've felt like a terrible, terrible betrayal."

"It did. And it changed everything for me."

"Did you report her?"

"Yes. Turns out, it's not impossible to hide in a world as big as ours. Especially with the help of organized cartels."

"She was involved with the timber mafia? God, Merr, how that must've made you feel." Evie refilled her glass.

The prosecco was catching up with her. Or maybe it had moved ahead. Either way, the conversation was easier. "I'm much more inclined to be suspicious of people."

Evie laughed out loud. "Yes, I've noticed." She genially swatted Merritt's hand.

"Well, I can't argue with the Dalai Lama. Once you have been bitten by a snake, you are very cautious even of a coiled rope."

Evie laughed again. "I doubt you're driven entirely by suspicion. I noticed at the casino that you seem to have a knack for blackjack. That alone suggests that you're willing to challenge risk and balance it with caution. You are a complex person, Merritt Shepherd. I'm guessing you'd be even better at poker because you're also hard to read."

Now it was Merritt's turn to laugh. "I could say the same about you. You're not exactly an open book. I don't know much about your romantic past. Care to talk about it?"

Evie stopped the swing with her foot. Merritt's heart bounced as Evie slowly smoothed a thumb across her lip. "Talking is not on my mind at the moment. How's your elbow-stopper?" She moved her other hand farther up Merritt's leg.

The wave of heat on top of Merritt's thigh was eagerly chasing Evie's stroke. She shuddered and stuck her tongue out just enough to touch the injury. She hadn't given it much thought since the hotel fracas, and when they'd kissed at the loft last weekend, the wound hadn't prevented her from pressing deeply into Evie's lips. She was confident it wouldn't now, either. She put a hand on Evie's cheek. "My lip may need a little rehab."

As Evie kissed her gently, Merritt sensed that any reservations she might have had about "what happens tomorrow" had been washed away and not solely by the drink. She reciprocated with her heart more open now than it had been in years. *Just think about today.*

"I'm sure the Dalai Lama would have something wise to say

about rehab," Evie said, standing and pulling her off the swing. "But your lips, you, feel pretty perfect to me."

❖

Evie grossly overtipped the rideshare driver in lieu of the apology for being wildly unable to maintain a sense of decency. He might even have broken a speed record on the way to the hotel from Bev's. She and Merritt had been so physically engaged in the back seat that time was no longer measurable, and decency was barely relevant. She barely noticed that she'd stepped into the elevator, pulling Merritt in with her. Her whole body was humming, and the tune was Merritt. The doors slid closed, and she pulled against her tightly. "Two," Evie breathed, nibbling playfully on her neck.

Merritt raised her hand in the direction of the buttons, paused, and then raised it higher. The fourth-floor bubble lit up. "With your permission, we're taking the scenic route."

Scenic route? It hit her, then. She was in an elevator, walking the very edge of annihilation but inexplicably not freaking out. Merritt, on the other hand, was categorically making her crazy. Her kisses were soft and insistent, landing at the base of her neck tickling their way to her nipples. Good crazy. Great crazy. Irrefutably and irresistibly crazy. "Permission granted. But you realize you're killing me, right? Don't law enforcers have a 'first, do no harm' policy?"

Merritt began kissing each of her fingers and stopped to respond only once each had been gifted. "That, gorgeous, is a doctors' directive. We swear to 'uphold the right.'" With that, she lifted Evie's right arm above her head and pinned it against the elevator wall. Merritt pressed against her, the kisses now more urgent. Her body and lips were hot and eager to press back. The doors opened on the fourth floor and closed. Merritt pressed the button for the second floor, and the car descended.

Too quickly, the doors opened again, and Evie spun out of the car with Merritt's jacket gripped in her fists. "Come with me. Right. Now." When they got to her suite, Evie fumbled for her key card, and Merritt gently took hold of her wrists.

"Are you sure you want to…"

Evie kissed her, fingers weaving in her short black hair, drawing her closer.

Merritt resisted and pulled away. "I need you to say it," she said. This time, her distinct, slow drawl flowed through Evie like a glass of whisky. She was completely disarmed. Only the pain of absence, the loss of physical contact, registered. *Please don't stop touching me.*

"Evie?"

It took a moment to realize Merritt had stopped in the doorway, apparently awaiting her consent. Permission. Even sexier, Merritt's entire being seemed focused on her. Unwavering. Demanding. Desiring. Like a lioness about to pounce, Merritt's restraint was hanging by a single thread. A split second. A heartbeat.

"Yes. Take me."

She had barely spoken when Merritt rammed into her. Legs and arms entangling, mouths searching necks, hands molding against backs and breasts. The urgency carried them into the room. The door shut behind them. Evie was driven by her need for Merritt and pulled her own blouse off while Merritt unzipped the back of her skirt. Evie's lips hungrily explored Merritt's, stopping only to let the shirt she'd untucked from Merritt's khakis pass between them. She heard a boot thumping against the wall, unceremoniously kicked off. Then another bounced off the luggage rack. She was lifted out of her skirt. Merritt's arms flexed as she pulled Evie toward the bed. Evie's breath deepened, desire welling up from a place she didn't know existed. A place that had never been touched until this moment.

By the time they landed on the pristine linens, nothing was

between them except a burgeoning tempest of passion. Evie pushed up on her elbows so that she could see past the hair that had fallen around her face. Merritt staring up at her was intoxicating. The intensity of her desire was palpable, and it penetrated any defense Evie could imagine mustering. Not that she would. She wanted Merritt desperately. In spite of their best intentions, in spite of how distracting it might be, in spite of the questions and concerns and danger, there was no space or time for caution. A storm gathered quickly in those dark eyes. Evie was not about to step out of its path.

With unsurprising ease, Merritt flipped Evie onto her back and pressed her into the bedding. A leg slid between hers, and she could feel her own wetness against it. She wrapped her leg around it, pulling herself into the thigh. She grabbed the sheets as a torrent of pure need knocked her back. A deep growl escaped Merritt's mouth. Evie's neck tingled where the warm exhalation fell.

"You feel so amazing," Merritt's words formed a momentary break in the storm. "Promise me you're not drunk."

"I'm not. You?"

"Stone-cold sober."

Probably not entirely true for either of them, but it didn't matter.

A hand slipped between Evie's legs, and long fingers found her center. The winds came up again, stronger this time. As Merritt stroked, Evie's mind exploded with bursts of light as the maelstrom raced unrelentingly toward her. Merritt pushed deeply, entering her with one finger, then another, and still swirling around her clit. Evie's hips lifted against the onslaught, the pleasure excruciating and wild.

"Yes," she cried, her head rocking against the pillow, glimpses of hair flying before her eyes.

Another explosion rocked her as Merritt bit firmly on her nipple. Evie could barely make out where the bed was anymore.

She could only feel Merritt, inside and out. All of her surrendered to the raging torrent, letting it lift her until she broke open and fell gently back to earth. Into Merritt's arms.

Exhausted, she floated in the sweet calm aftermath. She was reminded of the first time she'd heard her own heartbeat. Seven years old, a hot July day, and instead of swimming against the river current as usual, she'd let herself be buoyed by the water and carried downstream. Her ears had submerged, and she'd managed to quiet her mind against the fear of sinking to the point that she could hear the big thump, little thump, big thump, little thump of her own heart.

She was hearing it again now, nestled against Merritt in a field of white cotton.

❖

Evie woke up half-buried. One half beneath the comforter, and the other overlaid with an arm, a leg, and an exceptionally warm length of torso. She took a moment to enjoy the sensations, like how the goose bumps traveled across her skin, disappearing under the places where Merritt's body touched hers. How Merritt's breath touched her shoulder and moved her hair so that it drifted perceptibly across her nipple, causing it to tighten. That in turn reminded her of the moments before she'd slept. Was it last night? Or last hour?

She had as much an idea of the time as she had of her orientation in space. She slowly opened her eyes to discover that she was lying in the bed in her suite, her foot was on a pillow, and her toes dangled near the bedside table. The rest of her, and all of Merritt, was diagonally positioned. Naked. Naked in bed. Naked in her bed. Evie's other nipple responded and matched the one already perked up.

"Someone is up," Merritt said playfully, one finger casually circling the puckered areola.

"Someone is most definitely up…for a lot of things." Evie

stretched to take full advantage of all the naked contact. "I hope I didn't sleep too long. That certainly wasn't part of the plan."

"Oh, so this was all planned, was it?" Merritt laughed and propped herself up until her lips felt only inches from Evie's. "And here I thought it was spontaneous." She planted a slow, arduous kiss that crept directly downward.

Evie rolled into her until Merritt was on her back. Their lips were still joined, but now, their tongues were tangled. The salty sweetness excited a hunger in Evie. When it came to making love, she tended to follow, but there was something about the taste of Merritt that drove her to lead. Any insecurities she might have about her relative inexperience with women was steamrolled by the appetite growing inside her. She took possession of Merritt's breasts, molding them as if they were clay, rubbing her thumbs over the hardened nipples and drawing out a ragged moan. Taking the cue, she squeezed one while claiming the other between her teeth. Merritt arched against her, and she placed her free hand beneath Merritt's lower back, drawing her closer as she positioned both knees between Merritt's and eased them apart. The wet heat and perfume of desire was like an invitation.

Evie planted a series of light kisses on Merritt's lips, then up her jawline to her ear. "I want you so badly." The words must've come from somewhere deep because they sounded more like a groan than a whisper. A plea.

"Then touch me, Evie. Please. I need you."

Evie kissed her again as if sealing a pledge before moving down her body on a trail of kisses and nips. She filled her hands with Merritt, kneading and caressing each part of her. When she passed her belly button, she slowed to take in the scent. For a moment, her brain stalled as if waiting. But not waiting. Immersing. All senses immersed in the moment. She pressed against Merritt's muscled inner thighs before slipping her fingers beneath each cheek, moving her thumbs between satiny folds, opening them to reveal the thick shiny nectar.

Evie moistened her lips and leaned down to drink. At first,

she licked along each fold of the labia and vulva lightly, tasting each distinct and delicious offering before increasing her speed and pressure. As hungry as she was, Evie wanted to enjoy each and every moment. More so, she wanted Merritt to do the same. So when Merritt trembled and grabbed Evie's head, tangling fingers in her hair and pulling her deeply in, what else could Evie do but meet her demands? There was nothing more satisfying than pleasing Merritt Shepherd. She moved higher, and with the tip of her tongue, she pushed up the hood and swirled Merritt's engorged clitoris with the back of her tongue. She pulled it between her lips, sucking gently and then releasing it. Merritt gasped, and her cheeks clenched tightly. Evie repeated the pull and release. The response was a quake so strong, the headboard rattled against the wall.

"Fuck, Evie, please. Have mercy!"

Evie wholly claimed Merritt's vulva, rapidly stroking the clitoris and penetrating deeper and higher, using the increasing pitch of Merritt's gasps to find her core. Within seconds, Merritt's tremors became one, her hips thrust upward, her sweet juices released, and she collapsed to the mattress.

Evie exhaled as if she'd come along with her. And if the warm fluid cascading down her thigh when she moved to her knees was any indication, it seemed she had. She fell beside Merritt, pulled the twisted knots of bedding over them as best she could, and wrapped her in her arms.

CHAPTER FIFTEEN

For the tenth time since leaving the hotel, Merritt swallowed back the emptiness. Only one night with Evie had fulfilled her beyond anything she'd ever experienced, and she was painfully aware of how much she was missing her. Her body ached in other ways, too. In all the right ways. They'd maximized every minute together, from the time they crossed the threshold of Evie's room to this morning's shower. God. Merritt swallowed again, this time spurred by memories of the synchronous, standing up, soapy wet orgasms that had pushed her thighs and balance to the max. How they'd managed to dress afterward was an exercise in self-control and had taken a lot longer than expected, thanks to a bra that they'd found in the ice bucket after ten minutes of searching.

Neither wanted to leave, but both had to. Evie had to invigilate an exam in Saskatoon, and rescheduling wasn't possible. Dodging responsibility also wasn't possible for Merritt, who had more "fires to put out" at Farmexal, according to an abrupt, borderline snotty text from Kelly detailing the discovery of more totes. They took a rideshare back to Bev's. It was barely dawn, and they agreed not to wake her. Stealthily, with the help of an unconscionably stinky dried salmon treat, they managed to lure a still-drowsy Walter downstairs and into Evie's car. Merritt quietly closed Evie's door, then leaned down and accepted a lingering kiss through the window.

"Later," Evie whispered. "Not too much."

❖

Merritt searched her pockets for the fifth time without success before realizing that she'd left her wallet and passkey card for Farmexal's secured entrances at Bev's. Blaming post-sex-brain, but also celebrating the cause, she turned the Caddy around and headed back to retrieve it. How was it possible to have forgotten to take them with her not only last night but this morning? She shrugged it off as a minor consequence of living in the day. After the kiss on Bev's porch, nothing but being with Evie had been at the top of her mind.

Lost in musings of the previous night's surprising events, she arrived in what seemed like no time. She recalled setting it on the small entranceway table when she'd arrived for dinner last night, and since they'd left the door unlocked when picking up Walter, she hoped she could retrieve her things without waking Bev.

She smiled with the realization that sleep might be a negotiable commodity. She'd trade it any time for more of Evie. Soft and sensual. Tongue and touch. Merritt's eagerness surged. When would they see each other again? Was last night, amazing as it was, a good idea? Her desire flared again, and Merritt accepted it as the answer.

She found the card and wallet where she'd left them, but before she turned to the door, she heard Bev's voice behind her. "Look what the cat dragged in!"

"You're one to talk," Merritt said as she spun. "Where did you come from? I thought you were still sleeping. I hope you don't mind, but I forgot my passkey and…"

"God, don't worry about that. I figured you'd be back for it. You're just in time." Bev greeted her with a broad smile and pushed a brown bag into her hands. "Jammy doughnuts. Sit down, I'll pour you a coffee."

"No, thanks, I can't really stay. Work beckons." Merritt placed the weighty bag on the kitchen table, and it fell over. Several sugar-coated delicacies tumbled out, and purplish-blue jam bled out of a small hole in their sides. Her stomach growled. "The day after a Thanksgiving feast and you made an early morning doughnut run? You're my kind of woman, Bev."

"I doubt that, but you're sweet to say so. Seems to me, my sister is a bit more to your tastes."

"Guilty." Merritt shifted but caught Bev's friendly tone and sly smile and knew that no explanation was needed. She bit into the doughnut, and her mouth was filled with the almond, apple-like taste. "Saskatoon berry? Where did you find these?"

"Don't tell Max, but I traded my neighbor a piece of pumpkin cheesecake for these. She told me that Saskatoon is derived from a Cree name for the berry's bush. Mis-sak-qua-too-mina? I'm sure I mispronounced that. It's full of antioxidants…"

Bev's chattiness, pacing, and lack of eye contact alerted Merritt that something was up. *Of course it is.* She spotted a sizeable suitcase next to the door. *She's leaving Lonnie?* "Is there anything I can help with?"

Bev followed her gaze to the suitcase. "You've already done so much. Evie gave me that number. Your friend. Chantal." She pulled a paper bag out of a drawer and began stuffing it with doughnuts. "Robby is coming by in a bit. I'll be fine. And very soon, I'll be great. Take these for the road."

Merritt felt her phone vibrate and glanced at it. Kelly. *Relentless.* Part of her wanted to stay, but once Robby arrived, Bev would have all the help she needed. Merritt accepted the bag with a hug and walked to her car.

Whether it was the tempting aroma from the bag or the fact that she'd burned off the previous night's feast with Evie, Merritt was starving. She promised herself she'd do an extra, *extra* hour on the bike at the end of the day and pulled another jammy out of the bag before heading to Farmexal. She managed one bite before her phone rang. *Kelly again.* She set the doughnut on the bag and licked her sugary finger before clicking the steering wheel switch to answer. "Hello, Kelly."

"I sure hope you're planning to be here this morning." It was a demand, not a statement.

"On my way."

"Look, Mr. Chisley told me what you're really doing at Farmexal. You've got to sort this situation out ASAP."

Merritt grimaced. She hated when people said that as if it was a word. And she hated that Chisley had been indiscreet. But she could sense something else was on Kelly's mind, and a second later, it oozed out like the doughnut jam.

"We're hearing some pretty credible rumors that protesters are organizing another event just outside the company gates. He's furious because of how much worse this will make us look."

Merritt rolled her eyes. "Shouldn't his concern be on the potential for harm that his company's chemicals might cause? Rather than on how things look?"

Kelly hesitated. "Yes, er, of course, that's at the core of it."

Wait. What did she just say?

"Merr, are you still there?"

She hung up. Kelly's last words were smashing around her head. *At the core of it.* Merr looked at the doughnut again, and her mind leapt to Farmexal's shipping process. Specifically, how the orders were packed. With a hollow core. An idea began to take shape.

She was just about to pull into the Farmexal lot when she caught sight of a group of protesters filing out of a large school bus. She rerouted and headed for the washhouse to see if her new theory held water. As she drove, she gave thought to the nature of these protests. Was she being fair in her concerns regarding direct action? After all, she'd spent much of her twenties marching and standing in crowds, unified in the passionate purpose of demanding change. Of making a difference. Sometimes, it required civil disobedience. And sometimes, change came about. But as the forests had continued to crash down, Merritt had looked to the inadequate systems that had contributed to the problems. The corporate greed. The impossible consumer demand. Ignorance and denial. Nonexistent or untenable legislation and enforcement. She'd turned her passion into a promise to chip away at the veneer and help make sustainable change. She'd been pursuing that goal for the past ten years. Slowly, things were changing. But so slowly. Would it soon be too late? Was it already?

As she rubbed her chin in thought, she discovered an excess of doughnut sugar and as she wiped it away, she detected Evie's fragrance on her rumpled sleeve. The clean cotton perfume transported her back to the bed, to the smell and taste and touch of the good, very good, doctor. Maybe there was room for compromise where their political differences were concerned. Just maybe those differences weren't so great after all.

Once at the washhouse, she hesitated to put the car in park, trying to create a viable excuse to drive to Saskatoon. To Evie. But first things needed to be first. She took the Caddy out of gear and texted Evie a dinner invitation. Hopefully, she'd have good news to share if things in the washhouse were what she suspected.

Just as she was about to turn the ignition off, her phone blew up.

❖

Evie cruised into her parking spot at the university, feeling a bit like the cat who'd swallowed the canary. She could not and would not explain the goofy smile she'd seen reflected in the rearview mirror as she drove to Saskatoon, and she hoped no one on campus would ask her to. As she walked to her office, she tried her best to look cool, certain that her best didn't even touch cool. Just the thought of last night caused her stomach to somersault. Goose bumps piled on top of goose bumps. She pulled her thin sweater tighter and folded her arms so her nipples wouldn't betray how resoundingly turned on she was by the memories. But it was more than the sex. The great sex. The goofy-smile sex. Spending the night with Merritt was in so many ways transformational. That revelation was what she'd spent the two-hour drive from Regina thinking about. *Well, that and the sex.*

And the elevator ride. Very curious. Not for a moment had she experienced the disabling symptoms she'd struggled with in enclosed spaces since, well, since Mexico. Was it too much to hope that she'd finally shaken the claustrophobia? Did the simple act of Merritt pinning her to the wall and nibbling on her neck really have the power to exorcise that demon? She laughed at the thought. Of course not. Maybe not. It was hard to completely reject the possibility because as Merritt was fond of saying, things had changed.

Her phone dinged as she stepped into the lecture hall. She clicked it to mute before reading the incoming text from Merritt.

Great night. Great morning. Miss you. New ideas re: totes to share. Free tonight for dinner? I'll come to you.

Evie began to a response in all caps but managed only the *YE* before remembering that today was the day Bev was leaving Lonnie. She wanted to be available in case her sister needed her. Bad enough she was hours away, but that was unavoidable. There was no reason to think things would go other than to plan. Lonnie was out of town. Bev would stay at Robby's tonight and then come stay with her in Saskatoon until Lonnie packed his things and cleared out.

Evie stared at her phone and wondered what she could text. Maybe it was selfish, but she wanted Merritt's focus to be on the investigation. The *new ideas* sounded promising, and stopping the thefts had to be at the top of Merr's list, not the O'Halloran family crises. Besides, she had distracted her enough last night. And two more times this morning.

Better than great. Can't tonight. Explain later. Miss you, too.

She thought about the story Merritt had shared about

Natalie. The disclosure had drawn them closer emotionally, as disclosures often did. And what it eventually led to felt, well, perfect. But there was something still niggling at her as she set up the projector for class. Sitting on the porch last night, feeling safe and having Merritt open up about her life, Evie had been aware of a conscious decision not to reciprocate. Not that it was required. Building intimacy wasn't an obligatory transaction. The truth was, she'd only ever told her sister and niece the events that had unfolded in Mexico years ago. As best she could recall.

She'd returned from the research trip a complete emotional mess, and Bev and Alan had taken her in until she could look after herself. And she hadn't fully comprehended the whole of what had happened. How it had and would plague her. She still didn't. It was an incomplete story, and maybe that was why she had chosen not to share. Maybe.

Evie had done her best to manage the ghosts that had followed her to Saskatchewan, sometimes better than others. She didn't completely understand the source of the resulting behavior, one of which—claustrophobia—had been held at bay just last night. Of course, there were other symptoms. Blackouts. Flashes of anger. But she'd taken the easy route. Denial. Convenient and simple. Usually, sufficient. But the niggling continued.

As her students filed into the exam room, she decided to shelve any notions of sharing the details until things with Bev had settled. She texted one last time with a heart in response to the "disappointment" emoji Merritt sent before slipping her phone into her briefcase.

CHAPTER SIXTEEN

Merritt hoped the relentless beeps from her phone might be Evie saying she'd changed her mind about tonight. But they weren't. Far from it. She let the Cadillac's onboard system read the texts.

The first was from Steph: *Does Evie's sister live in Coventry Place? Near the park?*

Several more beeps sounded before the system read the next from Robby: *Can you come to my mom's house?*

At the next cluster of beeps, Merr pulled over and picked up her phone to read the rest. Another from Steph: *I got wind of a domestic. Call came in from the vic. O'Halloran. Isn't that your girl? Met at Régine, right?*

Intimate partner violence? What? Merritt felt her gut clench as another of Robby's texts hit her screen and might as well have been the only message: *Lonnie lost it. Police called.*

Merritt tried to call Max. No response. Robby's line went straight to voice mail. Steph was next. The panic was choking Merritt, and all she could do after a brief, "What the fuck?" was listen as Steph filled her in.

"Relax and breathe. Regina Police Service responded, coding it first as domestic violence. They added assault with a weapon. Three RPS cruisers and two ambulances are on scene. No status on the Com. Soc arrested and in the cage." Merritt mentally translated Com to complainant and Soc for subject of complaint.

Fucking Lonnie.

"I'll give the lead on scene a heads-up that you're coming. Just give him or her my name when you get there."

Still struggling to speak, Merritt forced out a thanks before hanging up and calling Evie. Was she in Saskatoon? Yes, she was, right? Yes. An exam. No answer. Merritt was shaking. "Dammit." She tore out of the lot and sped toward Bev's.

The scene was almost what she'd expected. Police cars were parked on the lawn at various angles. Ambulances parked on the driveway, one beginning to pull out. Lights off. Good sign. The remaining vehicles' flashing red, blue, and white lights bounced off the nearby houses and trees. What surprised her was Robby's car, headlights smashed in, large dents from bumper to bumper, surrounded by auto glass from the rear window, which was flipped like a mishandled pancake on top of the truck. Uniformed officers walked between the vehicles, notebooks out, marking evidence and taking photos. One was bagging a baseball bat. She found the officer in charge, who nodded and pointed to the remaining ambulance. She turned toward it, but before she could see who was in the wagon, Robby crossed the lawn and stepped in front of her.

"He's okay, Merr."

Only then did Merritt slow, and her heart skipped a beat.

"He?" *Not Bev? Maybe Lonnie. Hopefully, Lonnie.*

"Max. He's okay."

Max? Her heart jumped to her throat, damming her words. *What was Max doing here?* Questions screaming in her head, Merritt stepped around Robby and bolted to the back of the wagon. Max sat on a stretcher inside wearing his chef's whites, a foil blanket over his back. His whites were scuffed with grass stains and something red. Blood. Her mouth went Sahara dry. Her eyes fell to his motionless arm encased in an inflatable splint.

She stared for an extra-long moment, waiting to create saliva and swallow her panic so she could ask what had happened. She could hardly see his arm through the plastic squares of the splint. It reminded her, strangely, of the jammy doughnut. "Max, are you okay?"

"I'm fine, sis. Probably just a small break. Great meds, though, I don't feel a thing."

The ambulance attendant, a colorfully sleeved Gen Z woman whose body was proof of an intense dedication to her workout regime, chimed in. "I might've given him a bit more than protocol. I've eaten at Régine, and it's in my best interests to have him back at work soon." She smiled.

Her brother's welfare now no longer in question, Merritt turned to Robby. "What the hell happened?"

They sat on the bumper while the attendant began to strap Max to the gurney in preparation for transport. Merritt handed over a bottle of water she'd liberated from the med unit's supply. Robby chugged it and took a deep breath, then passed it to Merritt, who finished it off in one glug.

"Mom was leaving. She really was doing it this time. As we were heading to the car, Lonnie showed up. He wasn't supposed to be here." Robby was shaking. "I managed to get Mom into the car, but I dropped the keys in my hurry to jump in. Thank God, he didn't see them. Instead, he started beating on my car with a baseball bat."

Merritt put an arm around her, and she leaned in before continuing. "I'd been on the phone with Max, and he rushed over."

He'd arrived before the police. He'd tackled Lonnie but not before taking a bat to the arm. "The blood isn't even his own. It's Lonnie's." Robby seemed relieved but mostly satisfied as she described how Max had taken Lonnie down hard and "pummeled him pretty good" with one good fist.

Merritt's head was spinning. "What was he thinking? That so easily could've gone sideways." *Relax. It didn't.* "Your mom? Is she okay?"

"Mom is fine. She's in the house. Unpacking. It's her house, and today pretty much got Lonnie officially uninvited. I should go check—"

"I'll make sure your mom's okay. You go with Max." Merritt supported Robby as she stepped up into the ambulance with Max, who had a sideways grin plastered on his face. "He's probably developed a hero complex, but I think you can handle him."

When Merritt walked into the kitchen, Bev was putting the phone back in the old-school wall cradle, the cord dangling like coiled vine. "Just trying to reach Evie," she said as if nothing had happened. "She's invigilating an exam this morning, so the phone must be off."

Merritt exhaled, relieved that Evie hadn't been here when Lonnie showed up. Bev seemed to know what she was thinking and put a steadying hand on her arm.

"She'll be pleased to know you're worried about her." Bev opened the doughnut bag that was still on the table and waved it under Merritt's nose. "Last one. I eat when I'm stressed."

"Given the circumstances, you don't need to explain." Merritt smiled and politely waved off the bag but not before she noticed the purple jam oozing from the lone doughnut inside.

"I'm sorry Max got hurt," Bev said. "He really was incredibly brave."

Merritt only half heard. Her attention was still on the jam. Then it shifted to Max's inflatable splint. *The core.*

"Bev, if you're okay, I need to go." There were still so many unanswered questions, but Merritt had a solid theory about how the fertilizer was leaving Farmexal. It was a start.

CHAPTER SEVENTEEN

H ow is it you're both hot and smart?"
Merritt wrapped her arm around Evie's lower back and pulled her close. Walter waddled ahead of them as they walked to the parking garage. "I'm not sure how to respond to that, especially the hot part." A blush warmed her cheek. "As for the smart, are you talking about the totes?"

Merritt knew she was. She and Evie had spent the entirety of their dinner talking about little else. She'd hoped for a reprieve. The case had been all she'd been thinking about for two days, and she'd hoped that time with Evie would occupy her mind and body in a different way. Still, she was proud of her discovery and hoped it would bring about a resolution so her energy could be spent sorting out the next steps. What would those look like, and where would they lead? To Ottawa? She tried to hide the conflict that roiled at the thought by pulling Evie closer.

"Yes, darling, you know I am. Who else would've guessed that the pallet of empties had a core of filled totes? Correction. Who else would've figured it out because of a doughnut?"

"Well, doughnuts are inspirational." Merritt laughed. "But in this case, it was also Max's inflatable cast. My mind had been tinkering with the idea that if empty totes could be placed as a core in otherwise full pallets, then why couldn't empty totes disguise a full core? Seeing his arm wrapped in a hollow plastic sleeve solidified thoughts that, until then, had been unconnected. Maybe we should take Bev and Max out to dinner to thank them. When this is all over, that is."

Merritt was pleased that the question of how the fertilizer was leaving Farmexal's manufacturing facility had been answered. But there was a lot left to learn. "After all, we still don't know for sure who has been rerouting the nitrate."

"But there are hidden cameras now, correct? At the washhouse?"

"Yes. Well, almost. They're being installed tomorrow."

"I'll resist teasing you about bureaucracy's inordinate resistance to urgency."

"I'm grateful." Merr shook her head and smiled in spite of herself. "For now, we've replaced the filled core I discovered yesterday with totes containing an inert fluid. The hope is that whoever hid the totes will come to retrieve them, but liquid ammonium nitrate is unpredictable, and there's no need to put anyone in harm's way."

"I love…that about you."

Merritt heard Evie trip over her words. It was probably too early for either of them to say it, given the situation. But Merritt wanted to hear it as much as she wanted to say it, and that was probably not fair, regardless of how they'd spent the afternoon or her rampant attraction and affection for Evie.

Instead, she slipped a hand in hers as they walked toward the car. As competently as Evie wore heels, the cold often caused patches of ice to form on the parking garage ramps, and she'd hate for her to take a spill. She'd already confessed to Evie how her shapely legs, made even sexier by the stylish stilettos, ignited her libido. So as much as she was being chivalrous, she also had selfish reasons to want Evie on her feet. At least until she could get her off them. Again.

Their afternoon had been spent curled up at Max's unoccupied loft. He had been at Robby's for the last two nights, accepting her offer to care for him while his arm healed, and Merritt and Evie had made extensive and creative use of the space.

"It wasn't necessary to buy me dinner. I didn't do anything to help Bev or Robby, and Lonnie was in custody before I'd arrived. You were right, though, those casino chefs sure do know how to cook a steak." Merritt playfully rubbed her belly.

"I know, but Bev made it clear that I was smothering her and kicked me out for the day. Consider dinner a thank-you for taking me in this afternoon and for helping Bev."

"Taking you in was my favorite part of the day." Merritt squeezed her hand and smiled, recalling their afternoon's activities. "My only regret is that I can't spend tonight with you as well. I have some work to follow up on."

"And I still have exams to mark. But take the credit, Merritt. If you hadn't given Bev your friend's number, I'm not sure she would've been able to pull herself out from under Lonnie's thumb."

"I think her sister had a lot more to do with it." Merritt kissed Evie sweetly on the cheek, taking the edge off her desire to do more. "I'm glad she's found her feet. I hear Lonnie's being held until the court date. Steph tells me they've charged him with multiple counts of aggravated assault, issuing death threats, public mischief, and of course, drunk and disorderly. Bev has time to figure out her next steps. Are you still planning on taking her back to Saskatoon for a while?"

"I am. She needs to be out of her house for a bit. To regroup. She doesn't know it yet, but Robby is going to clear out Lonnie's stuff while she's with me. Give her a fresh start."

"Speaking of fresh starts, I've missed you." What was she saying? It had only been two days. Not even. She was saved from outright panic when Walter stood on his hind legs and put his paws on her thigh. "You, too, Walter." He seemed satisfied and continued to walk beside them. "I still need to push through the investigation, but I know some things for sure. I like you. I like us." Where had that come from?

Evie stopped and turned Merritt to face her. She took her face in her hands and ran her thumbs along Merritt's lips before kissing them. "I like us, too. Oh, hey, speaking of Max..."

Merritt bit her bottom lip. "Were we?"

Evie swatted her. "I found out that he and I are both Steelers fans. So once the Grey Cup is won by our beloved Roughriders, be prepared for a regular visitor in front of the big screen on Sundays."

"Done deal, provided you're prepared to stay over the night before."

"Is that an enforceable directive?"

"I'm not sure the ministry has any jurisdiction on that kind of thing, but I'd rather not resort to restraint."

"Too bad. I would."

Evie's comment took Merritt by surprise, and her nipples instantly and unnervingly responded to the suggestion. God, what this woman did to her. She'd wanted to maintain boundaries. *Not in the cards.* She'd hoped that their ideological differences weren't insurmountable. For now, those differences had been parked outside the bedroom door. What about tomorrow, though? Was she still going to be in Regina once her work was done? For Sunday's football and Saturday night's pregame? Yes, there would be paperwork. Lots of paperwork. How long could she stretch it out? Not forever. But possibly. Even she had to respect Evie's perspective on bureaucracy. It did sometimes contribute to the sluggishness of political action. Before she could formulate a response to the restraint comment, which still had her nipples on point, Merritt's focus was steered to the large iron door that Einerson's truck had been parked in front of last week.

There, just along the edge of its oversized handle, she could make out a lengthy scuff. A yellow scuff. Merritt stopped in her tracks. She had seen that color on two occasions in the past few weeks. Her phone rang just as if she'd hit the jackpot.

"Shepherd. Hang on." Merritt palmed and lowered the phone.

Evie bent and clipped a leash to Walter. "Clearly, my goal is to keep you in bed once I get you there," she said quietly, "but I'm aware you have other responsibilities. I promised Walter a walk before we go back to the room. I'll do that while you take that," she said, pointing to the phone. "We'll be back to say a proper good night in a bit." She headed for a stairwell and Merritt, raising the phone to her ear, walked closer to the iron door.

"Hi, Merr. Just following up on a couple of things." Kelly's tone was atypically professional but still friendly. Merritt had been seeing a different side to her in the past few days. She had maintained discretion where Merritt's true purpose at Farmexal was concerned, and she had developed some strong PR messaging that Chisley was surprisingly upholding during media interviews. "Mark's security card was used at the washhouse far more than the security schedule dictates. You don't think he's involved, do you?"

"Hard to say." Merritt didn't want to say what the cameras were soon likely to show. "I appreciate that you helped convince Mr. Chisley to go with my plan."

Chisley had balked at first, then agreed to installing surveillance and letting the process play out until they knew how the fluid was being transported out of the washhouse and how the empty totes were ending up in the fields.

"As you said, just loading a pallet core with filled totes isn't enough to prove much of anything," Kelly said. "I've got some more work to do before I can head home. Call if you need anything."

As Merritt hung up, she maintained her belief that someone would come to collect the purloined totes and that a breakthrough was imminent. She'd promised Chisley as much. With that assurance came mixed feelings. An end to the investigation also meant an eventual return to Ottawa.

She caught sight of Evie and Walter returning from their walk and pocketed her phone, Evie's eyes grew as she took in the door behind Merritt.

"Impressive, right?" Merritt tried to keep things upbeat, reading the wary look on Evie's face but needing to shelve her emerging fears about what their world would look like post-Farmexal. The yellow streak on the door near the handle was as close a match as she could imagine to the yellow on the dollies in the washhouse. The dollies that they'd hidden behind that day. And the same color as the ding on the bumper of Einerson's truck.

"It is." Evie's response was guarded. "I'd not noticed it before now. It blends in with the grime down here."

Merritt smiled and took hold of the oversized handle with both hands. Evie and Walter stepped back. She lifted and pulled. The door was heavy, but it opened without much resistance. The dim light from the parking garage barely lit the first few feet of otherwise pitch-black space behind the door.

Evie gasped. "Well, I'll be damned."

"I'm guessing this is one of those old tunnels you told me about?"

Evie moved in a bit closer. Walter was guardedly smelling the air emerging from the dark cavernous space. "It appears to be. I don't believe it's one I'm familiar with, though."

"No worries." Merritt took a step closer.

"You can't be serious." Evie grabbed her sleeve. "You're not going in there alone."

"I'd never ask you to join me. I just need to check something out." She put her hand on Evie's and gently extricated it from her jacket.

"Merr, no. Please. Can't you call someone?" Evie was shaking her head emphatically.

"I promise, I'm just going to see if I'm right. Give me five minutes?"

Evie was gripping her pendant so tightly, her knuckles were white. "Where have I heard that before? These tunnels aren't safe. Please don't."

Merritt hesitated, then put a hand gently on Evie's. She was going to check it out despite her protests but wanted to ease her concerns. "It's okay. I already have a pretty good idea where it leads." Walter was trying to follow, setting his paws on Merritt's leg. "See, even Walter is on my side. Five minutes. Set your phone."

Evie stepped back and pulled against Walter's leash until he sat beside her. "Be careful, dammit."

Merritt turned on the flashlight of her phone and stepped into the tunnel. Fifty or so meters in, she turned. Evie and Walter were a single silhouette in the open door. The tunnel curved, and they disappeared. There was no longer light from any source but her phone.

❖

The minute Merritt's phone light disappeared, Evie's apprehension spiked. She called out, but there was no response. She thought about phoning for help but could only stare at the stopwatch on her phone, which showed that only two minutes had passed since Merritt had headed into the tunnel. Too soon to panic. Right? Surely, she wouldn't put herself in any danger.

But she already had. The tunnels were no longer maintained, and who knew how stable the fault lines were? Or if they were still passable. Three minutes. Still no sign. Still too soon to panic. After all, Merritt wasn't just any woman tromping through an old tunnel; she was a competent investigator. But she was also Evie's competent investigator. Evie's Merritt.

Four minutes. Walter was fixed in place, ears and tail up, staring down the tunnel as if he was seeing a rabbit and straining hard against his leash. Evie rubbed his head to comfort him, aware of the reciprocity. As she stood, a flash bounced off the tunnel wall, accompanied by a loud crack that echoed against the cavernous space.

Walter tore the leash from her hand and bolted into the dark toward the sound.

"Walter, no!" Evie stepped over the tunnel threshold and tentatively took a step. "Merritt!" A chasm of conflict opened up in her chest, widening as one side urged her to keep going, while the other screamed at her to stop. Musty air swirled in her nose. The rock walls began to close in, and she strained to hear any sound coming from the blackness ahead, but it felt as if her ears had been plugged with cotton balls. "Merritt! Walter!"

Then a bark cut through the muted darkness. *Walter.* And another, this time a yelp.

Another flash. Another crack. A scream. Silence. Then a bark, this time throatier. "Merritt! Walter!"

Evie pushed against the panicky tentacles miring her in place. She flipped on her phone light and ran into the dark.

❖

Merritt figured she'd walked about two hundred yards since leaving Evie at the parking garage entrance. Outside of the light from her phone, the tunnel ahead and behind was as dark as night. Confident that her theory was right, she soldiered on. *This must lead to the washhouse.*

Another fifty or so yards in, she noticed a light ahead. A tall figure with its back to her, wearing a headlamp, was bent over and securing a tote to a dolly. A yellow dolly. *Yellow paint.* An LED lantern was propped on a nearby ledge. She tucked her phone into her back pocket and felt for her badge. The figure, who fit Einerson's height and build, did not appear to have a weapon. Good thing because neither did she. In deference to Evie's disdain for guns, she'd chosen not to bring hers to dinner. She hoped she wouldn't regret the compromise now, all the while hearing Steph cautioning her in her head.

She approached slowly, trying to confirm an identity, when a pile of loose gravel crunched beneath her feet. The headlamp turned in her direction, almost blinding her. But the adjacent lantern cast enough light for her to confirm that it was, in fact, Mark Einerson. He stood and stepped toward her. She raised a hand to block out his bright lamp.

"Merr? What the fu—"

She squinted into the light. "Mark, I already know what's going on, so please step back and—"

He knocked the lantern off the ledge. She was blinded by his headlamp. She reached for her badge, not taking her eyes off him. She caught a glint of metallic gray near his waist and the silhouette of the weapon rising in front of his chest.

Didn't see that one. Damn. She jumped out of the beam of light and moved lower to the ground, closer to him. He fired, and the gunshot echoed behind her in the cavernous space, deafening her.

She scrambled behind a stack of totes to his left. He headed down the tunnel, no doubt thinking she'd retreated. *Perfect.*

Her phone vibrated. A text from Steph: *Arriving at location. On standby.*

Not wanting to risk too much light from her screen, she clicked off without responding. Then she heard a bark from deeper in the tunnel. Walter? *Damn.*

Einerson headlamp created a surreal light show on the tunnel walls and ceiling, casting light in every direction as he tried to detach Walter, whose teeth were sunk into his pants. With every other step, Walter and the leash swung like a pendulum. "Fuck off, dog!" Einerson spun again and shook his leg. When he got closer to Merritt, she held back a gasp. He had his gun pointed down, taking aim at Walter. "Get the fuck—"

Merritt launched at him, wrapping her arms around his midriff and shouldering his ribcage. They fell against a semi-collapsed rafter, and she wrestled to restrain him as Walter provided a relentlessly toothy assistance. The leash wrapped around Einerson's and Merritt's legs as they tumbled on the ground.

Another gunshot echoed through the tunnel.

❖

Evie was still on her feet. Her breathing was rapid, but she was still moving despite the terror that clung to her. Ahead of her, shadows appeared on the tunnel wall, and soon, a light detailed the grimy walls. "Merritt? Walter?"

Within seconds, a large shadow appeared down the tunnel, quickly getting smaller as something ran toward her. She tipped her phone light down. "Walter!" One down, one to go. She scooped him into her arms and continued toward the light, desperate to find Merritt. She sank her fingers into Walter's fur, glad he was warm. And…wet? *Why is he wet?*

She stopped and looked at his coat and noticed much darker spots. Maybe grime from the tunnel? She turned her palm toward her light. Red. Bright red. Thick. Blood. The walls began to close in. The tentacles wrapped around her, squeezing and lifting her off her feet.

She landed in Mexico. Twenty-two years earlier:

Evie had spent weeks logging the samples and submitting the data at a remote cenote in the steamy Lacandon rainforest. Her survey book was often spotted with perspiration from her chin and nose, but she diligently inputted the smeared numbers at the end of each day. It wasn't long before they began to tell a story. Collapse was imminent. By the end of the first week of the graduate research project, she was ready to present her evidence and announce that the site was now too dangerous. The team should pivot and gather core samples from the surrounding stratum rather than in the cenote itself.

The team deliberated only a short time after hearing Evie's findings before reaching an agreement. All but one. The dissent had nothing to do with the data. No matter how compelling her evidence, Julianna was not going to concur. It was personal. Evie had ended their three-month relationship a week prior to the

Mexican research trip, and Julianna had been tediously contrary since. She had become increasingly vocal and disrespectful, undermining Evie's leadership at every opportunity. Evie suspected that she'd even gone so far as to falsify data to contradict the team's findings. If Evie said yes, Julianna said no. East? West. Stop? Go.

Julianna chose to go.

She was pulled from the water shortly after the predicted collapse, alive but unconscious and irrecoverably injured. Brain injury. Spinal damage. Against caution, she'd been on an unsanctioned, unaccompanied dive into the cenote. Evie believed she was attempting to find samples that would contradict the conclusion regarding its structural integrity.

In the hours afterward, Evie felt the weight of the accident on her shoulders. Ultimately, the team sided with her, but it was Evie who raised the flag. And it had consequences. For them both. If she'd paid more attention, if she'd recognized how reactive Julianna was, maybe she would've seen it coming. Stopped her. Her penance was to sit bedside at the hospital while waiting for Julianna's parents and the inevitable outcome. Mercifully, perhaps, it didn't take long. But it felt like eternity.

"Call 9-1-1, Evie."

Evie stared blankly into the thinning darkness of the tunnel. Walter was at her feet, bouncing and pushing his paws into her thighs. Clearly, he wasn't injured. *But the blood.* Confused but still standing, she found her breath. "Merritt?"

"Evie. Call 9-1-1." Merritt's voice echoed off the tunnel walls.

She forced herself to take a few steps and was confounded by what the light revealed. Merritt crouched beside someone. Mark, was it, the bodyguard from Farmexal? His headlamp was directed at a rag that Merritt was holding firmly against his thigh. He was leaning against the wall, his face contorted with pain, and his hands were tucked behind his back. As Evie moved closer, Walter took up a position between her and Mark, a low growl emanating from his core.

"Keep your mutt away from me!"

"Merritt, what happened? Are you okay?"

"I'm fine. Walter, too. Mr. Einerson is not. I don't think he expected Walter to redirect his aim, and he clipped himself in the leg. Please, call 9-1-1. With any luck, we're near enough to the end of the tunnel to get a signal. I dropped my phone somewhere. Be careful where you step."

Evie still felt a hum of panic coursing through her mind and body, but she cobbled together enough of Merritt's words and managed to do as instructed.

"Tell them to come to the Farmexal facility on Dewdney. Down the back stairwell."

Evie followed the emergency operator's request and handed her phone to Merritt. She looked around, trying to make sense of it all. There were several stacks of totes, all full of a yellowish liquid. A small lantern lay on its side on the ground. Within its circle of light, she noticed a phone near a fallen support beam. She picked it up and wordlessly brought it to Merritt, laying it carefully next to her.

Dewdney? They were near Dewdney Street? That was the other side of the tracks from the parking garage. They'd crossed under the train yard to… Her thoughts were muddy, but Evie tried to piece it together. The opening in the parking garage led to the Farmexal building she and Merritt had hidden in a week or so before. Now, a Farmexal employee had tried to shoot someone but had ended up shooting himself.

Merritt would explain it when she could. When Evie could focus. At the moment, she stood in the closeness, knees almost buckling. The dank smell of mildewy rock mixed with the sulfurous discharge of gunpowder, and on the periphery of the unpleasant odors was something familiar. Something that caused

Evie's mouth to go dry and her throat to constrict. Throwing up was imperative. And imminent.

"Evie?" Merritt's calm clear voice called her back. "We're not far from the other end of the tunnel. Would you please go and make sure the door is unlocked?"

Evie had just enough self-awareness to know that she'd been fading in and out of whatever was going on. She choked back bile and struggled to claim relief. After all, Merritt was safe. And Walter was safe. But it was that something else, something biting at her from somewhere beyond this cave, keeping her on edge. Gathering herself as best she could, she nodded toward Merritt, and with Walter at her heels, headed toward the tunnel's end.

❖

Merritt folded the rag to absorb more blood while maintaining pressure on Einerson's wound. He winced and moaned. Her compassion amounted only to what one human would extend to another injured human. Anything beyond that was abated by the fact that the bullet he'd been struck with had been intended for Walter. The next one, if he'd had the opportunity, would've been meant for her. She pushed slightly harder on the injury as she read him his rights.

Everything by the book, she thought before pressing record on her phone and beginning to question him. "Mark, I know about the filled cores."

His skin turned impossibly grayer. She kept a straight face, intent on letting him react to her statement. During her investigation, she'd noted that there were no cameras on the side of the warehouse where the totes going to the washhouse were stacked, so hiding filled totes in the pallets could be done with little oversight. Especially if someone had 24/7 access to the building. Merritt couldn't yet prove it, but a confession would solidify her hunch. And confessions always came easier when a suspect thought they were already in deep. Einerson had been caught with filled totes and had attempted to assault a peace officer. She smiled to herself, knowing that he would be feeling right up to his neck about now. He shifted uncomfortably, and she considered cutting off the zip ties securing his hands.

Before she could, he broke. "It's not what you think. This isn't about blowing anything up. My grandpa uses it. On his farm."

"That seems exceedingly risky, Mark, don't you think?"

"Yes. He's crazy."

"Then why help him?"

"He promised to help me. Financially. Said he'd pay for my truck." He explained that his grandfather would also leave the farm property and operations to him as an inheritance in return for his help.

"Why dump the totes? There was no reason for you to do that."

"I didn't dump them. Grandpa did. He hates Farmexal. Blames them for shutting down the supply of liquid. I know it was a government thing, but his bottom line doesn't know the difference. It costs money, ya know, to change out a spreader. Anyway, he was hoping to make them look bad."

Voices were coming from the direction of the washhouse. She recognized Steph, and the others were likely EMT. She figured that either Einerson wanted a deal or thought his injury was worse than it was because he continued to divulge the details of the operation as if he was on his deathbed, even as the EMTs began to treat and transport him. His great-grandfather had apparently helped build the tunnels, and when his grandfather had found some old maps and discovered that one of them led to a Farmexal property, he'd broached the deal with Mark. It had seemed so easy but had gone so wrong.

"I told him not to dump the empties. I could have easily snuck them back the same way I snuck them out. Stupid old man."

Merritt had more than enough. His taped confession would

be shared with police, who had arrived in accord with an officer-involved shooting. Merritt filled in Steph, who didn't technically have jurisdiction in the matter, but she'd arrived in response to the text Merritt had sent before she'd encountered Einerson, the one saying she was chasing down a lead that would take her to the washhouse.

"I'm glad to see you're okay. Still pretty dumb, heading in here by yourself. I have a lot more to say, but we'll need beer. You'll need a few. How's his injury?" Steph asked.

"He'll be fine."

"You might want to make sure she is," Steph whispered, gesturing to Evie, who'd returned on the heels of the first responders. "Your protester gal pal doesn't look so good. Even her dog looks more pulled-together at the moment. Let me know how she's doing, okay?" After a quick, one-armed hug, she headed back toward the tunnel entrance.

Merritt approached Evie with concern and caution and gently guided her to a ledge that would suffice as a seating area. She was holding Walter, and Merritt could feel her hands shaking. She seemed unbalanced and needed extra support to stay upright. Strange that she'd seemed to regain her composure when going to ensure that the ambulance crew found their way to the scene. Now, her equanimity seemed wholly impaired. She was rocking as she sat, cradling Walter and gasping for breath. She appeared worse than when they'd first met minutes after being stuck in an elevator. But that hadn't lasted. Whatever Evie was going through now was different.

Merritt feared for her. Shock could do terrible things, and there was no question that shootings often caused severe emotional trauma for victims and witnesses alike. Merritt took a seat and put an arm around her to keep her steady. "Evie, I need you to look at me, okay?"

"I'm not sure I care what you need, Merritt. Merr. Whatever." Evie's words flew out with the force of a missile, and she pulled away as if Merritt's arm was burning her. Her frail mood pivoted completely, and Merritt felt as though she'd been slammed in the chest with a hammer. She was at a loss for words.

But Evie wasn't. "You're wrong, Merr. And you've just proven my point. No matter how many laws are put into place, people will always do what they want."

What? "I don't understand, Evie…"

Evie's voice raised to the point that it echoed down the tunnel and back. "No. *You* don't." Merritt gulped. Evie continued, relentless. "People don't care about data. Or policy. When they're told no, they'll do it anyway. They'll break laws. No matter what audits show." She said the word "audit" like it tasted bad. "You can count as many beans as you want and push paper from here to the moon, but people will always do as they want. They'll steal deadly chemicals. They'll race into tunnels. Damn near get shot. Jesus, it could've been you just as easily as him! And it could've ended up much worse, Merritt. Much, much worse."

She cast a glance at Walter and paused only long enough to take a shaky breath and wipe the tears from her cheeks. "People will do what they want no matter what it does to themselves, their communities, or their planet. And don't kid yourself, people who drop in to patch up a problem and then disappear are not doing any favors for those who are left to pick up the pieces when the Band-Aid falls off."

Her voice broke, and tears broke from the anger. She hugged Walter closer, and smears of blood transferred from his soaked fur to her cheek and chin.

Merritt didn't budge. Against what had long been her nature, she didn't react. At least not outwardly. On the inside, she was rocked, struggling to keep her heart open and her head clear so she could take stock of the situation, deescalate, and figure out what exactly had happened. Clearly, Evie was rattled. Not without reason. Merr was her target, fairly or not, but there was more to this. She carefully weighed her observations of Evie's behavior from the elevator incident, to the panic she'd witnessed at the washhouse, to the manner in which she'd just expressed herself. Not the words. Just the manner. Merritt had seen this, or something very close to this, before. With a colleague a few years ago.

Merritt looked at Evie until she had her full attention and tried to speak with a gentleness that could only come from an open heart. "I know something is going on with you, Evie. I think you're in trouble. Please tell me. What can I do to help you right now?"

CHAPTER EIGHTEEN

Merritt walked into the loft and threw her keys on the counter. Autopilot kicked in, and she began grinding beans—lots and lots of beans—and boiling water. Once they were steeping in the French press, she sat at the island and stared at her phone. Lots of new texts but none from Evie. She reread the messages she'd sent over the last day and a half. Asking how Evie was feeling. Asking how Walter was. Asking if Evie could send up a flag so Merritt knew she was okay. Asking if she would please text back. Then the same queries by voice mail.

Two days and nothing. No response to the texts. No response to the calls. No response to the last question Merritt had asked in the tunnel. The last she'd seen from the belly of the ambulance, a second team of EMTs were checking Evie out, her diminished affect raising their concerns as well. Merritt hadn't had a choice but to leave. She'd needed to give her statement to the police and begin the onerous task of documenting the events of the investigation. But she had called Bev, who'd arrived to take Evie home. Had she gone home? Was she okay enough to go home? For all Merritt knew, Evie could be on a psych hold. That might explain the radio silence.

She stirred the ground beans and threw a towel over the carafe while picking away at the parts of Evie's tirade that still hurt. She did believe that protest could bring about social change, though policy changes were more effective. And protests could so easily become dangerous, and their legacy, more times than not, did not have staying power. Merritt knew from experience in the field and in Ottawa that legislation, enforcement, and managed public pressure had longevity, but part of her could see Evie's point. Was she overly concerned about the risks of active protest because of her feelings for Evie? It could easily have been Evie taking an elbow to the lip. Or worse. Then again, time was of the essence when it came to redirecting the increasingly difficult environmental challenges away from irreversible catastrophe. Ultimately, they were on the same side. Right now, though, it didn't feel that way. She stared at her phone, willing a text from Evie to pop onto her screen. Nothing. She plunged the coffee, her spirits equally depressed.

Moments later, Max and Robby showed up and helped themselves to coffee before taking a seat in the sunken lounge with her. She'd filled them in briefly yesterday by phone, explaining that Evie had been present at a shooting and had experienced some difficulty. Now that she'd surfaced from the mounds of paperwork that arrests and shooting generated, Merritt hoped that Robby would be able to allay her concerns.

"Robby, she's not returning my calls. Neither is your mom." Merritt's guilt began to surface. "You know that if I'd had a choice, I never would have left her on the scene."

Robby put a hand on Merritt's. "It's not your fault, Merr. Mom called yesterday afternoon to let me know that she was at Auntie E's house in Saskatoon. And she called this morning to say they were still there and that Auntie E was still sleeping. She asked me to tell you."

Merritt felt instant relief. Evie was safe and with her sister. She still had plenty of questions, and now that the lid was off the worry pot, she let herself wonder about what had caused the breakdown.

It must've read on her face because Robby seemed to zone in on her mood within seconds. "She didn't tell you, did she?"

"Tell me what?"

Robby sized her up and smiled. "You really like her, don't you?"

Merritt looked accusingly at Max.

"Don't look at me," he said, shaking his head, "Seriously, just look at yourself in the mirror. It's written all over your face."

"He's right," Robby added matter-of-factly.

Merritt's defenses dropped. "I'm worried about her. She really flipped out, and I know she's not a fan of small spaces, but it seemed like she was struggling with much more than claustrophobia."

Robby opened her mouth, then shook her head and stayed silent. Merritt could tell she was struggling with loyalties, sorting out what would be okay to divulge and what should be held back, presumably to protect her aunt's privacy.

After a few minutes and several pensive sips of coffee, Robby drew a breath. "I can't say for sure how much of what I'm about to say is true because I heard it from my mom, and you know what they say about third-party intel. Auntie E doesn't like to talk about it. Remember that story she told us a few weeks ago? About the cenote?"

Merritt's mind was rapidly trying to put pieces into place, to anticipate what Robby was about to say. She willed her to speak faster. "Yes. In Mexico."

"When she was in university, Auntie E was dating a fellow grad student. Julianna something, I think my mom said." She shrugged. "Anyway, they broke up during a field trip to Mexico over a plagiarism issue on some shared research. A few days later, while still on the research trip, Julianna was killed when a cenote collapsed and crushed her underwater."

Merritt held up a hand to process what Robby was saying. The student killed was Evie's girlfriend. *No wonder.* She nodded as she let things sink in.

"Auntie E had been gathering data that led her to believe something was unstable, and she warned her team not to swim into the cavern. Julianna shouldn't have made that dive. Mom thinks she was doing so out of spite. To prove a point. But Auntie E is such a softie. She felt *so* guilty. When she came back, she was acting differently. She had blackout episodes. Once, when I was a kid, I cut my hand falling off my bike. I thought she was having a stroke while she bandaged me up. Either I got used to her episodes over the years, or she sorted things out—"

"Or she learned to hide it effectively," Merritt added. "As a coping strategy."

"Likely. I've tried to talk to her about it, but she always manages to change the subject."

Merritt went to the kitchen and poured them another cup of coffee. "I appreciate you trusting me with this. I have a few ideas that might help."

"Be careful, Merr, she's a different person on this subject. And Mom says you're top of her naughty list right now. Like, very top."

Merritt's heart dropped. "I'll be discreet, and I'll give her all the space she might need." Her phone buzzed, and she snatched it off the counter, almost spilling her fresh cup in the rush. It was a text from Steph; she was downstairs. "Not Evie," she announced, trying to hold the disappointment from her voice as she tossed the phone on the island.

"It'll be okay, Merr. We're heading out. We've had a run on our hot-chocolate entremets. Thanks for that, sis." Max hugged her with his good arm, holding her that extra second longer. "Hang in there, okay?"

She nodded and gave him an additional squeeze. "I promise I'll let you know if I hear anything new. She'll be okay. You will be, too." Robby hugged her and they left.

Steph sat close beside Merritt, shoulder leaning into her. She liked having someone else to focus on, though Evie still played around the edges of her conscious mind. She brought Steph up to speed on the charges she could support against Einerson. He would be in hospital for another day and held until the Crown sorted out the formalities. Her voice trailed off when she finished. The investigation was almost over. Her time in Regina was coming to an end. She began to feel it all. Exhilaration. Exhaustion. Sadness.

"Fish 'n, I can tell you're hungry." Steph picked up an avocado from the fruit basket on the island. "You can't live on coffee alone, and I'm guessing that's all you've had since Thursday. I'm making you some eggs."

Merritt liked that she didn't expect or need permission. She simply headed to the fridge, bundled a bunch of ingredients into her arms, and put herself to the task.

The promise of food helped Merritt find another gear. She explained about the abandoned tunnels and how the yellow paint from the washhouse dollies had ended up on Einerson's truck and on the door edge at the parking garage. She went on to talk about the jam and the pallet core and how she'd pieced together the illusion. "The empty pallet going to the washhouse wasn't exactly empty. Einerson was loading full totes into the core of pallets going there. They were surrounded by empties, and the return pallets don't get weighed, so no one was the wiser."

Steph shook her head and smiled as she whisked a bowl of eggs. "And you made the connection because you were eating a doughnut? I hate you, girl."

"Well, the critical part is that it was a filled doughnut. And when I saw Max's inflatable cast, that sealed it. Einerson had weekend access to the facility, and eventually, the cameras would've caught him in the act. The fact that we ran into each other in the tunnel was dumb luck."

"Dumb is right, my friend. You took a risk that you shouldn't have."

"Yes, but I did text you partway in. Points for that, right?"

Steph grumbled and stirred the eggs. Merritt was always amazed by her. She was a phenomenal multitasker who could listen to each detail as she opened an avocado and made toast, all while making sure the eggs didn't burn in the pan. "So you think the money was his only motive?" she asked, setting two plates of scrambled eggs on the island. She then expertly carved the avocado, putting a fan of the green fruit across the top of an egg mound.

"Put mine on the side, please," Merritt asked before picking up the thread about Einerson's motives. "That and family pressure. He had no idea his grandfather was pissed enough at Farmexal to start dumping totes in obvious places. By the time he realized it, his truck payments were due."

Steph sprinkled a generous portion of Himalayan salt on the eggs and set the plate in front of her. Steph began eating, the only activity Merritt knew of that drew one hundred percent of her attention. Soon, she'd finished her eggs and toast and was sitting back on her stool. Merritt was still mindlessly picking away at the eggs but sensed the change in Steph's demeanor and prepared for whatever was about to come.

"How is Evie? Have you figured out how you feel about her yet?"

Merritt kept her eyes down. "I thought I did. And I thought she felt the same. Now, I'm not sure I know who she is, let alone how she is." She scraped some of the salt off with her knife.

Steph sat back. "People aren't eggs, Merr."

"What?"

"You can't always scrape the salt off. True, you might not see who people are off the bat. Sometimes, for some reason you may never come to understand, they don't make it easy. It may not be intentional. They just come with stuff in the way. Stuff that you can't easily push to the side. But Fish 'n, that doesn't mean that the layers below are unstable. Or rotten. Or expendable. You've got your own stuff, you know?"

Merritt looked at the salt and avocado, both pushed to the very edge of her plate. "What are you talking about?" She wasn't sure she was going to like the answer.

"Seriously? We're going to go there? Okay. You won't eat anything that has sauce on top. That includes spaghetti. You pull every sheet off your bed before you get in. You won't eat a sandwich until you've pulled back each layer to make sure you know what you're biting into. Max even told me that you returned a pizza because they hadn't followed your specific instructions to put the cheese under all the other toppings. And just the other day, I watched you scrape chocolate off a pastry. Who does that, Merr?"

Merritt shifted in her seat, searching for a defense against an indefensible truth. "But I…"

"Just you, that's who." Steph didn't slow. "And it's quirky, and harmless…when it's pizza or linens. But when it's people, well, we're just not perfect. And I know that you know that, but you have to stop peeling back the layers looking for faults. Because soon, my friend, that's all you'll ever see."

Merritt was struck silent. Her chest sank, and her throat constricted. Then, for the first time in years, the pain she carried inside was too much to hold. Tears welled, her shoulders dropped, and everything hit her at once. The magnitude of the investigation. The shooting. Evie's tirade, followed by her silence. Leaving Regina. Big things. Little things. Even the salt on her eggs. She grabbed Steph's hand and let the tears fall. When nothing was left, she told Steph what had happened with Evie.

"Merr, I'm going to say this as gently as I can because I know you're hurting. Not every woman you're attracted to is going to fuck you over like Natalie did."

The words hit home. Steph was right. She sat up and took a cleansing breath. Then she nodded, smiled, and pointed her knife tip at the salt pile she'd created on her plate. "This much salt is not healthy."

Steph laughed and threw her head back hard enough that she almost fell off the stool. "You're some stunned, Fish 'n Game."

Merritt laughed at the phrase, thinking fondly about the first few times she'd heard the Newfoundland vernacular brightly color Steph's language. When they'd first worked together, she'd wished she'd had a glossary to help interpret Canada's easternmost province's expressions. But endearing idioms aside, Steph was probably right about her being "some stunned." She had been clueless. Not just about Evie but about how deep her feelings for her were.

It couldn't be too late.

Merritt's stomach growling alerted her to the fact that she was still hungry. Weary as she was, she needed a burst of energy. She lifted up the fan of avocado with her fork, plopped it on top of her eggs, and dug in.

CHAPTER NINETEEN

After a whole day spent lying in bed, Evie felt like she was in a movie theater with the reel spinning the same show over and over. She'd replayed every bit of the incident in the tunnel. If the bits had been glass lenses, like the kind on an old projector, some would have been crystal clear, others covered with a film. Foggy. Distorted. She clearly remembered picking up Walter when she'd first seen Merritt and Mark. She had a visceral memory of a deep and almost toxic anger churning in her belly before it had broken free in a vicious rant directed at Merritt. The anger and guilt could've been directed at just about anyone. It had just needed a target. Did an out-of-body experience feel the same way? Floating farther away from oneself but also seeing everything with a peculiar, haunting clarity? She prayed that one day, she would forget the shocked expression on Merritt's face when Evie's panic had exploded and launched a volley of verbal shrapnel. At the woman she loved. God, what she wouldn't do to reel those words back frame by frame. To splice out Merritt's confusion. Her pain. Damn. Too far.

The anger and guilt were not unfamiliar monsters. Any psychology student could probably guess what she already knew: her demons had been born in Mexico on that steamy terrifying day in her mid-twenties. Just a child, really. And they'd come to life, to rule her life, because she was the one who'd broken up with Julianna. She was the one who'd refused to accept Julianna's excuses for a research paper with serious integrity issues. Unforgiveable issues. And Julianna had dived into the cenote mostly out of spite for Evie having broken up with her. When Evie had run toward Merritt in the tunnel, not knowing if she was dead or alive, it had done more than scare her. It had reminded her.

Through a crystal-clear lens, Merritt's expression had replayed in Evie's memory a hundred times since she'd crawled into bed and a hundred times while her sister had driven her to her house in Saskatoon. In the tunnel, in that single moment when her monsters had ripped control from her intellect, she'd fucked up and lashed out so unforgivably cruelly. After the outburst, things got fuzzy. One minute, she remembered trying to gather back her words as if they were gumballs liberated from an open dispenser. The next, she couldn't recall if she'd actually said anything out loud. She remembered Walter. And blood. Lots of blood. Sticky. On her hands. There were EMTs. She recalled watching Merritt step into the ambulance with Mark. She remembered looking down the tunnel, wondering if she'd have to go back. Alone. From there, the belowground theater that was her memory went dark. No projector. All light absorbed by the coal-black walls of the tunnel.

When she'd surfaced—minutes, maybe hours later—Bev had been in the driver's seat, and they were on the road. She'd stared blankly out the car window with Walter snuggled on her lap, relieved that Bev gave her space to talk when she was ready.

That might take a while. Then, like now, clarity was as ethereal as the tiny lights from distant farms dotting the limitless horizon.

Evie slept restlessly until daybreak, then accepted a mild sedative from her sister. She awoke around dinnertime but wasn't hungry. Jittery, perhaps. Numb, certainly. She didn't want to pick up her phone, let alone answer the texts and messages amassing. She cried often. Uncontrollably. Maybe she really was losing it. The EMTs had suggested she give herself some quiet time to process things and talk to her family doctor if things hadn't resolved in a day or so. Instead, Evie had diagnosed herself. Her anxiety was abnormally high. But there was a rational explanation. Intellectually, she understood the parallels between Julianna's death and the panic she'd succumbed to in the tunnel. She'd been aware of her claustrophobia and had connected it to the cenote incident. She even thought, hoped, that she might have conquered the intrusive behavior. With Merritt. But the closed-in feeling had come back in the tunnel, and joining it, a new disrupter. Something different. Maybe it was a companion of the usual monsters. Guilt and anger always seemed to lurk inside her. She tried to pin it down, but this new sensation was evasive.

It visited her again when she was bathing Walter that evening. This time, whatever it was spun her sideways. She slumped against the tub, and Bev scooped her to her feet. Once she was settled in a chair at the kitchen table, Bev insisted she eat.

"I made you some steak soup and dumplings. Your favorite. I expect you to eat every bit. I'll look after Walter, poor wet soul. He's so cold, I can hear his tags jingling from here." She pulled Evie's phone from her apron pocket and set it on the table. "You might want to check your messages. Seems some folks are concerned."

As Evie made her way through the classic Saskatchewan stew, she realized that the episodes she'd experienced more intensely over the past weeks should have been reminders of why she shouldn't let herself get involved intimately with anyone. She still wasn't quite right. Emotionally. Psychologically. Maybe she did need to seek help. When she'd returned from Mexico, she'd gone to therapy and had been diagnosed with PTSD. But at the time, she'd been trying to finish her master's and hadn't committed to a treatment plan. She had no excuses now. She'd lost Merritt. She didn't expect to be forgiven, and she couldn't ask to be. But ultimately, hopefully, she could find her healthy self.

The doorbell rang when Evie was halfway through the impossibly large bowl, and with Bev upstairs, she forced herself down the hall to answer. A round young man who looked like a new recruit in the local Beard and Mustache club handed her a vase.

"Dr. Evie Evelyn O'Halloran?" he said, reading the card stapled to the plastic stick poking out of the middle of the gorgeous bouquet.

Merritt? "Yes, that's me. Uh, thank you."

"No worries. G'night."

Evie carried the flowers into the kitchen and set the vase on the table. Her heart was hammering. She stared at the colorful assortment until their fragrance was irresistible. She opened and read the card. Merritt. Evie loved her but had never said it. Instead, she'd treated her like an enemy. *Idiot.* Without taking her eyes from it, she laid the tiny card open on the table and picked up her cell phone.

CHAPTER TWENTY

Evie stared into the closet. Satisfied it was empty, she turned back and watched Bev jam the last of her clothes into the suitcase. It was clear from the inefficient, or more precisely, absence of organization, that Bev hadn't done the amount of traveling Evie had in her lifetime. But that might change soon. Over the past two months, they'd spent time planning future "sister-trips." Nothing firm, but it was a good first step in Bev's new Lonnie-free life, and it gave her something to look forward to. Not that Evie wasn't looking forward to a trip abroad, but her heart didn't flip the way it used to when traveling was on the horizon. Not much lately made her heart flip, to be honest.

While Bev carried her suitcase downstairs, Evie went back to her room and began packing her own clothes for this week's stay in Regina. Lonnie's case was going to court next week, and she wanted to be there. Bev had been so good to her since her... what was it, breakdown? Yes. It was. *Own it. No reason to feel shame.* She was learning. As she transferred a stack of underwear from the drawer to her bag, a small card slipped out and landed on the bed. Evie stroked the white linen paper lightly and opened it, reading it as she had almost every day since she'd received it.

Lori Paskell, B.A., M.Sc., Ph.D.
Clinical Psychologist

And a phone number.

She turned the card and read Merritt's careful handwriting:

I know there's no magical cure, but finding good people to talk to can be hard. Dr. P. is very good. Please consider calling her.

Evie had.

And call me when you're ready.

Evie wondered if she was or if she'd ever truly be ready. Or if she ever could be. And she certainly couldn't expect Merritt to call her. If Evie had been on the receiving end of the litany of allegations she'd spewed in the tunnel, she'd likely have kept her distance, too. She'd been so panicked that emotion had overtaken her. She still didn't remember exactly what she'd said, but it was abusive. Of that, she had little doubt. Its magnitude had become painfully clear as she'd worked through the event.

There was a small probability, when she allowed herself to consider it, that Merritt was simply giving her space. She'd needed it. Especially in the days following her race to rock bottom. And the ultimate crash. Those days were nothing but a jumble of hours; she hadn't been able to pull herself out of the bed, let alone the house. Dr. P. had helped. Reframing and processing were her expertise, and she was a persistent and intuitive psychologist. For almost two months now, Evie had gained a much better perspective. It saddened her that so much time had passed before she'd invested in a healthier mindset.

Thanks to therapy and time, she was coping. With the help of a junior faculty member who'd taken over her mid-semester coursework, she'd taken time off work and decompressed. She planned to return for the January semester better able to manage her trauma symptoms. The hope she felt about her future was dulled by the sad truth that she'd pushed Merritt too hard, and all she could do was respect her need for distance. Lost in her thoughts, she didn't hear Bev enter the room until she spoke.

"I texted Max Shepherd this morning. He asked about you."

The mention of Max caught in Evie's chest and stopped her where she stood. Try as she might, she could not separate herself from the feelings that the Shepherd name evoked in her. Dr. P. was in her head for the second time in as many seconds. *Unresolved things can have that effect.* Words stuck painfully in her throat as she sat on the edge of the bed.

"I suspect he's asking on Merr's behalf," Bev said, picking up the white card and sitting beside her, followed by Walter, who squirmed against Evie's leg as if urging her to react. It worked.

Evie's voice was so tight, the words almost squeaked as they came out. "How is she?"

"Evie, honey." Bev wrapped an arm around her shoulders, which began to shake under the embrace. "Ah. There it is. It took you long enough. I was hoping you'd eventually get through the thinking part. To the important stuff. What you feel."

Evie wiped her tears on the back of her sleeve. "It doesn't matter how I feel. I mean, it does, but not where Merritt is concerned. I don't have a right."

"Baby sister, listen to me." Bev squeezed her closer and sighed. "I didn't get enough time with Alan."

More tears fell as Evie remembered her sister's first husband. Such a sweet man.

"But I wanted it, Evie. I wanted to have that man forever. I never thought for a moment I would only have him for a fraction of that. And I never thought I'd waste so much time with the likes of Lonnie. We all make mistakes in times of crisis."

"It's too late. I said such terrible things, Bev. There's no way I can take them back. She's young." Evie paused, knowing that was a convenient excuse and tried for something more real. "I'm not what she needs right now."

"You're hardly old. And you're not too late. People are capable of forgiveness. Including forgiveness of oneself. You're just afraid because you love her."

"Love her?" Yes. She did. The words curled up against her chest, and she wanted nothing more than to embrace them. Was she afraid? Was it too late? Why did it still hurt so much? "She needs someone steady. Someone more put together…"

"Stop right there. You are not broken, Evelyn Margaret O'Halloran. You just got nicked a long time ago, and it has taken you a while to heal." Bev turned the card over and handed it to her. "You're on your way now, though."

Evie stroked Merritt's words on the card. "I…I'm sorry I didn't tell you. There has just been so much on your plate and—"

"Come on now, sweetie. How could I not notice the department meetings you've had between ten and noon three times a week for the past couple of months. No department is that bureaucratic," Bev said. "I figured something was up but didn't want to push you, baby sister. Even though I probably should've done so years ago."

Evie blinked. "What do you mean?"

"I should've pushed you. To see someone. A professional. I'm sorry I didn't." Bev's voice softened, and she again picked up Evie's hand. "What happened in Mexico was awful. When you came back, you weren't yourself. You'd check out at times. You were quieter. I was raising a teen at the time, up to my eyeballs in angst and drama. But I noticed. After a while, it seemed you'd turned a corner, and the episodes got further apart and, well…"

Evie could hear regret in her voice. "You don't have to explain. I just wasn't ready to see things objectively. Dr. Paskell helps. It's still hard. Maybe because I'm more aware of what I've lost."

"I don't think you've lost her, Evie."

"I wish that were true, but it's too late."

Bev shook her head. "Do you see the way Max and Robby look at each other? And do you remember how Alan and I used to look at each other? That's the way Merr looks at you. I've seen it. And if that's the way you look at Merr, Evelyn Margaret, and if you love her the way I think you do, then you must stop wasting the only thing you can never get back. Time."

Evie wiped the tear-stained ink on the card with her thumb. The blue streak reminded her of the river from her childhood. Of floating. Of Merritt. Her heart, filled with possibilities, felt buoyant. It couldn't be too late. She wouldn't let it be.

CHAPTER TWENTY-ONE

The weather had turned cold and drab, but inside the Regina courthouse, it was quite the opposite. Fluorescent lighting bounced off the speckled marble floors and rebounded off the maple-paneled walls, the brightness causing Merritt to squint as she walked toward the hearing room. It was coming up on Christmas, and while most people might've expected the heating system to come to terms with the freezing outside temperatures, the 1960s had not been any heating-and-cooling system's best decade. Today, the courthouse was sweltering, which Merritt guessed was better than freezing for most. She preferred it cool, but after a week or so working with the Crown Attorney's office on the third floor—dubbed "the Trombone" because its temperatures slid up and down the scale several times a day—she'd adapted by wearing layers that were easily doffed or donned, depending on the building's whims.

Usually, this was her favorite time of year. But even the arctic cold that blanketed the city fell a bit flat. Like most things lately. Regardless of how well the investigation had gone. The required independent agencies were still doing due diligence regarding the tunnel incident. Her gun hadn't been with her, let alone fired, but as with any officer-involved altercation resulting in injury, her actions needed to be above reproach. There was still a lot to do before she could complete her reports. Once they were submitted, she would head back to Ottawa. No point staying through Christmas, despite her family's expectations. *Maybe distance will help with the cold and the flat.*

Rounding the corner on the floor below, she found Max where he'd said he'd be: sitting outside of the courtroom. Inside, a judge was presiding over Lonnie's case. Merritt felt a bit estranged from her brother since she'd been trying to keep her own pain over one O'Halloran from harshing his clear buzz over another. He and Robby had been inseparable since they'd met in early October, and between that and the amount of time Merritt had spent wrapping up the details of the Farmexal case, she and Max had rarely seen each other. He stood when he saw her, and his eager embrace told her that he had missed her, too.

"Back in uniform, eh, sis?"

She tossed her James Bay storm jacket on the chair and sat next to him. "Yeah. Makes it easy to pick out the day's outfit." She glanced at the green-gray khaki pants and linen shirt and smoothed her gray-black tie. "Where are things at? Are you nervous?"

"Nah. Robby already testified, then stayed in the room to support her mom. Evie is in there, in case you're wondering."

Merritt flinched. She hadn't stopped wondering about Evie in the past two months. "You're up next?"

Max didn't miss a beat. "You're not fooling me, ya know. I know you miss her."

He was right. She was curious about whether Evie had received the flowers, but there was no reason to believe she hadn't. She wondered if Evie had called Dr. Paskell and hoped she had. Almost every day, Merritt picked up her phone, hoping to find the nerve to call, wanting to hear Evie's voice. She fought the urge to drive by Bev's, hoping to see Evie's car, as if just that would comfort her. But she didn't, worried that if they did encounter each other, it might undermine Evie's healing. Yet, here she was. At the courthouse. Knowing Evie was also here.

"I think it's too soon."

"Bullshit." He didn't need to say it. She didn't believe any of her own excuses either.

She just didn't want to know for sure that things were truly over. She didn't want to believe that Evie meant what she'd said in the tunnel. That Merritt had been reckless and had put herself and Walter in harm's way. That Merritt's work on behalf of social policy was foolish and futile. And that she represented an opportunistic bureaucracy that didn't care about the deeper issues.

Some days, the criticism was hard to ignore. Even if Evie's words did come from a very deep pain. Merritt didn't know exactly the source of that pain, but she hoped that Evie might someday resolve it. The flowers and note were intended to be helpful, but with so much silence since, she couldn't help but wonder if the note had been too intrusive.

"Get your ass in there. I can't go in until they call me." Max pushed her gently on the shoulder.

Would her presence be perceived as a step over the line? *Only one way to find out.*

Merritt swallowed, gathered up her jacket, and stepped into the courtroom. She removed her peak cap, tucking it under her arm with her coat, and lowered her head as a sign of respect for the proceedings. Then she stepped to the right of the doorway, choosing to stand against the back wall rather than interrupt the room. Only then did she look toward the bench. To the left of the judge sat Bev, who was engaged in a dialogue with the questioning attorney. It was more of a monologue, actually, with the lawyer asking carefully constructed questions requiring only a yes or no. Typical. Bev was holding her own, maintaining her composure in the presence of not only the adjudicators but also the accused. Merritt could make out the back of Lonnie's head at the defense table. His orange prison outfit suited him. Hopefully, that would be his everyday fashion going forward. She caught herself smirking.

She continued scanning the court until she spotted Evie. Her blond hair was up in a loose bun, curled tendrils hanging down each side. Merritt must've subconsciously willed her to turn. They locked eyes, and Merritt tried to read the expression on her beautiful face. Sad? Surprised? Anxious? Disappointed? A mix. Merritt's heart was in her throat. She swallowed hard against her own emotions. God, she was beautiful. Evie's eyes did not leave Merritt's as she reached to her chest and picked up her treasured pendant, rubbing the bluish-black stone as if to glean comfort from it. Perhaps magic.

The thump of the gavel broke the spell, and Merritt almost jumped. The opposing attorneys approached the bench for a sidebar, probably to caution the defense. As Bev stepped down, she caught Merritt's eye and smiled. The gavel pounded again, and the judge ordered a five-minute adjournment. Merritt looked toward Evie, but she was already out of her seat, crouching over Bev's shoulder and gently rubbing her back. Robby had moved to join them.

Merritt put her hat on and stepped back into the hallway. She was shaking and gritted her teeth against the flood of emotion. Tears threatened her. People began to exit behind her, and she was eager to find an escape. Max was engaged in conversation with an assistant from the Crown's office, so she decided to head back upstairs to dig through a bit more of the mountain of reports that towered on her temporary desk in her temporary office. *Nothing like paperwork to ease a broken heart.*

She was about to push open the stairwell door when a hand gripped her elbow.

"Hey there, you."

Evie. Merritt's cheeks burned, and her pulse quickened. It was as if she had inhaled a sack of sand.

"Just on my way to the ladies'," Evie said. "It was very nice of you to come. I know it means a lot to Bev."

"I was here. Working. I mean, I work here." She gestured to

the ceiling with a nod, hoping Evie would understand. Her mouth was still so dry. "For now. Temporarily. I mean, I'm putting the case to bed." *What? Who says that? God, Shepherd, get a grip.*

Evie's eyes widened, a smile forming on her full lips.

Merritt recovered, barely. "I thought I would check in." *Lie. Stupid.* In truth, she'd planned to be there for the whole of Lonnie's hearing and would've been if her work hadn't detained her. Evie was assessing her uniform, giving her time to sneak in two breaths—the second less ragged than the first—and managing to wrangle her jumbled thoughts. "That's not true. I wanted to be here. For Bev. And for you."

Evie tilted her head and bit her lip. "I don't really have to go to the bathroom."

Her words landed on Merritt like a butterfly, fluttering in her chest. "How are you?"

"I'm better. Much better. And you? You look great."

"Okay. Yes. Good." *Lying again.* "Not good, really. How's Walter? Rumor has it he's getting a citation of some kind?"

"True. From a dog food company." Evie paused, apparently to let the coincidence register. Merritt felt herself blush. "Of course, he now considers himself quite the hero, so he's come to expect an extra level of personal care. I still can't believe he barked in the tunnel that day. I've never heard him do that."

Merritt nodded, relieved that Evie was able to touch on the subject, even if it was just the edges. "The hero picks his moments, I guess."

Their mutual amusement gave way to awkward silence. Evie stared at her feet, then shifted. Merritt steeled herself, preparing for the inevitable.

"So." Evie sounded tentative. "Max invited me to watch the Steelers game with him and Robby on Sunday. At the loft. I wanted to make sure…"

Merritt interrupted to spare her the awkwardness and take the sting out of the slap of rejection. "I'm sure I can find somewhere else to be."

Evie took Merritt's hand between hers. "No, Merritt. No. I wanted to make sure…I was hoping, well, that you'd be there. I'd really like to find time to talk."

For the second time in minutes, tears threatened to breach Merritt's carefully constructed walls. A squeeze of Evie's hands tore them down as if they'd been made of tissue. She wiped her cheeks, remembering she was in uniform and should look composed, even as she crumbled with happiness inside. This was not the good-bye she'd been dreading. Maybe it would come later, but this was not it. "Come early on Sunday? We'll have lunch."

CHAPTER TWENTY-TWO

Evie was having a great day. She'd been staying at Bev's house in Regina since mid-week, Lonnie's aura now vanquished. That morning, they'd gone for a walk with Walter that had been long enough to warm their souls but not so long that it froze their feet as the snow crunched beneath them. Winters in Saskatchewan were especially cold, the unbroken surface of the prairie landscape giving free rein to arctic winds that roamed across them with endless will and abandon. Afterward, they had indulged in coffee, with a respectable Sunday-morning dollop of cream liqueur, and oatmeal with blueberries and walnuts. Evie let herself appreciate the moment, a practice she'd been consciously working on as part of her therapy. She'd noticed it was helpful in keeping intrusive thoughts from hijacking her mind, but it didn't work in every circumstance. This morning, she could only try her best to avoid thinking about Merritt and their pre-football lunch.

She fully expected that, after months focusing on recovery, the dynamic between them would be different. New. Clear. No longer lovers but maybe still friends? Yet, since seeing Merritt at the courthouse, maybe there was room to hope. Merritt's honesty and vulnerability had come through with painful clarity. So did an immovable, unwavering sexual energy. If Merritt felt the same, maybe there was a chance for them. Two things needed to happen before they could move forward. Forgiveness for herself. And forgiveness from Merritt.

Evie spent the rest of the morning rehearsing what she wanted to say and anticipating how Merritt would answer until she'd covered all possibilities. Except during her shower. During those long, hot, wet twenty minutes, she'd indulged in memories of when they'd made love. And about how good Merritt had looked in her uniform. The khaki shirt pressed and perfectly tucked into matching cargo pants that tapered at the waist. The black leather belt with holstered sidearm. Even the baseball-style cap with the yellow ministry insignia had looked cute atop her head. She'd realized that, by the time Merritt had asked her to lunch, she was so turned on that she'd almost asked if she could come for breakfast. The night before. "Good" and "cute" were inadequate words for the feelings Merritt elicited. Sexy, no question. Desirable. Luscious. Butch. Breathtaking. All much more accurate and, as her time in the shower proved, powerfully inspiring as well.

By the time she arrived at the loft, Evie had almost rubbed the blue specks off the larvikite in her pendant. And all thoughts of Merritt in uniform vanished when she opened the door, offering a warm hug and looking fifty-plus shades of incredible in a pair of jeans and a navy hoodie. Her short, almost-black hair was slicked back, but the longer strands on top were loose and messy and absolutely adorable. It was all Evie could do not to run her fingers through it.

She kept herself in check long enough to notice the insignia on the hoodie. She pointed at it and shook her head. "Broncos? Really?"

"I can't help myself. The Comeback Kid and the Orange Crush were the bomb back in the day."

Merritt smiled, and despite the rivalry with her Steelers, Evie still found her irresistible. "I'm surprised you're old enough to remember Elway."

"Are you kidding? Imagine coming back after three Super Bowl losses in the late '80s and winning not one, but a second at age thirty-eight. What was it you said in your office that day? About the rock layers in Scotland? That many of our ideas about time and age have yet to be discovered?"

Evie was not surprised that she remembered. There had been a time when all she'd wanted was Merritt's attention. But right now, knowing she'd lost that chance, she wished Merritt's memory wasn't as good. She took a cup of coffee and a seat on the couch. "Merritt, I can't possibly apologize enough for what I said in the tunnel. I don't remember everything. Just enough to know that I hurt you."

"Please, Evie, you don't need to. I owe you an apology, in fact, for leaving you there. I knew you were in trouble, but I chose to—"

"To accompany your suspect? To make sure he was processed properly so that there would be little interruption in the chain of custody?" Evie smiled at the look of surprise on Merritt's face. "Yes, I watch TV. British procedurals, mostly, but the principles apply. And you didn't leave me alone. Bev materialized at your request. She looked after me. And Walter."

Merritt relaxed, sinking more deeply into the couch cushions, coffee mug resting on her thigh. "I'm glad the investigation is over. Successfully. But I'm mostly glad I don't have to continue lying. It's not a comfortable state for me, and I'm ashamed I kept things from you for so long."

"I hope you can let that go. Everyone has layers. We can use them to cover up our past, or we can use them to hide ourselves. But we can also get over them."

"Is that some nerdy geologist reference to Knockan Crag?"

Evie processed the comment, initially confused, then delighted that Merritt had remembered the story. Over them. Like the plates. Clever. Emboldened by the ease of the exchange, she moved a bit more closely and put a hand on her knee.

"Thank you for the flowers, and Dr. Paskell's contact info. I gather my sister told you."

"She was worried about you. Robby was, too. But I'd already guessed what was going on." Merritt cocked her head and leaned toward Evie before explaining, "One of my colleagues in Flin Flon tried unsuccessfully to pull a kid—a protester—out of the way of a wayward logging skid. For months afterward, he couldn't smell fresh-cut pine without blacking out. His reactions reminded me of yours. In the elevator. The first time. I know you were scared...who wouldn't be. And in the washhouse that day, I could feel your heart hammering and see that little spot on your neck pumping wildly. I thought you might explode. Then there was the tunnel..." Merritt paused, shaking her head. "Dr. Paskell worked with my colleague. In fact, she works with a lot of first responders who suffer from PTSD."

"Well, I'm not a first responder, but she has been incredibly helpful. Given how long the guilt and fear have physically and emotionally manifested, it's miraculous. Once the triggers were sorted out, we were able to make huge progress."

"Triggers? Like confined spaces?"

"That was one, yes."

"You had more?"

"Yes, and that's the one that really tripped me up that day in the tunnel. I was able to manage the claustrophobia. Not well, but at least enough to function. The second trigger was a mystery until then." It had become so much easier to talk about her struggles. Therapy had helped her release much of the guilt and shame that had plagued her for so many years. And Dr. Paskell had encouraged her to talk about her feelings with people she trusted as part of her healing process. People like Merritt. "Blood."

"Blood?"

"Technically, the smell of it. The ferrous, almost astringent quality it has. Unmistakable. Indelible."

Merritt put her arm on the back of the couch and laid a hand on Evie's shoulder. "Why that trigger?"

Evie's thoughts turned to Julianna and Mexico. This time, they didn't drag her under. She'd been working on detaching from the trauma associated with the memories, reprocessing them so that they didn't have the chronic and debilitating impact. "I didn't tell you this part of the cenote story, but the friend who died in the collapse was my girlfriend. Ex at the time. But regardless, there was a day or two after the collapse when Julianna was comatose. The doctors had her on a respirator so that her parents could say a proper good-bye. I stayed with her at the hospital, waiting for them to arrive, and at some point, probably to distract me from the sadness, a nurse asked if I would like to wash Juli's hair. She'd had multiple scalp lacerations, some pretty deep, so it wasn't surprising that when I poured water through the tangled and matted strands, streams of rusty red fell into the basin." Evie swallowed, noting that her breath had quickened. She gripped Merritt's arm and focused on the story, waiting for the emotion to subside before continuing. "The smell of the water, the smell of blood, well, it stuck with me."

Merritt moved close enough to hold her. She snuggled in and felt a gentle kiss on her forehead. "And it all came back when you picked up Walter?" Merritt asked while twirling Evie's hair. "He was soaked in Einerson's blood."

"I'm not so foolish as to think that I've got it all figured out. There's a long therapeutic road ahead of me. After all, I've carried the trauma for twenty-plus years. But I suppose I should thank you. You couldn't have known it at the time, but following you and Walter into the tunnel forced me to hit rock bottom, no pun intended." She was happy she'd been able to tell the story and had even found humor in it until she noticed a look of consternation cross Merritt's face.

"Please don't thank me, Evie. You were somewhat right about my reaction. It wasn't well thought out. I had ordered backup, but I honestly didn't think I'd need it. I didn't foresee danger. That was my mistake. Evie, I'm sorry. Then afterward, the distance between us for two months…also not well managed. I have my own triggers, I guess. I'm not sure I realized that until a good friend pointed it out. Staying away from you wasn't what I really wanted, but I was ashamed. Afraid to face you. To admit I was wrong. About a lot of things, really."

"No one expects you to be above fault. It's an impossible standard. But I hear what you're saying about shame. I felt like I couldn't run far enough away after my outburst. Someday, when I'm feeling stronger, you can walk me through the parts I can't remember."

"I'm hoping I'll have forgotten by then. Besides, it wasn't you lashing out. It was just a ghost from your past."

Evie smoothed the worry lines from Merritt's brow with her thumb. "If it makes you feel better, my reaction in that Farmexal building corner wasn't solely driven by PTSD. It was a reaction to you. Your proximity. It took most of my energy to resist kissing you. You have that effect on me."

"Have?" Merritt's face brightened like a child's on Christmas morning. Then her eyes took on the smoldering quality Evie had first seen at the precinct the day she'd rattled Farmexal's cage. So she hadn't misread the signals after all.

"Yes, Investigator Shepherd. Maybe we should ease up on the pressure we feel and just let the earth move beneath us for a while." She winked and ran a finger along Merritt's lower lip. Evie steeled herself against the possibility of rejection.

Merritt leaned in and kissed her gently on the cheek. Big thump. Little thump. Merritt smiled suggestively. "How much time do we have before kickoff?"

❖

"Enough," Evie pleaded. "God, Merritt, please. Enough!"

Merritt slowly unwrapped Evie's legs from around her shoulders and fell sideways to the mattress. "Which is it? God?

Or Merritt?" She propped herself up on an elbow to watch Evie as she regained her faculties post-orgasm. Her body was still quivering, seemingly with smaller orgasms nipping on the heels of the one that had almost snapped Merritt's head off. Her cheeks were flushed, and her eyes were closed. Her mouth, plump from the hungry kisses they'd shared, was open in the shape of a small O while her diaphragm pushed short gasps through it. When Merritt put a fingertip near her belly button, Evie's eyes flew open, and she twitched.

"Stop that."

"Or?" Merritt couldn't help herself. Since racing to the bedroom and abandoning any notion of lunch, she and Evie had teased each other into an alternating series of orgasms. Each time they'd proclaimed an end, their "enough" was soon followed by another passionate kiss. Another perfectly placed touch. Then another indulgent round of bites and nips. Usually, screams and laughter. Sleep was expendable. *Sunday afternoons are the best.*

"Football."

Merritt feigned confusion. "If I don't stop, you're going to use a football on me? Is that some sort of kink I don't know about?"

"Don't be ridiculous. You have more than a passing knowledge of kink."

Merritt smiled and looked toward the knotted piece of silk that hung from the headboard, then stared into Evie's eyes. "Is that a…"

"Complaint? No. For certain, no. A compliment. And a commitment to spending a lot more time exploring our preferences. You might be surprised at what lurks beneath this shy and demure exterior."

They both laughed, and Merritt rolled onto her back, pulling Evie with her until she was seated like a rider in a saddle. She put her hands on Evie's thighs and roamed back and beneath her, squeezing the soft and ample cheeks until Evie tilted her wetness hard against Merritt's pubis.

"I have a fairly good idea what's lurking, love." *Love.* She sighed and opened her legs just wide enough that Evie's mound pressed more deeply into her own. Evie leaned down and placed her elbows on each side of Merritt's head before kissing her. Soon, Evie's fingers wove into her hair and pinned her head firmly against the pillow.

"You might think so," Evie whispered in her ear, "but I'm about to make things abundantly clear." She punctuated the promise with a small lick of Merritt's ear and a commanding squeeze of her hair. "Does that sound good to you, sweetheart?"

Merritt's throbbing center melted. "Very good." She smiled. "My safe word is Elway."

"Of course it is."

Evie smiled and pulled Merritt's head back before claiming her mouth. The kiss was so powerful and urgent, it generated a hot flow that Merritt feared could quickly and easily erupt. But Evie left her on the edge, and the sex that followed was diabolically, delightfully slow. Expert and methodical, as if she knew each inch of Merritt, Evie gently and intently shifted pressure and places within her. Merritt lost all space, all time, had nothing to measure the moments. When she found herself at the edge, Evie mercifully and tenderly opened her up so she thrust upward in momentous climax before tumbling happily from peaks she'd never climbed before.

When she woke, Merritt was curled tightly against Evie's chest. The beautiful pendant had settled in the crevice between Evie's satiny breasts, and the blue flecks of feldspar flashed with each sleepy rise of her chest. Merritt thought about untangling her arms so she could rub the stone, then quickly reconsidered. *Nothing at all to worry about here.*

ANNIE MCDONALD

EPILOGUE

The Outreach Center was empty except for the volunteers who'd helped cook, serve, and now cleaned up after the Christmas Eve dinner. Evie and Merritt had answered Bev's call for help and then pulled in a few extra hands, including Max and Robby; Steph, Angela, and their kids; and a small crew of trainees from the RCMP's Depot.

As the volunteers packed up boxes of leftovers for the RCMP crew, who promised to deliver to shelters and to those living on the streets, Evie marveled at Bev's resiliency. Now that Lonnie was a guest at the Department of Corrections for two to five, Bev had more energy to give to the community and was dedicated to cooking three meals a week for Reginans in need.

Evie had a lot more energy, too, but that had more to do with Merritt. They were both on a holiday schedule, so when they weren't hiking with Walter, they were curled up in bed enjoying other pursuits. *Enjoying them very much.*

"Hey there, sexy," Merritt said. *Speak of the devil.*

"Hey, yourself." Evie pulled her in for a long, sexy kiss. "Good news. Bev insists on driving herself home. Last-minute gift-buying, I'm guessing."

"Hey, get a room, you two," Steph said. "What did I tell you, Angela, they're sickening, right?"

"They are." Angela was helping the boys into their coats and boots. "Evie, I have your word that Fish 'n Game there will show up to council in the new year, right? Our band is eager to put her to work."

Angela was descended from First Nations Denesuline, a Chipewyan branch holding lands in Fond du Lac, in the northern part of the province. She'd introduced Merritt to her band chief because he'd approached the ministry for help training his own environmental enforcement team. Illegal logging had struck even their northernmost areas of boreal forest, and as a result, waterways were being compromised. The band had initiated an organized movement to grant one or more of the main rivers in the territory preeminent rights to curb the illicit practices.

Evie was excited about the prospect because establishing personhood with the Chipewyan as guardians would protect not only the river itself from pollution and hydroelectric development, but the way of life for those depending on it. With the ministry's approval, Merritt had already been green-lit for a February start on the training project in Fond du Lac and would stay in Regina as the Farmexal case wrapped up.

Evie would have her close until then. After that, well, she had a plan.

When Merritt was called to help package the meals, Steph gave Evie a hug. As she did, she asked quietly, "How goes that bit of Christmas shopping you mentioned?"

"Good. I got exactly what I needed. In fact, I think Merritt is going to like it."

Steph released her and patted her on the back. "I think old Fish 'n Game is going to love it. We'll see you for dinner tomorrow, and you can let me know how things go."

Merritt returned and grabbed Steph from behind. "Philly, I love you, but I am pretty sure if you hang around much longer, Angela will leave you to walk home."

Steph turned and trotted off after her crew, yelling over her shoulder that she'd see them tomorrow and that they'd bring a cheese tray.

Merritt turned to Evie with a look of mock horror. "No way we could politely say no?"

Evie laughed and kissed her. "Did you finish the packaging? That was so quick."

"Max and Robby powered through it. I hope you don't mind walking back because they need to sign papers for the new space, and I gave them the car."

Evie was thrilled that Robby was not only still dating Max but had decided to start a side business with him. When the building next to the Boulangerie came available, they had submitted an offer, with plans to create a carbon-neutral coffee shop. "Real estate transactions on Christmas Eve?"

Merritt raised and lowered her eyebrows comically and winked. Evie set aside her surprise about the papers and paid attention to a very deep and distinct yearning. *The loft will be empty.* "We'll take the shortcut through the park," Merritt whispered in her ear.

It was bitterly cold, but the dry air kept the misery at bay. Besides, the moon was full and the sky clear, stars shining even through the city lights. They walked mitten-in-mitten, and Evie's heart was filled with a joy she'd never imagined possible. Or gratitude? A seasonal mix, most likely. "I hear through the grapevine that Mark Einerson pleaded guilty for the thefts. Are you to thank for sparing me having to testify about the tunnel?"

Merritt squeezed her hand. "I'd like to take the credit, especially if it means you're in my debt." She winked. "But Mark knew he had few options but to plea. His grandfather was charged as a party to the offense, and he's also fully cooperating. It might've helped that the word 'terrorism' kept coming up in my reports."

Evie stopped and swallowed. "The chemicals weren't being stolen for that purpose, were they?"

"No." Merritt tugged her back into stride. "But once off Farmexal's site, the liquid could've been co-opted. And even in transport, the potential for harm might've been catastrophic in many ways."

Evie maintained her pace, refusing to let fear overcome reason. "Is Farmexal going to be charged for their failure to prevent the thefts? I mean, they must share some responsibility, no?"

"They have, and they've already paid the fines for failing to adequately secure the shipping and receiving docks. They are also working with colleagues of mine in Ottawa to formulate tighter regulations around the industry's recycling processes."

"Do you mean the totes will be single-use going forward? They won't be refillable?"

"No, they'll still be refillable. No one wants more plastic waste in our landfills. The goal, in its early stages as I understand it, is to remove the separate washhouse from the supply chain. Farmexal isn't the only company that off-sites their cleaning. Moving the process into the manufacturing facility will eliminate the opportunity for redirection of the liquid product. You know, you're very cute when you flip into environmental-warrior mode."

Evie slapped her arm playfully. "It would be nice if you could use your superpowers to push that pencil a bit faster. Tighter policies to protect viable land, waterways…"

"…forest, and air. I know, baby. The more partners we can pull into the environmental fight—and that includes industry and activists, especially the sexy ones—the more quickly and efficiently we can turn the negative trends around."

It was obvious that Merritt was in stride with Evie's passion. In many ways. As the loft entrance came into sight, Evie wondered how many new directions that synchronicity would take them. "So you now agree there is room for protest?"

"At times, yes." Merritt stopped on the steps and pulled Evie close, placing her mittened hands beneath her ears and under her hair. She smiled suggestively. "Right now, no. Because I would very much like to kiss you." Her words slowly melted the cold Regina air between them. "And I'd prefer you didn't resist."

❖

Several hours later, Evie put another log into the lime-green cone fireplace. The vintage metal piece suited Max's loft and was his most beloved recovered treasure. He used it rarely because of the emissions but had granted them a Christmas fire and had stocked up on sustainably harvested wood. She returned to the couch and nestled beside Merritt, pulling a portion of the large Hudson's Bay blanket over her legs. Walter was curled up on Merritt's other side, an empty puzzle toy under his crossed paws. He was snoring softly, contentedly taking full advantage of the warmth emanating from her body and the fire.

In fact, since hearing that he would indeed be receiving an official police commendation for his part in the tunnel arrest, Walter had been taking advantage of a lot of things. Most especially, attention. *Just like a Cairn.*

Through the large factory windows, Evie watched fat snowflakes fall from above. "Looks like we're going to have an extra-white Christmas, sweetheart."

"Good thing we don't have to go anywhere tomorrow."

"True, but we have a few people coming over for dinner."

"We could cancel."

"Merritt Shepherd, we absolutely cannot cancel Christmas dinner." Evie pulled on Merritt's pouty lower lip and kissed her. "But I admire your effort. In fact, it deserves to be rewarded."

Merritt's pout turned to a smile, and she threw a leg over Evie's. Obviously, Walter wasn't the only soul in the room with an appetite for attention.

"Soon, baby." Evie slipped her hand beneath the throw pillow, pulled out a small gift-wrapped box, and set it on Merritt's knee.

"It's not quite Christmas yet," Merritt said. "Do I have to wait?"

Evie laughed. The time they'd spent together over the past weeks had convinced her that despite the sexy, slow pattern of speech, patience was not Merritt's greatest asset. "Is there any way I could stop you? Besides, it's not technically your official present."

Merritt efficiently ripped off the paper, reminding Evie of how Walter had earlier attacked his puzzle toy. She slowed, though, the minute she saw the hinged felt box.

"Baby?"

"Just open it," Evie said.

Merritt flipped open the lid carefully, revealing a small, dark gray stone. Evie worried she'd be disappointed, but her expression was one of marvel.

"It's larvikite, from the same place I found this one," Evie said, fondling her pendant.

"It's beautiful, like you. What a great Christmas gift. Thank you."

"Nope. Remember, this isn't technically your gift. Your actual gift will be a piece of jewelry that incorporates your stone or part of it. I've never seen you wear a pendant, so I thought it might be nice if you picked something to set it in." Evie leaned in and kissed her as she was examining each facet of the stone. "A bracelet, perhaps? Or maybe some other sort of circular-shaped jewelry?"

Merritt caressed her hair, running long fingers slowly along her neck. "Whatever it is, I'll happily wear it."

Evie's heart thumped. She hadn't been sure how much talk of their future Merritt was comfortable with, but it seemed they were on the same page. She'd realized her own feelings for Merritt that day in September while standing in the parking lot. "I think it will be a nice reminder of your days working in the dog food industry in Flin Flon."

The thinly veiled story Merritt had told to impress her, and then stumbled over to maintain the pretense, was a source of much good-natured teasing. Merritt blushed as she set the larvikite back into the box and balanced it on her knee.

"Since this isn't my official gift, you'll have to wait for yours until morning. But I'll give it to you before the family descends." She ran her fingers the length of the box. "Speaking of the family, are you ready to meet the Shepherds?"

Evie's stomach tensed. She hadn't met a girlfriend's parents except for Julianna's, and that was under very different circumstances. "I'm looking forward to it. Just promise they won't all have Max's quirky sense of humor."

"Sadly, they do."

Evie shook her head and stared into Merritt's loving face. She'd put up with all the dad jokes in the world if Merritt was by her side. "I have something else for you. It's under the stone. Again, not technically a Christmas gift."

Merritt picked up the box, palmed the larvikite and pulled on the small felt tab. The cardboard base lifted, and below it was a folded piece of paper.

"Go on, open it." Evie could hardly keep from doing it herself.

As she'd expected, the more the unfolding revealed, the more confused Merritt looked. Evie had become tuned in to Merr's habit of taking a moment before speaking, hoping to find the right words. She loved watching it transpire.

"Baby, I think there's a bit of confusion. Maybe I didn't let you know that the ministry pays for my transportation costs to Fond du Lac. As generous as it is, I don't, well…"

Much as she enjoyed the diplomatic effort, Evie couldn't let it go on. "Sweetheart, the ticket is for me."

More confusion. Evie smiled. Then, realization.

Merritt's eyes flashed, and the gold flecks glistened. "You got the project? Really, Evie, tell me. You're coming with me?"

"I am, yes. The dean approved my proposal. I will start a month after you, and I have a six-semester sabbatical."

Evie was proud of herself. Her plan had come together exactly as she'd hoped. As soon as she'd heard from Angela that the Chipewyan were unsettled about how to begin cleaning up several dozen abandoned mineral claims, Evie had recognized the educative opportunity for her grad students. And a change of pace for herself. Many of the exploratory holes would serve well for structural analysis, and in return for the lessons learned, the Dene council would have the data necessary to determine an appropriate dispensation plan for the claims. She'd put together a proposal to the dean with the help of the council and had hoped for the best.

Merritt's pout returned. "How are we going to manage a month apart?"

Evie was pulled closer. "Much better than we could've managed a year apart."

She could not take her eyes off the woman she loved. Her heart kept her warmer than the roaring fire ever could. A lightness of being that she had never experienced blanketed her. Perhaps it was a realization that over the past few months, she'd freed herself from so many of the anchors that had held her down for too long.

The kiss that followed ignited a desire to press more deeply into Merritt. Her attempt disturbed Walter, who sought out a new warm spot, wedging more deeply between them. They laughed, and since accepting was simpler than resisting, Evie pulled Merritt, and they comfortably sandwiched Walter deeper into the couch.

The next morning, she woke up still nestled in Merritt's arms in front of the fire. She didn't have to look to know that one hand was on Walter, the other flat against Merritt's chest. Big thump. Little thump. Big thump. Little thump. Fingers twirled in her hair. She opened her eyes.

"Merry Christmas, baby." Merritt spoke slowly and softly, the way she always did. The way Evie loved to hear it.

Walter stirred, and she felt something odd against her hand. Or was it in her hand. On her finger. Hard. Smooth. *Oh my God.* "Oh my God. Merritt."

"Which is it?" Merritt laughed at the running joke. "And is that a yes?"

Evie stared through tears at the ring Merritt had placed on her finger while she'd slept. Stylistically, the setting was similar to her pendant, but the stone was a striking shade of blue that perfectly complemented the feldspar in the larvikite.

"Yes, of course it's a yes. Merritt, it's lovely. You're lovely. Merry Christmas, my love."

It was still Christmas day. The snow was still falling in fat white flakes outside the window. The coals still shimmered in the fireplace. But things, well, everything really had changed.

About the Author

Annie McDonald wrote her first novel, *Where We Are*, in 2019 to kick off her retirement. In 2020, her second, *When Sparks Fly*, was a Golden Crown Literary Society finalist in the Short Contemporary Romance category.

Born in Montreal, Annie migrated a wee bit west until recently taking up residence on the south shore of Nova Scotia. In between rounds of golf, biking, hiking, and kayaking with her wife Sandy, she's kept busy by her Labradors, Scapa and Rey, who retrieve only on their own terms. She plans to celebrate her country's incredible diversity by writing novels set in each of Canada's ten provinces and three territories.

Books Available From Bold Strokes Books

Almost Perfect by Tagan Shepard. A shared love of queer TV brings Olivia and Riley together, but can they keep their real-life love as picture perfect as their on-screen counterparts? (978-1-63679-322-1)

The Amaranthine Law by Gun Brooke. Tristan Kelly is being hunted for who she is and her incomprehensible past, and despite her overwhelming feelings for Olivia Bryce, she has to reject her to keep her safe. (978-1-63679-235-4)

Craving Cassie by Skye Rowan. Siobhan Carney and Cassie Townsend share an instant attraction, but are they brave enough to give up everything they have ever known to be together? (978-1-63679-062-6)

Drifting by Lyn Hemphill. When Tess jumps into the ocean after Jet, she thinks she's saving her life. Of course, she can't possibly know Jet is actually a mermaid desperate to fix her mistake before she causes her clan's demise. (978-1-63679-242-2)

Enigma by Suzie Clarke. Polly has taken an oath to protect and serve her country, but when the spy she's tasked with hunting becomes the love of her life, will she be the one to betray her country? (978-1-63555-999-6)

Finding Fault by Annie McDonald. Can environmental activist Dr. Evie O'Halloran and government investigator Merritt Shepherd set aside their conflicting ideas about saving the planet and risk their hearts enough to save their love? (978-1-63679-257-6)

The Forever Factor by Melissa Brayden. When Bethany and Reid confront their past, they give new meaning to letting go, forgiveness, and a future worth fighting for. (978-1-63679-357-3)

The Frenemy Zone by Yolanda Wallace. Ollie Smith-Nakamura thinks relocating from San Francisco to her dad's rural hometown is the worst idea in the world, but after she meets her new classmate Ariel Hall, she might have a change of heart. (978-1-63679-249-1)

Hot Keys by R.E. Ward. In 1920s New York City, Betty May Dewitt and her best friend, Jack Norval, are determined to make their Tin Pan Alley dreams come true and discover they will have to fight—not only for their hearts and dreams, but for their lives. (978-1-63679-259-0)

Securing Ava by Anne Shade. Private investigator Paige Richards takes a case to locate and bring back runaway heiress Ava Prescott. But ignoring her attraction may prove impossible when their hearts and lives are at stake. (978-1-63679-297-2)

A Cutting Deceit by Cathy Dunnell. Undercover cop Athena takes a job at Valeria's hair salon to gather evidence to prove her husband's connections to organized crime. What starts as a tentative friendship quickly turns into a dangerous affair. (978-1-63679-208-8)

As Seen on TV! by CF Frizzell. Despite their objections, TV hosts Ronnie Sharp, a laid-back chef, and paranormal investigator Peyton Stanford have to work together. The public is watching. But joining forces is risky, contemptuous, unnerving, provocative—and ridiculously perfect. (978-1-63679-272-9)

Blood Memory by Sandra Barret. Can vampire Jade Murphy protect her friend from a human stalker and keep her dates with the gorgeous Beth Jenssen without revealing her secrets? (978-1-63679-307-8)

Foolproof by Leigh Hays. For Martine Roberts and Elliot Tillman, friends with benefits isn't a foolproof way to hide from the truth at the heart of an affair. (978-1-63679-184-5)

Glass and Stone by Renee Roman. Jordan must accept that she can't control everything that happens in life, and that includes her wayward heart. (978-1-63679-162-3)

Hard Pressed by Aurora Rey. When rivals Mira Lavigne and Dylan Miller are tapped to co-chair Finger Lakes Cider Week, competition gives way to compromise. But will their sexual chemistry lead to love? (978-1-63679-210-1)

The Laws of Magic by M. Ullrich. Nothing is ever what it seems, especially not in the small town of Bender, Massachusetts, where a witch lives to save lives and avoid love. (978-1-63679-222-4)

The Lonely Hearts Rescue by Morgan Lee Miller, Nell Stark & Missouri Vaun. In this novella collection, a hurricane hits the Gulf Coast, and the animals at the Lonely Hearts Rescue Shelter need love—and so do the humans who adopt them. (978-1-63679-231-6)

The Mage and the Monster by Barbara Ann Wright. Two powerful mages, one committed to magic and one controlled by it, strive to free each other and be together while the countries they serve descend into war. (978-1-63679-190-6)

Truly Wanted by J.J. Hale. Sam must decide if she's willing to risk losing her found family to find her happily ever after. (978-1-63679-333-7)

A Good Chance by Ali Vali. Harry, Desi, and Desi's sister Rachel are so close to getting everything they've ever wanted, but Desi's ex-husband is coming back to get his revenge and rip apart their chance at happiness. (978-1-63679-023-7)

A Perfect Fifth by Jaycie Morrison. Streetwise pianist Zara Keller and Lady Jillian Stansfield couldn't be more different, yet their connection brings a new awareness of who they are and what they truly want in their lives—including each other. (978-1-63679-132-6)

Catching Feelings by Ana Hartnett Reichardt. Andrea Foster expected to catch a lot of pitches from the Alder Lions' star pitcher, Maya, but she didn't expect to catch feelings. (978-1-63679-227-9)

Defiant Hearts by Lee Lynch. In these stories, you'll find your lovers, friends, and lesbians you wish you knew—maybe even yourself. (978-1-63679-237-8)

Love and Duty by Catherine Young. All Princess Roseli wants is to marry her three lovers, but with war looming, she must instead marry Princess Lucia to establish a military alliance between their planets. (978-1-63679-256-9)

Serendipity by Kris Bryant. Serendipity brings jingle writer Annie Foster and celebrity pop star Bristol Baines together, and their undeniable attraction keeps them close, but will their different paths drive them apart? (978-1-63679-224-8)

The Haunted Heart by Jane Kolven. A ghost, a ring, and a quest to find a missing psychic—it's a spell for love. (978-1-63679-245-3)

The Rules of Forever by Nan Campbell. After reconnecting at their high school reunion, Cara and Lauren agree to embark on a textbook definition friends-with-benefits relationship, but trying to keep it uncomplicated is harder than it seems. (978-1-63679-248-4)

Vision of Virtue by Brey Willows. When virtue and desire come together, be prepared for sparks in this next installment of the Memory's Muses series. (978-1-63679-118-0)

The Artist by Sheri Lewis Wohl. Detective Casey Wilson and reclusive artist Tula Crane are drawn together in a web of passion, intrigue, and art that might just hold the key to stopping a killer. (978-1-63679-150-0)

Cherry on Top by Georgia Beers. A chance meeting leaves Cherry and Ellis longing for a different life, but when Ellis's search for truth crashes into Cherry's insta-filter world, do they have any hope at all of a happily ever after? (978-1-63679-158-6)

Love and Other Rare Birds by Angie Williams. Ornithologist Dr. Jamie Martin and park ranger Rowan Fleming are searching the Alaskan wilderness for a bird thought to be extinct, and they're about to discover opposites really do attract. (978-1-63679-108-1)

Parallel Paradise by Mayapee Chowdhury. When their love affair is put to the test by the homophobia of their family, community, and culture, Bindi and Rimli will need to fight for a chance at love. (978-1-63679-203-3)

Perfectly Matched by Toni Logan. A beautiful Cupid named Hannah, a runaway arrow, and just seventy-two hours to fix a mishap that could be the best mistake she has ever made. (978-1-63679-120-3)

Slow Burn by Missouri Vaun. A wounded wildland firefighter from California and a struggling artist find solace and love in a small southern town. (978-1-63679-098-5)

The Inconvenient Heiress by Jane Walsh. An unlikely heiress and a spinster evade the Marriage Mart only to discover true love together. (978-1-63679-173-9)

The Value of Sylver and Gold by Michelle Larkin. When word gets out that former Boston Homicide Detective Reid Sylver can talk to the dead, the FBI solicits her help on a serial murder case, prompting Reid to assemble forces once again with Detective London Gold. (978-1-63679-093-0)

Wildflower by Cathleen Collins. When a plane crash leaves seven-year-old Lily Andrews stranded in the vast wilderness of Arkansas, will she be able to overcome the odds and make it back to civilization and the one person who holds the key to her future? (978-1-63679-244-6)